STRENGTH

JANE WASHINGTON
JAYMIN EVE

Copyright 2018 © Jane Washington and Jaymin Eve.
All rights reserved.
The authors have provided this ebook for your personal use only. It
may not be re-sold or made publicly available in any way. **Copyright
infringement is against the law.** Thank you for respecting the hard
work of these authors.

Washington, Jane
Eve, Jaymin
Strength

www.janewashington.com
www.jaymineve.com

Edited by David Thomas and Josephine Banks
www.josephinebanksofficial.com/editing

ISBN-10: 1723324426
ISBN-13: 978-1723324420

For Jaymin: Stop trying to use em-dashes.
Also for Jane: Stop trying to censor the sex scenes.

GLOSSARY

dormire – **server residence**

howler – **wolf**

longneck – **flamingo**

sleeper – **spider**

click – **minute**

rotation – **hour**

sun-cycle – **day**

moon-cycle – **month**

life-cycle – **year**

ONE

T he greatest thing about being dead was the food. I mean, *sure*, I had to endure a knife in the chest and a creepy death-cuddle from the worst being in all the worlds to *get* to the food, but I couldn't help but feel it was all worth it. Every sun-cycle I woke up, I pressed a panel on the wall, and a server appeared on the table.

On the table. Like a menu.

The server I was currently looking at was short, with a bald head and pale, grey eyes. I knew that it was a woman because her weird little skinsuit covered the chest. The skinsuits of the male servers only covered the hips.

"What's your name?" I asked her.

It was my favourite game—asking their names. I'd been hiding out in Cyrus's sterile white residence for almost seven sun-cycles, and in that time, I'd had seven different servers. After asking one of them why there was a new server each sun-cycle, I had discovered that a certain number of servers were assigned to the different sections of Topia. They were on a regular rotation because of the high volume of servers that ended up dismantled or banished when the food wasn't exactly right. In reply to that, I'd asked if they were the ones cooking the food, and she had replied that *no*, they weren't.

The servers that attended food calls had a relatively simple schedule: they were assigned to a section of Topia for the sun-cycle, and they answered the food call of every being in that section. After receiving the order, they went back to their *dormire* to fetch the food and deliver it. I hadn't had a chance to ask who or what the hell their *dormire* was, because the server that I had been questioning had been called away to answer another food call.

"Bush," my current server answered me, interrupting my thoughts and reminding me that I had asked for her name. "I am called Bush, Sacred One. What can I get for you?"

Bush. I cringed. "I'll have some bread, and some cheese, and some milk ... and I suppose I should have some chocolate, just in case. And some of that iced nectar drink, to wash down the chocolate. And some crumbed swimmer cakes, because you should always balance out too many sweets with other things that aren't sweet. And some chocolate milk, because you should always balance out too many savoury things with other things that aren't savoury. And some apple pie, with the frosted crust. And some—"

"That's probably enough for breakfast," Yael drawled, walking into the room.

The server snapped her head to Yael, and then switched her eyes back to me. Then back to Yael. Back to me. Back to Yael. She needed some sort of confirmation.

"That's enough ... *for now*," I told her.

She nodded quickly, looking relieved, and then disappeared.

I twisted in my chair to narrow my eyes on Yael. "I wasn't done ordering," I grumbled.

"Yeah you were. You told us you needed to leave the cave or else you would *wither and die ... again*, so Coen organised a little outing. We leave in one rotation and there's no way you can eat that much food in one rotation."

"Try me." I huffed a little, but it was hard to stay angry when they had finally decided to let me out of the cave.

I turned back around as Yael took the seat to my right. I was sitting at the head of Cyrus's dining table, clutching the knife and fork in front of me and leaning over my empty plate. It was the same way I had greeted the past seven sun-cycles. I called it my *power stance*: back straight, head up, cutlery ready. If I was going to have to be dead, I was at least going to spend my afterlife eating cheesy bread and gulping chocolate milk. I deserved it. Dying was hard.

Yael leaned back in his chair, smirking at me as Aros came into the room. I could sense him rather than see him, the smell of burning sugar plants drifting faintly through the air, so faint that I could barely catch it. A touch drifted across the back of my neck. He took the seat next to Yael. They knew the drill: *breakfast first*.

Aros *tsked*. "Actually, the family motto is *safety first*."

"I'm the one who died, so I get to pick the family motto," I countered. "It's breakfast first."

"We're all undead, technically." This had come from Rome, who had entered the room far too silently for his massive frame.

His hands gripped the back of my chair and I could feel him hovering over me, his breath against the top of my head.

"You were born already dead." I toyed with the knife in my right hand. "That doesn't count."

Instead of answering me, Rome straightened away and spoke to whoever had stepped through the doorway after him. "Willa changed the family motto."

"It's not safety first anymore?" Coen asked.

"Nope." This had been from Siret—the last to enter the room. "It's dinner first. We spoke about this last night, did you all forget?"

"*No*." I dropped the knife and fork, spinning around to face their little group, since Yael was the only one who had actually taken a seat. "It's breakfast first."

"I swear it was dinner first." Siret seemed confused. "Did it change?"

I didn't answer, because Bush had reappeared and was laying down dish after dish. I quickly picked up my knife and fork again. The appearance of food also seemed to clear up all the confusion in the room, as the guys claimed seats. Coen ended up on my left.

"We're going somewhere this sun-cycle?" I asked him hopefully.

He wasn't by any definition the 'leader' of our group, but he was the grumpiest and the most responsible, so that somehow translated to him policing most of the rules ... but he definitely wasn't the leader. *If the leader was anyone, it would definitely be me—*

"We're taking you to see our mother," Coen said, interrupting my thought, and I suspected that it was deliberate.

He leaned forward, piling his plate with food. I quickly began to fill up my own plate before all the dishes emptied out. I had only ordered *my* part of breakfast before Yael had cut me off—I hadn't had a chance to order for all the rest of them, too. Luckily, the server had brought several servings of each dish and several jugs of each beverage. She was now standing off to the side, I noticed.

I was torn. Coen had mentioned his mother with

such a lack of care, as though we went to see her once every few sun-cycles for family dinner. The rest of the Abcurses went on eating as though nothing was happening. None of them were acknowledging the strangeness of the *outing* he was suggesting, which meant that they had all planned it without me, and definitely had ulterior motives. On the other hand, I really wanted to ask the server where she managed to get all this food from if she wasn't cooking it herself, and what the hell *dormires* were.

Putting aside the mention of the Abcurses' mother for now, I turned to Bush before she was called away to serve anyone else.

"So who makes all this food?" I asked her.

She blinked as though she had heard me, but her face remained stoically facing the table, waiting for any further orders.

"Bush," I prompted, forcing her head to snap up and turn my way. "Who makes this food?"

"The pool," she told me. "The Platter of Staviti is used for the food, and the Cup of Staviti is used for the beverages."

"You mean the cup that—"

"Yes," Rome cut across me. "That one."

"But if we stol—"

"It's a copy," Aros answered, glancing up at me from his plate, his golden eyes holding mine, warning me to drop the subject in front of the server. "Staviti lost the original cup after being tricked by Abil—and then the original cup was stolen from Abil. *Nobody* knows where it is."

I snorted, turning my attention back to my plate. "So mysterious. But—" I looked to the server again. "How can the pool and the platter and the cup make all this food?"

"The platter is placed in the pool and we ask for the food. It is the same with the cup."

She flickered out, then, leaving her words behind for me to ponder.

"*That's* what the cup does?" I asked the others. "It gives you ... stuff to drink?"

"It holds the power of Creation," Siret replied. "*And* it gives stuff to drink."

"Okay then, so what is this pool?" I couldn't let it go. I had been asking them questions for sun-cycles, about everything. Everything and anything that popped into my mind.

Maybe it was because I had become accustomed to just letting things go for most of my life. Especially the things that made no sense, despite how often *senseless* things happened, like clumsy curses colliding with my chest and the daily threats to my life. Not even my inability to conform and dwell in the dirt with the rest of my people made sense.

"It's just water, Will," Rome answered. "Staviti uses it to channel his Creation to make all our lives easier."

"Not *all* of our lives," I muttered back.

Siret chuckled. "It's Topian water; it only works

inside Topia. If he tried to use it for the sols in Minatsol, it wouldn't work." His calm voice was enough to capture my full attention.

My mind immediately forgot about dwellers and focused on another word ... *water.*

That word had so many meanings to me now. Firstly, there was the mystery behind the sacred waters of Topia. The panteras had taken me to the stream and had asked me to drink from it, telling me that it would enhance my powers. They had also told me at the time that I'd been given the water before, that it wasn't my first time. They were really cagey with the information, which meant that I was definitely taking a trip back to visit them as soon as I could.

"What's on your mind, Soldier?" Siret asked, not picking up on my thoughts.

I blurted, "Water."

There was a beat of silence, which gave me a click to look between my guys. The five Abcurses: five specimens of perfect, over-sized, godly sexiness—

"Your thoughts came back at a good time," Coen remarked, as varying shades of amusement fell over each of their faces.

I glanced to my left, where Yael sat. There was something behind the amusement in his eyes. Something heated. I swallowed and glanced at the seat next to his, where Rome sat. The same heat was there, boiling behind his expression and setting my insides to squirming. The dark green depths were mesmerising, swirling as they watched me from across the table. Suddenly, my mind jumped to a very different kind of water.

I'd recently learned how to swim with Rome and Yael. There had been *a lot* of swimming, among other things, going on that night. None of us had acknowledged the fact that the pact had been broken. It didn't seem like a breach in our friendship, but more of a natural progression in our relationship. I had acted out of character, spurred by grief over the death of my mother, but I didn't regret it. Not for a click.

I kind of wanted to do it again. *Keep it even, Willa:* that's what they'd said to me. I was technically *obliged* to do it again. With each of them.

"Can you go back to having no thoughts?" Yael's voice was strained.

I didn't blush. For some reason I couldn't conjure up the slightest embarrassment about being with Rome and Yael, at the same time. It felt natural, and it wasn't anybody's business but ours.

"Do you think it's time we chatted about what happened?" I asked, looking between them again.

I wasn't sure where this new streak of maturity was coming from, but I knew that Emmy would be so proud. I had always told her that she wouldn't regret saving my life. Several times. Now, finally, I was proving it with sex discussions. Coen crossed his arms over his chest, leaning back in the chair, still wearing a somewhat amused expression. I liked it a lot more than his *death*-eyes, but since I didn't see it much, I was completely unsure about what might come out of his mouth.

"What exactly do you think we should chat about?" he asked, a twitch at the corner of his mouth.

My eyes went very wide. I quickly stuffed two swimmer puffs into my mouth so that I didn't have to answer immediately, because I had no idea how to properly start the conversation. So far, we had all been sleeping in the same room like a pack of howlers, seeking comfort through close proximity after everything that had happened. None of the Abcurses wanted to let me out of their sights, and I didn't want to be away from them either. An asshole had put a blade through my chest the last time I walked away from them ... it was enough to deter me from ever doing it again.

So, we definitely weren't going to be having any more swimming lessons in the near future. Our focus had been on each other: on growing closer, healing, and treasuring a brief time of comfort and safety. I wasn't eager for things to go back to how they had been with our pact in place—I was finished with being their girl-brother. And I didn't want to pretend that I hadn't shared that experience with Rome and Yael. I wanted to continue moving forward, so it felt like something had to be said.

Siret's grin was so wide that he looked to be moments from laughing. If anyone was going to find our situation amusing, it would be him. I focussed on chewing as I searched for what to say, because I had no idea what would happen if I choked as an un-dead dweller.

"Don't hurt yourself, dweller-baby." Coen took pity on me. "There are no rules, no need to check that our feelings are hurt. Just …"

"Keep it even," I mumbled, interrupting him.

"Exactly," Aros agreed. "Now that we know our powers *shouldn't* have a negative effect on you, there doesn't seem to be a reason to police your intimacy with us anymore."

I nodded. "Like the bullsen during mating season."

Siret snorted and shook his head. "No, Willa, not like the bullsen. This is more than mating season for us, you know that."

Right, I forgot they didn't like me to use the domestic labour beasts as a reference point for relationship development. Unfortunately for them, my influence in this department had been limited to my mother's relationships, growing up. Unless they wanted me to start charging them tokens for swimming lessons, they needed to let me pull references from wherever I wanted. Although, the 'Abcurse' way of mating sounded a lot nicer. The bullsen grunted too much, and I didn't even want to think about what kind of noises my mother had made.

Siret lost it then, his laughter setting off the rest of the guys at the table. I tried not to laugh—because I was significantly more mature than them—but a sound escaped anyway. Luckily, I had a goblet raised to my lips, so I passed it off as almost-choking. After that, our conversation drifted to topics unrelated to water sports, and as we finished up the food and moved to stand, I realised that I hadn't asked them about their mother.

"You're pretty easily distracted," Yael agreed, answering my thoughts as he so often did.

That's not the point. I took a deep breath. "So, your mother ... Adeline, goddess of beauty ... who has been missing for how many life-cycles .... feel free to jump in at any time here, guys ..."

I felt like I had missed the first part of the story: the part where they explained why their mother had been 'travelling', and where she had been 'travelling' to. Also, who she had been travelling with, and what kind of clothes she took travelling. Admittedly, I was a little too invested in exactly how the Goddess of Beauty handled long stints of travel, because I was sure that she didn't sit at the back of a bullsen cart, sweating and fanning her face to drive away the stench of the beasts. There likely weren't even bullsen on Topia, they probably had winged, sparkly beasts.

"We don't even really need to distract her," Yael muttered lowly to the others. "If you let her go off into her own mind, she distracts herself."

I shot him a scowl, which quickly melted as he returned it with a grin. I would learn how to stay mad at them later. For now, I needed to learn more about Adeline. Clearly, she was back, but ... *shouldn't there have been a lead-up to this moment*?

"Mother has returned from her journey, and she would like to meet you." Aros managed to summarise the situation brilliantly, with as little information as possible.

"You wanted an outing," Coen added. "We figured that it was a safe place to take you."

"She should have some advice about the best way to deal with your presence here in Topia," Siret finished.

I was in hiding because no one here knew that I was un-dead yet. Our entire group—barring me, their leader—had decided that it was better for Rau not to know. Cyrus was sure that I wasn't the Beta of Chaos, but he didn't know exactly *what* I was, and it would be too risky to alert Rau to the fact that I was still alive ... or, not alive, but still *living*. We were also attempting to hide the recent events from Staviti, since he had killed my mother and actively tried to capture me. His interest was a huge concern, because no one had any idea what he wanted, though we mostly assumed that it was because he had found out Rau's plan, and he had actually believed that I might become the Chaos Beta. Staviti wouldn't have wanted to assist Rau in his scheme for ultimate power.

Whatever the reason, we all knew that I couldn't stay hidden forever. Eventually, we would have to deal with certain gods finding out that I was alive, or un-dead—however we managed to present the situation. All we knew for certain was that I had died with Rau's curse still affecting me. *What did that mean for me? Was I a Beta, but not of Chaos? Could Cyrus be lying to us, and I was the Chaos Beta?*

Maybe I was just a Jeffrey with hair.

The power inside of me, the energy I had been trying to control, was quiet now. Almost as if I was no more than a normal dweller again. But … I *had* died.

"So, no sol can just become a god, right? Staviti is always involved?" I asked as we began to move toward the exit of Cyrus's secret lair.

Siret wrapped an arm around me and my body sank into his. One thing that hadn't changed was the absolute bliss I felt at the touch of an Abcurse. Somehow, our soul-link was in full effect, which made me think that only my body had been affected by the blade, and my soul had stayed intact.

"Like we've told you multiple times over the past seven sun-cycles," Siret said, "Staviti is involved in every new god ascension. His process is a well-guarded secret: only he is allowed to visit the temples where the strongest sols are taken to die. Many of them kill themselves at their peak of power, and then lay in wait. He only comes for some of them."

"So nobody knows how he does it?" I asked.

"He anoints them with water, or at least that's how he tells it. He breathes life back into them. After that, he brings them across to Topia. They go through a change, waking in a few sun-cycles as new, powerful beings."

Coen's voice was gruff. "We were prepared to search out the water he uses to anoint the new gods, but you had already healed yourself by the time Cyrus got you back here, so it was clear that you were transforming."

I fought the urge to bury my face into Siret's chest and hide from the world. This was too much for my poor dweller brain, which was probably why, generally, upon death, we were lobotomised and turned into Jeffreys. We couldn't handle knowledge of the divine.

"Bush is the worst name so far," I murmured, distracted again. "You gods really need to stop sending the servers to the banishment caves, because you've clearly run through all the good names."

Being so close to the banishment cave meant that it was often on my mind. It felt wrong, knowing that all of the wraiths were trapped there. Wraiths I had promised to help.

Yael laughed, and I managed to push my guilt into a box again.

"I don't know, Willa-toy. Wasn't one called Mole a few sun-cycles ago?"

I returned his smile. His sarcastic amusement was one of my favourite things. "You're right, Mole might be the winner. But Bush is a close second."

"Are you coming?" Coen called. He was already out

of the white room we had dined in, standing near a secret exit that Cyrus had created for our use—a secret exit he'd made clear would cease to exist when we no longer needed his hideout. As a general rule, Cyrus would kill to make sure that no one knew about his secret home, his secret exits, and the millions of other secrets he kept. He was the scary Neutral God and he *hated* his space being invaded. Even so, I had been using the convenient fact that he had brutally murdered me to get all the things I wanted from him. As I kept repeating to everyone: dying was hard work. I was well within my un-dead rights to claim compensation.

We reached the unmarked door toward the back of the dining room and climbed the stairs up to a stone landing. The appearance of this space was sudden and jarring, compared to the rest of the impeccable white home. It was just a cave: unrefined, damp, and cold. There was a ladder resting on the stone, leading up to a trap door. Our exit. It was covered in grass on the other side—making it almost impossible to find without stomping around the place and waiting for the *thud*. Luckily, it was located to the side of the banishment cave, so there wasn't much of a chance that anyone would stumble over it by accident.

Siret climbed up first, followed by Coen, who then reached back in for me. I was a few rungs from the top, but he apparently wasn't going to wait. His hands gripped my biceps, pulling me clear into the air. My feet hit grass and I found myself standing much closer to him than I had expected. I was staring at the black robes that clung to his body, revealing a simple, embroidered undershirt that did a terrible job at masking the formidable muscles lining his chest. Not that it was *trying* to mask them. If I was a simple, embroidered undershirt, I'd be clinging hard to those muscles, too. Coen smirked down at me and I heard Aros laughing as he emerged behind me.

"Stop laughing at me." I forced the words out through a grimace. "And stop listening to my thoughts while I'm complimenting you."

"Wasn't laughing," Coen countered, the smirk still in place.

"Neither was I," Aros lied. I could feel him behind me now, one of his hands landing on the curve of my hip, his breath against my ear. "I was agreeing. In a way. I'd kill to become your robes right now, to cling to your—" His hand had inched higher, slipping from my hip to my waist, and then to my ribcage, before Coen was suddenly leaning forward and yanking it away.

"That's enough of that, Seduction," he ordered.

I could feel Aros tensing behind me and knew that another fight was about to break out, so I quickly slipped out from between them, marching off in the direction of a grouping of trees close by.

"Where are you going?" Yael called out, a few clicks later.

Away from you assholes! I shot back in my head.

"Willa!" Siret yelled. "Where the hell are you going?"

"Oh *now* they can't hear my thoughts?" I grumbled, spinning around and cupping my hands over my mouth to shout back at them. *They weren't even that far away, so why the hell was it so hard to hear them?* "I'm going to find your mother!" I informed them all. *Why weren't they moving?* "And when I find her, I'm going to tell her that you're all assholes!"

"How are you going to get there?" Rome shouted back, his voice strangely drowned out. "Are you going to swim?"

"Swim?" I replied, in a normal tone, before the roaring of noise behind me finally registered.

It had been a dull but constant sound back where we'd emerged from the secret door, but now that I was closer to the trees, it was deafening. I spun around, facing the small and scraggly woodland. The sound was familiar, now that I paid attention to it, and I ducked through the treeline to come alongside the top of a *very* steep waterfall. I glanced down and then took several hasty steps backward. Those rocks didn't look comfortable. I quickly walked back to the guys and then ... walked straight past them, marching in the other direction.

"Can you just admit you have no idea where you're going?" Yael groaned, following behind me.

"I could," I returned thoughtfully, as though

actually considering his feedback. "Or you could just *tell* me where to go."

He reached out and snagged an arm around my waist, pulling me in against his side in a quick and efficient movement. I dangled there, my feet above the ground, somehow managing to cross my arms stubbornly over my chest.

"We need to go through a pocket," he told me, twisting on the spot and disappearing with me. I ended up clutching at him, my fingers tangling in his dark green robes.

Over the last seven sun-cycles, they had begun to wear their god-colours again, while I mostly just wore white. I was a *neutral*, without the neutral powers, or the neutral badassary—

"Not a word," Yael interrupted my thoughts, setting me back down on my feet.

I glanced around us briefly, taking in—*you guessed it*—another marble platform, before snapping my attention back to his face. "Not a word *what*?"

"Badassery." His eyes rolled briefly as the others all popped into existence around us. "It's not a word."

"Amended," Siret broke in.

"Amended *what*?" I asked him, beginning to get frustrated.

"The legitimacy of badassery being a word. I just amended it. It's now an official record in the tome of *Known Words and Meanings*."

My smile was so sudden and so wide that it

actually started to hurt my face. I ran the few steps toward where Siret stood, flinging myself against him. He caught me easily, chuckling as he drew me up against his chest, his arms tight around my back.

"Added," Rome grunted moodily.

"Added *what*?" I asked over Siret's shoulder. "And can you guys speak in full sentences *please*?"

"Added to the *Known Words and Meanings* record." He was still talking moodily. "I added shweed."

"How did you?" I broke out of Siret's arms, happiness and disbelief bubbling up in me. "Your power is Strength!"

"I know." He reached out, grabbed Siret by the back of the neck, and squeezed. "Add it," he ground out. "Don't make me look bad."

Siret shrugged out of the hold, shoving his brother in the chest, though Rome didn't budge much.

"All you had to do was *ask*," he groused.

Love. This was without any doubt my definition of love. My fabricated words were something that frustrated even Emmy, the way I made up words and messed with the original meanings of everything. The Abcurses, however, barely even blinked an eye. They just rolled with whatever came out of my mouth.

"You guys love me," I chirped, overly happy. My moods had been fluctuating quite widely, and it looked like this sun-cycle's emotion was *euphoria*.

Before any Abcurse could speak—and I was really curious to know what they were going to say because a range of emotions were written across their faces—a light purr of a voice drifted across the marble platform to us. "Well, *hello there*."

If seduction had a sound, it would have been this women's voice. Smooth, slightly rich and throaty. This was a person who could hit the high and low notes in any ballad. Reaching out, I pushed Rome and Siret to the side, standing there like a moron. All I could do was stare at the god before me.

TWO

Adeline was everything a God of Beauty should have been, plus more. She was just over six feet tall, her hair a mass of golden waves, stopping right above her tiny waist. Her flawless skin was somehow both pale and golden at the same time, as though she had never been touched by the sun, but still a healthy glow wanted to shine through from the inside out. Her eyes were a pale amber; golden, like the gold of Aros's eyes, but with a hint of pink, making the colour darker and deeper. Those eyes fixed on me, making me feel both terrified and welcome all at once—but maybe I wasn't so much *welcome* as I was going to stay anyway because she was pretty amazing to look at. She had a perfect hourglass shape, and it seemed to be accentuated by the way her robes draped about her; I wasn't even sure that her shape would have been possible for any of the mortals to obtain. It was magical, in the literal sense.

Basically, she was every male's fantasy ... except for the five men around me, because they were her sons. *Thank the gods.*

"Hello, Mother." Coen's voice was ... softer than usual. Gentle, even. He was the first to move, crossing the two steps to her side and wrapping her up in one of his amazing hugs.

The rest followed soon after, all of them standing close to their stunning mother. I remained apart from them, staring at the six of them together. Adeline was definitely where the golden sheen of my Abcurses came from. Abil was the dark and ruby tones.

It would have been impossible for Adeline and Abil to have ugly children.

"Willa," Aros called to me, holding out a hand.

Swallowing roughly, I nervously smoothed my white robe down, crossing to where they stood. I wasn't the girl you took home to meet the parents. In my village, it would have been considered the worst luck ever to end up with me as part of your family. It had been suggested more than once that I should refrain from sex forever, just in case I accidentally procreated. One of me was enough. This was the first parent I had met in this sort of situation, and I had no idea how I was supposed to react.

"Willa." The way she said my name evoked so many warm, fuzzy feelings inside of me.

Her power was Beauty, and there was something utterly enchanting about seeing something so perfectly beautiful.

"Yes," I said. "It's really nice to meet you ..." *What the hell was I supposed to call her? Adeline? Tower of Perfection? Mumma Abcurse?*

"Adeline," she finished for me, sensing the unasked question. "Please, call me Adeline."

"We need to get Willa out of sight," Rome told her. "Let's not linger up here any longer."

She nodded, and with a sweep of her robes, she spun, leading the way to one of those white stone doors. Unsurprisingly, it opened into a living quarter, though this one was even more spectacular than the others that I had seen. The first room was white, with very pale splashes of colour tastefully scattered around.

I had a feeling that I might be able to get along with this woman, and by 'a feeling' I meant that I was *sure* I was going to follow her around with my mouth hanging open, on account of how perfect she was. I was also pretty sure that she wasn't going to like me very much, especially when I inevitably knocked over one of her pretty vases or bled on one of her perfectly woven rugs, or set fire to the fluttering tapestry covering one of the walls.

Everyone filed into the main seating area and I ended up squished onto a couch with two giant gods. Siret had claimed one side, with Aros claiming the other. As usual, they immediately invaded my space—also as usual, I loved every click of it.

When the seven of us were seated, Adeline leaned back into her chair and took a moment to cast her gaze over her five sons.

"I have missed you all immensely," she said in her sultry voice. "Abil filled me in on what you've been going through." She leaned forward in her chair then —some of the demureness disappeared and I was almost a little surprised to see a flame burning in her eyes. "I am so sorry I wasn't here. Rest assured, you now have my full support for whatever you have planned next."

Her gaze flicked to me for a moment, that look measuring and assessing, before she turned to Coen, who had started to talk.

"Our main priority right now is Willa," he was saying. "Whatever we decide to do, there can be no fallout for her. She remains safe, or things will get very messy."

Adeline was looking at me again, and this time there was more than a little assessment in her expression. Before I could blink, she was out of her chair, standing right before me. She held a hand out, and even though my brain was screaming at me to pretend I didn't have a hand, I couldn't stop from reaching out and touching her.

The moment I did, I was hit with the sensation of a warm breeze drifting along my body. My curls even felt like they lifted up, before they rested against my shoulders again.

"You are a special one, Willa." Adeline was talking to me, so I figured I should pay attention. Siret snorted from beside me, but I ignored him. "What is it about you that has captured the interest of my sons so thoroughly?"

I sensed nothing malicious in her gaze, despite how much she frightened me: she was actually one of the kinder gods I had met so far. Even so, her words raised every insecurity I had ever had. I blinked a few times, trying to clear my throat of the emotions suddenly lodged there.

How was I supposed to answer that question?

"You're right, Willa is special," Siret inserted. "A being born a dweller, though she's more powerful than a sol. A being cursed, though she's immensely gifted. She's smart and resourceful. She has sacrificed for us ... and she's our family."

"That's right," Yael added. "We'll kill anyone who hurts her, that's a promise."

Adeline didn't show an ounce of concern at those words, even though they could have been construed as a threat. Instead she smiled, which had a small gasp slipping from my lips. I was pulled up then, and she wrapped me up in a firm embrace. The warmth of her touch spread right to my toes, which were encased in smooth white slippers.

She stepped back, still keeping both hands on my shoulders. "Welcome to the family."

I gulped in some air. "Uh, thank you ... happy to ... be here." *You're an idiot, Willa.*

I'd spent every sun-cycle in Topia lately, and yet for some reason, this one god in particular had me completely losing my mind. I'd just turned into a blathering moron.

Before I could do something completely embarrassing, like cry, or vomit on her, she released my shoulders and turned back to take her previous seat. "Okay, I think it's time you tell me everything that has happened. Abil is woefully ignorant of the finer details, we all know that man is interested in himself first, and everything else in the worlds second."

I had no clue if Adeline and Abil were still a couple, or if they had been together to have their children and now just caught up only in regards to co-parenting situations. Something to ask later.

Siret began to explain the prank that had gotten them punished in the first place, forcing them to weaken on Minatsol for such a long time. Coen told her about how I ended up as their dweller attendant, and how I helped them retrieve something from Abil, which he shouldn't have had.

The explanation went on and on for some time. Rau, the curse, Staviti, and the attack on Blesswood. Adeline listened intently, only interrupting to ask the occasional question. I was beginning to gain a new appreciation for her intelligence. It started to occur to me, though, that it was strange she hadn't bothered to check in on her sons, since she seemed to care about them so much—at least based on what I was seeing. How could she not have known about any of this? Surely someone would have informed her that they had been banished to Minatsol?

Unless … they *often* got banished to Minatsol.

"Where is the cup now?" Adeline asked. She was directing the question toward Aros, which surprised me.

I would have thought that Coen would be the one to hide the cup, since he stepped up to be the 'responsible' Abcurse in most situations.

"Sienna's vault," Aros answered, casting a sideways look at me.

Don't ask, I told myself, just as my mouth blurted out the question, "Who's Sienna?"

Coen coughed.

None of the others answered.

Eventually, Adeline stood from her chair again and moved to a sideboard, pulling out a tray of crystal bottles and tiny crystal glasses. She quietly poured out seven precise measures of yellow-gold liquid into the tiny glasses, arranging them all on a smaller tray and carrying them over.

"Sienna is the Beta of Revelry," she told me, holding the tray with one hand as the guys all reached over to grab their drinks.

She took one of the glasses and handed it to me, before claiming the last one and returning to her seat. She sat back, lifting the glass up to the light and casting refracted golden patterns on the wall behind her.

"She made this wine—named it Tears of the Sun." Adeline smiled at me again, and then tipped the glass to her perfect lips, downing the liquid in what seemed to be an entirely *ungodly* way.

I just sat there and blinked at her, before turning my attention to my own glass. It didn't feel warm. I would have thought that the sun would cry little teardrops of fire or something.

"They aren't *actual* tears of the sun," Aros told me. "Sienna is a glorified tavern-keeper. The main God of Revelry is an immortal named King. He hosts a dinner party every night on his platform."

"And a breakfast party every morning on his platform," Rome added, with a grin.

"And a lunch party." Yael tipped his glass toward me with a brief smile before he drank the whole thing down the same way his mother had. I now assumed that it was just the proper way to drink the stuff.

Adeline was laughing now, the sound a tinkle of perfection. "He actually has a party on the rotation, every rotation," she explained to me, shaking her head. "His system can't process alcohol the way the rest of us do, so he is forever sober while his companions grow more intoxicated around him—that's why the parties are so short and so frequent."

"So, Sienna made this stuff?" I asked, swirling the liquid around a little bit before tipping it to my lips and drinking it all down.

I had expected it to taste terrible, to burn or tingle or coat my tongue in fire—but that wasn't the reality. It was *amazing*. It was like breathing in the purest form of air and feeling it melt into liquid across your tongue. It was cool and sweet, silkily slipping down my throat and alighting all throughout my body.

"Whoa." I set the glass clumsily aside, bringing my hands up before my face, expecting them to be glowing or something. "So Sienna can make heaven in your mouth. Is that why you gave her the cup? So she could make the sun cry?"

Coen cleared his throat again. I was beginning to interpret that sound as *don't ask, Willa, you don't want to know.*

Adeline jumped in to explain. "Sienna had a brief liaison with Aros." She shot Aros a look that seemed oddly disapproving, but Aros had wiped his expression blank, and was looking from me, to Coen, and back.

Oh.

OH.

Him and Coen. Seduction and Pain working together. Suddenly, everything made sense.

"You hid the sacred and special and irreplaceable —" I began, before Siret cut me off.

"It's very much replaceable, Staviti could make them all sun-cycle long—"

"*You gave the very sacred and special and irreplaceable cup that* I *stole,*" I barrelled over Siret, "*to your ex-girlfriend. That makes sense. I mean, why wouldn't you? That makes sense. That's okay. I'm okay with that.*" I reached out, snatched the glass off Coen that he hadn't had a chance to drink yet, and tipped it down my throat.

Siret didn't even wait—he just handed over his glass as soon as I was done with Coen's. The barest arch of Adeline's perfect right eyebrow was the only reaction she showed.

"I'm really not okay with it," I told her, practically bouncing out of my seat at this point. I felt like my slippers had grown wings. That even *I* had grown wings. I suddenly felt as though I could have stepped into the *actual* burning sun and it wouldn't have been able to harm me at all. I was light. I was fire. I was invincible.

"She thinks she's light," Aros muttered to Siret. "If she jumps off the platform, it's on you."

"I'm not okay with that at all," I continued, speaking only to Adeline. "She sounds irresponsible, with her ... name. It's an irresponsible name. She shouldn't be in charge of the cup. *Sienna*," I mocked, making a face. "Terrible name. Never trust a *Sienna*. I bet she doesn't even know how to cook a fowl."

"You don't know how to cook a fowl either," Rome

told me, sounding like he was holding back an unwilling laugh.

"I cook a *great* fowl," I lied, springing out of the chair and planting my hands on my hips. "I bet she can't even make her own animal-conscious jewellery—"

"What," Coen interrupted, "the *hell* is animal-conscious jewellery, and when have you ever made it?"

"This one time I found some shackles in an old bullsen stable and I sold them as bracelets to one of the boys in our school—he wanted a gift for Emmy. She made him return them to me though, and I had to give back the sweets he gave me. Anyway, *stop trying to change the subject*. I bet *Sienna* can't even make a bed."

"I've seen you try to make a bed." Yael decided to join the conversation. "You put the pillows down the wrong end."

"I thought you would like to sleep and look out of the window at the same time." I pouted a little bit at this, crossing my arms over my chest.

"You're lying, aren't you?" he returned, standing and cupping my arms, drawing me in against his chest. "You really got confused about which end to put the pillows."

"No," I lied in a huff, breathing out against his robes.

He squeezed me in with a chuckle, and then turned me around, so that he was pressing up behind me and I was facing Aros. "Why don't you tell her why you gave the cup to Sienna and put her out of her misery, Seduction?"

Aros settled his golden eyes on me. "I knew where she has hidden the key to one of her vaults. I stashed the cup in there and changed the location of her key. She won't even notice, and it was the only place I could think of that our father wouldn't look."

For some reason, I calmed then. Sienna didn't even know about the cup. She wasn't special enough to know about the cup—*my cup*. I stole the freaking thing so at least seventy percent of it was mine. I nodded at Aros to acknowledge his job well done, and then I retook my seat on the couch. Everyone else was standing—probably because of my brief freak-out— but I felt like my knees needed a moment of rest. They were wobbly.

And was it really warm in here?

I fanned at my face and Aros looked at me with concern. "Uh, I think Willa might be about to do her fire thing."

Adeline's concern matched her son's as she peered closer to me. "Fire thing? What fire thing?"

Everyone was gathering closer. I ignored them in favour of fanning my face, because it really did feel extra warm in the marble house.

"She sets things on fire," Coen announced without preamble.

"All the time," Siret added.

Rome shrugged. "It's her thing."

33

I really wanted to argue with them: it was *not* my thing. If anything was my thing it was ... swimming. *Arghh.* Of course that would be the first thing on my mind, because I was addicted to se—swimming now.

No, Willa! For gods' sake, this was not the time.

My thing was being naked, which was marginally better.

Yael laughed out loud, which had a perfect O forming on Adeline's full lips. I wasn't surprised: Yael wasn't really the laughing kind.

"The fire thing again?" Adeline asked, trying to figure out the inside joke.

My eyelids clamped shut, because the last thing I wanted to be discussing with this perfect being of beauty was my relationship with her sons. Nope. *All the nopes right there.*

Thankfully, Coen jumped into his role as 'responsibility guy', and changed the subject. "Willa can't stay hidden forever, so we're trying to figure out the best way to present her to Topia. Staviti is going to lose it, no matter what we do, because he never approved her as a god. She didn't go through any of the steps that would normally be required. Somehow, Willa died, but didn't, and we have no explanation for it."

Everyone returned to their seats then, Siret and Aros re-claiming either side of me. Their heat added to the inferno inside of me, but I was pretty sure that it was actually dying down. Maybe whatever that wine had done to me was subsiding, which hopefully meant no fires this sun-cycle.

"Do you know what I am?" I asked Adeline. I could have phrased that better, but I was pretty much sick of being in the dark. I had been a freak for my entire life: an outcast, a menace that people shunned because I didn't fit into the proper dweller mould.

I wanted to know my mould.

Adeline stood in a single graceful movement. She glided over until she was positioned right before me. Reaching out, she took my face in her hands and I tensed. When Aros and Siret remained relaxed on either side of me, I figured that she wasn't about to rip my head off, so I released some of the tension I was holding.

Her touch sent small tingles across my skin, as though she had a low level of electricity running through her veins. It had the feel of Coen's Pain, but his went straight into my body, whereas Adeline's energy skimmed across my skin.

She pulled back and part of me was bereft. Her power was so warm and loving, one could easily grow addicted to that feeling. As she returned to her seat, I leaned forward in mine, waiting for her to speak. Her face was expressionless, but there was a flicker of something deep in those blush-coloured eyes.

"Well ..." Rome got in before me.

The goddess shook her head. "I have no idea what Willa is now. She has energy like a god, but it's different. I'm not a Neutral, so there are limits to what I can sense, though there's no denying the power inside her. It seems to be trapped, or dormant. She needs to figure out how to set it free or utilise it. Once she does, she will have a better idea of who, or what, she is."

Great. Unleashing my power was just about the last thing I wanted to do, especially if it meant that the horrible fires I caused weren't the full extent of it. Maybe there were *bigger* fires waiting inside of me. Or earthquakes. Swarms of crawlers. Wind-storms. *Twisting wind-storms that tossed fire around.* The horrific possibilities were endless.

Abcurses. My eyes flitted over to the huge gods sprawled around me, their giant bodies spilling out over the sides of Adeline's delicate couches. Maybe I'd have to recreate the kiss with Coen and Aros, where my 'beta' power had been released.

"I volunteer," Siret said, hand in the air.

My smile could not be stopped ... I was barely able to stop from throwing myself into his lap.

Adeline just shook her head. "It's very peculiar that you can hear Willa's thoughts still." We'd told her all the details about this particular quirk of our group earlier. "The original soul-link came about because Willa could not contain the curse, it was too strong, and would have fed on her energy until she was nothing. But death should have destroyed the link and the curse. Willa was ..." She scrunched her face slightly, as if searching for the right word. "Reborn. Her rebirth is a renewal. As we see with the few rare sols who have made it to Topia. They shed the old life, scars, disease. So why …"

"They have a soul-bond now," came a deep voice, suddenly. "The link was transformed, clearly long before the dweller died."

The voice had the five Abcurses on their feet in a single beat of my heart. They were positioned in front of me and their mother, backs rigid with tense muscles.

Jumping up off the couch, I peeked my face between Rome and Coen's arms, and a familiar god came into sight. *Abil.*

"What are you doing here?" Adeline asked, stepping around her sons to stand before the God of Trickery.

Abil shrugged, his purple robes shifting across his broad shoulders. "I came to tell you that Staviti has called a meeting of all the gods, at the crest of the sun this afternoon. He wishes to discuss the new protocols for Betas. He wants the worlds back in order."

It felt like Minatsol was so far removed from my current world, but I still had Cyrus checking on Emmy for me. I knew that she was safe—though he hadn't reported about the rest of Blesswood. I had no idea what was going on back there. I expected that things were going to be rough while the sols tried to exert their dominance. Dwellers were rebelling, servers were attacking, gods were acting out of character. Elowin had been right when she had told me that I was upsetting a balance that could destroy everything.

She had been right, but I couldn't help but feel that the worlds needed some upsetting. Things hadn't been functioning well for a long time. The old way only worked for a small percentage of the population. I hated to think of everyone who was being caught up in this anarchy.

"When you say everyone is called for this meeting ..." Adeline distracted me from my worried thoughts.

Abil nodded. "Yes, every single god must attend." He turned to his sons. "There's no hiding from this, you need to go and deal with whatever Staviti has planned. He won't try anything with all of us there, especially Adeline." His eyes flicked across to her. "But we need to know what he has planned, and there is only one person he will possibly give that information to."

The goddess in the room let out a breathy sigh, before she schooled her face back into pure, calm perfection. "I will see what I can find out. We will protect our family." She smiled at me. "Every single member of it."

My chest got tight and I struggled to suck in my next breath of air as I tried to make sense of the emotional overload I was experiencing. There had been something just before that too, something that Abil had said ...

"What the hell is a soul-bond?" My words seemed

extra loud in the silence that followed Adeline's statement, but I wasn't letting anyone leave this room without an answer.

Because I could totally stop them, I thought wryly.

Adeline spoke first. "It's a rare connection that only gods can share. It's rare because we don't like to share our power or energy with anyone, we're greedy that way. A soul-bond ties you to someone, giving you access to their energy and life-force. Abil believes that the link you share with my sons has transformed into something deeper. More permanent. Something that cannot be broken in death."

No one around me looked to be worried, but for some reason I felt like freaking out. *Unbreakable.* That was ... a big deal. Like *big* big deal. What if we all got sick of each other one sun-cycle? What if I tripped and headbutted Yael in the bal—

"Breathe, Will." Rome's huge hands were on my shoulders, his thumbs lifting to trace gently across my cheeks.

"Did you all know about this?" I asked, still breathless.

Five heads shook, and I suddenly felt terrible because none of them appeared to be upset, and I was clearly having a breakdown. I'd been tied to them for so long now that I couldn't imagine my life without them, but in the back of my mind I had been operating under the knowledge that Cyrus would be able to break the bond if we needed him to.

"That's why I don't have to be near any of you now, but I can still always feel my connection to you," I said slowly. "It has nothing to do with the semanight stone."

Abil gave me a look that was similar to the way I imagined he stared at a bug. "You should consider yourself absolutely blessed to be tied to my sons. There is no other in any world like them. You need to start learning your place, dweller."

THREE

I was still processing this new development when Abil gave his next command.

"You know what you have to do."

He then strode out of the residence, only pausing halfway through the doorway, looking back at Siret.

"I'll get it done," Siret replied, nodding once.

He didn't look particularly excited; his face was utterly blank, his arms hanging down by his sides and his posture casual. He looked so utterly *unexcited* that I started to grow suspicious. The only time Siret looked like he wasn't up to something was when he was up to something *big*.

The other guys all began to stir into motion as Abil left. They stood and muttered to each other, Coen and Yael crowding their mother and arguing over the details of what sounded like a plan of action on how to extract information out of Staviti. Adeline looked like a woman who was very good at pretending to listen. She was nodding and making small sounds of understanding at all the right moments, while expertly examining the sleeve of her robe. I was pretty sure that she had a plan figured out before they even started arguing, but she was trying to be sensitive and humour them. *Or* she knew that they weren't going to entertain any plan but their own.

Well ... she wasn't wrong about that.

As for me, I was fixated on Siret.

Mostly because Siret was fixated on me.

Whatever his father had told him, it had something to do with me, because he had turned his gaze to me almost immediately after Abil left and hadn't shifted it since. Rome was standing just behind me, his hand low on the curve of my back. I had no idea when he had put it there—even though that was something I probably should have noticed. I had probably been too busy having a staring contest with Siret, but now I was completely aware of the big hand burning through my robes. I couldn't actually see him, since I was still turned toward Siret, but I could hear him grumbling things that might have passed as contributions to Coen and Yael's discussion, so he must have been turned to face them.

"What did Abil mean?" I asked Siret. "Why do you have a secret mission that nobody else has? And why are you staring at me?"

Siret grinned, and the others stopped talking for a click.

"He's supposed to disguise you," Rome said, turning so that more of his body heat fell across my back. "So that we can bring you to the meeting."

"Disguise me as what?" I asked, growing a little bit nervous.

"Anything." Siret shrugged, claiming the distance between us in a single, casual step, stopping in front of me. His hands lifted to my cheeks, tilting my head up to his. "Just as long as Staviti doesn't recognise you."

"I could be a tree," I blurted, without thinking. Siret's eyes were close. Way too close. He was so close I was blurting things about trees and thinking about kissing him.

"Trees don't move." His smile had grown. "We need you to stick with us. That requires moving."

"I could be a robe." This had been another idea blurted without thinking. *Okay.* That was a lie. I had thought about it. I had thought about *sticking with them*, which had led me to thinking about *sticking on them*, which had led me to thinking about *stripping them naked and touching everything on them* ... and now I was off-topic. I could admit that.

"You can't be a robe," Rome grunted, in the same voice that a mother used while telling their child that they weren't allowed to stay up past bedtime.

"Way to ruin all my fun," I groused quietly.

"Trust me." Siret grabbed my arm, drawing me away from the others. "This will be fun."

I glanced back at the others, as though I needed to say a proper goodbye to them even though I was only being dragged out of the house to get a disguise ... and not going on a perilous quest that I may never return from. They looked back at me as though they felt the same way, though, so I didn't feel as pathetic when I gave a little finger wave just before I was pulled through the door.

"I could be a bug," I told Siret. "Those are small, and they can move."

"They can also get stepped on," Siret reminded me.

"Yeah but you're not actually turning me into a real bug. So I can't actually get stepped on."

Siret wasn't pulling me into another stone house, as I had expected. Instead, he was leading me into a marble gazebo with vines snaking up the pillars and covering the three stone benches within. There was a small marble fountain at the centre, with a few birds perched on the edge, grooming themselves in the spray of water.

"If I turn you into a bug and someone runs into you, they're going to realise there's an invisible force walking around, and they'll set off an alarm." Siret sat me down on the bench and stood before me, unnecessarily trapping my knees between his legs, as though I would try to escape at some point. "That's not something we want right now."

"What do we want right now?" I asked, crossing my arms over my chest and arching a brow at him.

"We want *subtlety*." He grinned, planting a hand on the back of the bench, beside my right shoulder, bending over until his face was looming over mine.

"And you're the King of Subtlety," I snorted.

"You're going to be a goddess." He ignored my insult altogether.

"Maybe I'm already a goddess," I murmured, pushing up on the seat a little bit and brushing my lips over his with the words.

He grunted, his hand shifting from the back of the bench to my shoulder, his fingers somehow finding their way beneath my robe to the skin of my collarbone.

"A specific goddess," he clarified, his thumb tracing the outside of my collarbone before dipping down further, the rest of his fingers digging into my skin.

"You already know who you're going to disguise me as ..." I was working to keep the accusation out of my tone, to keep my voice soft and breathy as I continued speaking against his lips.

His thumb inched down lower, almost pressing into the top of my breast now, his breath heavier against my lips.

"Yes ..."

"Asshole!" I declared, pushing him away. "What the hell are you assholes hiding from me?"

He groaned, falling back from me and slumping

into the seat opposite mine, putting the fountain between us. "That was mean."

"Who did you pick and what are you hiding?" I demanded.

"Don't be mad okay, Will? It was the only way."

"*What* was the only way?" I was standing now, my hands planted against my hips as I stared down at Siret over the top of the fountain. "Why did you take me out of the room to disguise me? I swear to the gods ..." I was already striding from the Gazebo, ready to storm back into the marble house, but Siret was quicker.

He grabbed me, pulled me back into his chest and lifted me until my feet left the ground. "Calm down, Soldier. Just calm down and I'll explain everything."

"You have until I count to five, *Five*."

"You can't be serious." He froze, his frustrated breath rushing out against the top of my head.

"One," I replied.

"Willa."

"Two."

"For the love of Staviti. Rome taught you this trick, didn't he?"

"Three."

He jostled me further up and then suddenly tipped me over his shoulder, his hand coming down hard on my ass. A loud *smacking* sound assaulted my ears, and I could almost *feel* his sudden grin.

"You hit me," I said, dumbfounded. "On my ass."

"I spanked you," he clarified, "and I'll do it again if you keep counting."

"I can't believe you—"

"Or talking," he added, cutting me off. "In fact, I might do it again regardless of what you do or say."

"I'm going to kick you right in the—" I started threatening, but he cut me off again.

"You can't; you're hanging over my shoulder."

"RIGHT IN THE BALLBAGS!" I shouted out, probably loud enough to alert the next floating platform. "Just as soon as you put me down. So ... put me down!"

"Not a chance." There was a definite smile in his voice, and that was all the warning I got before his hand was coming down on my backside again. Hard. "Now here's what's happening, before you threaten me again. Aros is ... persuading ... a certain goddess to stay on her platform for this meeting, so that you can attend the meeting as her."

"I was pissed off before. Now I'm ... worse. Now I'm dangerous."

"Cute." His hand landed on my ass again, but this time it was soft. A caress. The skin there was burning slightly, and I might have been wiggling against him as though I wanted his hands beneath my robe, but that had nothing to do with anything.

Because I was pissed.

Dangerous.

"So fucking cute," Siret muttered, and then he was

setting me on my feet and pushing me back against the fountain.

I had barely a moment of warning before his mouth was on mine, his fingers moulding to the side of my face. He drew me up, into the kiss, and then sent me down, spiralling with a need that was almost too much to control. His tongue was against mine, claiming my mouth and scattering my attention. I was pressing into him, needing to have every inch of myself covered by him.

I couldn't remember what we had been fighting about anymore.

I couldn't even remember why I was there.

Siret was kissing me and I needed more. I needed the robes gone. I needed skin against skin. I needed ...

I needed ...

"Wait a gods-dammed-click," I growled out, tearing my mouth from his. My breaths were only small, gasping noises. I could feel my face growing hot. I could barely stand. My mind was muddled, but a growing fury was pushing its way back in. "*How* exactly is Aros persuading this goddess to stay on her platform?"

He didn't answer me, he just recaptured my mouth and I was still disorientated enough that he managed to distract me again. In moments of clarity, I decided that whilst finding out Aros's plan was very important and pertinent, I could wait another few clicks.

I opened my lips further and at the same time

pressed my body up and into Siret's. We were so close together, I could feel every hard line. Every muscle. His strength was almost overwhelming, and it reminded me of how very different I was to the Abcurses. A difference I was starting to like ... a lot. Because they might be physically stronger than me, but I had my own strengths, and ... I was not letting any of them get away with their underhanded bullsen shit any longer.

It took every ounce of my strength to push through the fog in my mind and formulate a plan. One which involved me being able to continue this very enjoyable task of kissing one of my boys. I was starting to think I'd do anything to always be kissing one of them.

There was no space between us, so I let one of my hands trail down his side, pushing and gliding across his robes, feeling the lines of his body. Siret made a sound from deep in his throat, and I forgot for a micro-click where I had been going with my plan. His arm was wrapped tightly around me and all I wanted was to taste and breathe in the scent of him.

Plenty of time for this later, I forcefully reminded myself, regaining some of my focus. My hand continued down, over his hip and along the top of a rock-hard thigh. My centre ached, I wanted him to shift his position and place that thigh between my legs ...

Focus!

My hand snaked between us and just as I was about to wrap my fingers tightly around him, he let out a low laugh against my lips and twisted his body out of reach. I gasped and fell forward, completely missing my mark. We were standing a few inches apart now, our breathing hard, his eyes burning into mine with a glowing intensity.

"How did you know?" I pouted between the deep breathing I was doing.

He laughed again, but those eyes remained at almost full glow. "We're connected, remember? Not to mention your first instinct when you're cornered is to fight dirty ..."

"I only have so much power to use against you," I admitted.

Siret made that noise again, although this time it sounded like it came from even deeper. I stepped into him, needing to feel his body against mine. This time there was no ulterior motive—I clearly couldn't hide my intentions from these five, they knew me too well. Nope, all I wanted was to touch him. He lifted me against his body and I let out a low breath, melting against him.

"You're wrong, you know," he murmured close to my ear.

"Huh?" I had absolutely no idea what he was talking about, my brain was mimicking my body. Both were mush.

"You have more power against us than any other being in the worlds. It's almost scary the things we would do for you, Willa. You never have to worry about

Aros and what he's doing right now. Everything we do is to keep you safe."

"So he's not over on some marble platform seducing a goddess?" I'd been planning to force the information from Siret, but now I hoped he would just tell me.

Our bodies shook as he laughed hard.

"How about I change you first, and then we can go and see," he suggested.

That seemed like a great plan to me, so I nodded, and he pulled back. Just as he was about to set me down, I lifted my upper body and settled my lips against his again. This time it was short and sweet, the kiss just a brief touch of skin before I pulled away.

"That power goes both ways," I told him. "I won't let anyone hurt you five. I promise."

The certainty of that statement came from deep in my ... soul, maybe. There was a ring of finality about it, like a promise that I could and would not break. I didn't know what my new energy was, the one that was lingering just below the surface, but whatever I ended up being, I would use that power to keep my family safe.

Siret didn't say much after that, but his face was different than usual. No less beautiful. No less god-like. There was just a softness there as he cupped my cheeks in his hands, a softness that I hadn't seen before. No laughter, just a lot of emotion.

His energy washed across me; it was similar to the

way it felt when he changed my clothes, but so much stronger. My head went shaky ... almost fuzzy for a moment, and it felt like I was swaying on my feet, even though I knew I wasn't moving. Mild pain rocked over my skin, like he was inflicting a billion little cuts across my body. The very fine kind which took a click to hurt.

Heat grew with that tingling pain, and just when I was worried that it was going to be too much to handle, Siret let out a grumble of annoyance before releasing my face.

"That will do, even though I much prefer you in your original form."

Opening my eyes, I realised that he didn't tower over me quite as much as he had before. So, I was taller. My fingers looked long and slender, and my skin was very pale. Normally I was a golden tan, because I had been outdoors most of my life, but whichever god I was now disguised as had that sort of porcelain perfect skin that didn't have a birth spot or blemish to be seen.

Siret noticed me trying to inspect his disguise, so he led me a little further along the platform, to a section of marble so polished that I could see my reflection in it.

I blinked a few times. "Whoa."

Siret moved closer, standing next to me, both of us reflected in the marble. "You're now Sienna, God of Revelry."

I'd guessed as much. It certainly explained the new

attire I wore, which was very reminiscent of the robes my mother had favoured when she was heading out for the night. White, with a strap on one shoulder, the other bare. It was cut tight across my breasts, half of my very slender waist was showing, and the short skirt swished high on my thighs. I wore flat shoes at least, but they had laces that crisscrossed right up my calves.

"Where are the rest of my clothes?" I demanded.

"This is what she wears," he told me. "We can't have Staviti being suspicious of us yet, so the details have to be exact. We need to figure out what he's up to, first. Let mother work her magic on him."

I knew that wasn't magic in the god sense he was talking about.

"Tell me why Staviti will not be suspicious of ..." I threw a hand out, waving it toward the marble. "All of this."

Sienna had straight, black hair that hung to just above her butt. It was thick and shiny with a fringe cut above dark, rich blue eyes and to-die-for cheek bones. All of the black hair should have clashed with the white skin, but it didn't. She was stunning, exotic, the exact sort of woman that men around the two worlds would fall all over themselves to touch.

I didn't like it. It made me feel insecure, needy, and pathetic. I wanted to rip every strand of her black hair out and that was insane, because this wasn't even really her. It was me ... disguised. Ugh. Stupid men.

Siret seemed to choose his words carefully. "She is

the one god who is overlooked a lot. Treated almost like she's nothing more than a ..."

"Whore?" I guessed as he trailed off.

He nodded, not looking all that happy about it. "Because life is a party for her, she doesn't take things very seriously. That's her power. Revelry. Flitting between whatever she feels like at any given moment, never settling down."

None of that sounded any different to the rest of the gods. They were always having parties, randomly killing dwellers like my mother and disposing of their servers when they sneezed at the wrong time. Sienna didn't seem any different.

I was starting to feel a little sorry for her, though. They called my mum a whore in our village, and I always thought it was an unfair label, considering she wasn't having sex on her own. The men on Minatsol never seemed to get the same labels, and I had no doubt it was going to be the same in the god world.

"Ready to go and find Aros?" he asked me, and I remembered that the Seduction God was off doing something to keep the real Sienna from attending Staviti's call.

Spinning away from my reflection, I nodded jerkily. "Yes. Take me there now, and don't you dare tell him I'm coming."

I'd work on my trust issues another sun-cycle, right now I needed to see with my own eyes what they had planned. Siret pulled me in, but his touch wasn't the same. It was a little colder, a little more distant. He wasn't holding me against him, but simply ... holding onto me. I glanced up at his face, but he wouldn't meet my eyes. I wound my arms around him to get closer and caught his cringe. He didn't like my new appearance.

He turned on the spot and everything blinked out of existence, materialising around me again a micro-click later in the form of yet another marble platform. This one was more cluttered, with furniture strewn everywhere—both whole and broken—along with contained fire pits scattered about and sparkly matter flitting through the air, collecting on the marble ground. It looked as though a party had torn through the platform and disappeared, leaving behind only chaos. There was a single stone house directly in the middle of the platform, surrounded by odd-looking statues and animal ornaments. My mouth fell open a little as I gazed up at the design of the residence. It was in the style of the skyreachers back in Minatsol, with level upon level stacked up toward the sky—except *unlike* the Minatsol skyreachers, each level was a different shape, making the design impossible to achieve without some kind of magic.

The first level was a simple square shape, with windows and doors. The second was perfectly round, and the third was a perfect triangle. The fourth was a long, thin rectangle, barely high enough for one of the Abcurses to stand in, but long enough to fit a crowd. It was difficult to tell the shapes of the others, beyond the long platform, but I could count eight levels in total.

"Holy god-balls," I breathed out, taking in the beautiful monstrosity.

"God-balls?" Siret questioned, pulling me toward the residence. "Why not, I guess. Try not to touch anything, Sienna likes her pranks and illusions, even if they're at the expense of someone losing a hand."

"That's not very nice."

"She's not a very nice goddess. A god once tried to feed one of her *longnecks*—" he motioned to one of the pink bird statues out the front of her residence. It had a long, slender neck, topped by a tiny, mean-looking face with a sharp orange beak. "He thought the bird was real," Siret continued, pushing open the door and pulling me into the first level. "It grew a giant snapper jaw and took his arm clean off. There was blood everywhere. I've never seen Sienna more pleased by anything. She couldn't stop laughing. When people started slipping over the blood, I thought she would piss herself."

I snorted, but quickly tried to mask it. That was *not* funny, not even a little bit. Except for the part where—

"Nope," Siret broke into my thoughts. "There was nothing funny about it. I was having a perfectly decent night until that happened. The gods didn't know what to do with all the blood—metals and such are usually unable to pierce our skin, unless we've been severely weakened by Minatsol. Sienna had to especially enchant the prank with some of Death's magic so that it would break the barrier of our skin and draw blood. Everyone was freaking out about it. They all tore their robes off, but kept getting covered in blood. I think she must have come up with some kind of bleeding enchantment because I'm sure that amount of blood was unnatural."

I was standing still in the middle of the room, Siret two steps ahead, tugging on my arm. He turned around when he realised I wasn't walking, and took in my expression.

"That's disgusting," I finally said. "No wonder you didn't want to touch me. I'm a maniac. A freaking blood-crazy maniac."

"Technically, *Sienna* is a blood-crazy maniac," he corrected me. "You're just ... a normal maniac."

I shook my head to dislodge the images in my brain, casting my eyes about the room. The inside looked very similar to the outside: random and weird trinkets and pieces of furniture placed carelessly about. Different coloured robes had also been discarded here and there, some of them torn and some of them folded. Plates of food had been left out, and many *many* pitchers of drink were standing at one of the tables. The room was also devoid of people, just as the outside had been.

"Is everyone at the meeting already?" I asked, as we headed for the stairs.

"Yes, that's why Aros needed to leave immediately."

We climbed up to the second level, but Siret quickly stepped in front of me before I could clear the top stair, blocking my view of the room.

"What have you done?" he asked, his voice weirdly toneless.

"It wasn't me," Aros's voice answered, before I could open my mouth. "I found her like this."

I tried to push past Siret, but he was faster, tucking me behind him again. I was just about to make another escape attempt when his story from earlier came back to me, forcing me to hesitate.

"Oh gods," I stopped, taking a step backwards. "There's blood everywhere, isn't there?"

"Let her see," Aros spoke up, as Siret turned to face me. "She's as much a part of this as we are."

"She's not," Siret replied, his eyes on me, a frown weighing heavily at the sides of his perfect mouth. "She didn't know what she was getting into, she didn't know what stealing the cup would mean."

These were too many riddles for me, so I sidled closer to Siret, plastering a confused look over my face, and then quickly slipped past him, evading the arm that he shot out to catch me. I paused after clearing the top step, shock forcing me to lock into place. There was a woman sitting in a wide, high-backed chair, a set of chains binding her wrists and ankles. Her hair was long and shiny, an ebony curtain that fell over her front to tickle her lap. Her skin was sickly pale, her eyes wide and unseeing.

"Is she d-dead?" I stuttered, when the goddess made no movement. "I mean, dead...er?"

"Worse," Aros replied, the same frown on his face as the one marking Siret. "Her soul has been separated, locked into torment in another realm."

"What realm? Minatsol?"

"Not a realm in the sense of another world, as you know Minatsol and Topia to be," Siret began to explain, stepping up beside me, "but more like a pocket of existence where only bad things exist."

"Like hell?" I flicked my attention from Sienna to Siret, to Aros, and back again. My horror over this situation was a slow build, starting somewhere in the base of my stomach and slowly travelling to my mind.

This wasn't good.

A goddess was dead.

Goddesses weren't supposed to die. They were supposed to be *un*dead, immortal.

"Not quite like the myth of hell." Aros stepped to my other side, his fingers reaching through mine, locking our hands together strongly. "It's a prison-realm where things get trapped, and because they're trapped, they're in torment. There's nothing there but torment and the inability to escape it. That's where her soul is, and once it's been sent there, we can't get it back. She's as good as gone."

"But gods can't die," I spluttered, panic building. This wasn't a good sign for me. This meant that I could die again—probably *would* die again.

"Not without the assistance of Crowe—the God of Death, or the Creator," Siret agreed, motioning toward the chains that bound Sienna.

I glanced down, noting the dark metal, the tiny inscriptions that covered each link.

"But Crowe helped her with pranks." I sounded petulant, upset about people and relationships I had never even encountered. Crowe and Sienna were supposed to be friends. Friends didn't send their friends' souls into torment realms. It should have been the first rule of friendship.

"You're actually right." Siret bent down to inspect the shackles. "They were friends, and they have been for hundreds of life-cycles. It would have taken something significant to turn Death against her."

"The cup," Aros actually sounded panicked. "Rau figured it out, somehow."

"We need to check the vault," Siret agreed, standing and taking my arm.

Without further warning, the room was disappearing around me and I was being pulled from the platform and into a dark space flickering with the barest hints of orange light. The ground was smooth beneath my feet, but the air felt heavier. I could feel the two guys pressing in against me from either side, and when they started moving toward the light, I followed alongside them. As our surroundings became more illuminated, I started to realise that we were in some sort of cave again—I recognised the dank, heavy feeling of the air. It was a different sort of cave to the others, though. This one was coated in marble, with flat marble floors and a marble ceiling. The walls were still stone, but they had been treated in some way, turning them smooth and shiny, almost giving them a shimmer. Alcoves had been cut into the stone walls to house torches, with each alcove appearing closer together the further in we travelled. Aros stopped at a bench set beneath one of the alcoves, our tunnel now well-lit, and bent to work one of the planks loose from the seat, pulling it up and out. There was a tiny compartment set beneath that plank, with a single golden key laying inside.

"Sienna is a little dramatic at times," Siret explained, as we followed Aros further down the hallway to a set of vaults set into the stone wall.

He moved to the last one, but the key dropped from his hand before we even reached it. The door was hanging open by an inch. He pulled it wide, spilling light into the shadowy depths. Inside, there was a blade set into a holder, propped up so that it looked as though it were standing on its own tip.

"Fucking Rau," Aros growled, his body lined with tension.

"The cup is gone?" I was pretty sure it was gone, since Aros was standing in front of a cup-less vault, saying 'fucking Rau', but I needed clarification before I could get angry.

"Yes," Siret confirmed.

"Fucking Rau," I growled, before pausing for a click. "How do we know that Rau did this?"

Aros was still staring at the knife. "This is a message. He thinks you're dead, not *un*dead, just plain dead. He wants revenge."

"Why does he need to torture Sienna and steal the cup to get revenge? Why does he need revenge on you five at all?"

"He knows we care about the cup—otherwise why would we have snuck back into Topia to steal it? Why would we have taken this much effort to hide it? And he clearly thought that torturing Sienna to get it would be a good message to send us."

"But why does he need revenge on you five? Cyrus is the one who killed me."

"Under his apparent orders. He wanted you dead so that you would join him. You died, but didn't join him."

"And that's ... *your* fault?" I was confused.

"The curse was meant for us. You got in the way and were somehow affected by it." Aros slammed the vault door and moved back to me. "We treated you as one of our own from then on. We protected you, treated you as something special, something precious. We basically told him that the curse succeeded in turning you into the Beta, as it was supposed to turn one of us into the Beta. We fooled him—not deliberately, but I am sure this is how he's twisted it. We made him believe that you were the Beta, we made him turn his attention to you while we stole the cup and hid out on Minatsol, and it was all for nothing. He has no Beta, and we're back in Topia. We're no longer weak enough to infect with another curse. His whole plan has been ruined, and it's our fault. Now he wants revenge."

Aros shook his head, his hand lifting up as though he would touch my cheek, but he dropped it again, his eyes moving up to Siret's, over my shoulder. "Can we have our girl back now? Whoever did this is going to know that Sienna shouldn't be at the gathering."

Siret didn't answer with words, but I could feel his fingers on the back of my neck, and the trickle of his magic passed through me. I didn't need to pull my hands up before my face to make sure that I was a healthy, golden-brown again. I could feel how my two guys suddenly pressed closer, how their hands suddenly reached for me and their heat suddenly surrounded me. It was the only confirmation that I needed. I was me again.

FOUR

I was seduction personified. The *meaning* of seduction. Seduction was me. I was seduction.

"Make her stop," Aros begged. "She's going to give us up. Look at her. She keeps doing that weird thing with her hands and talking about how she's seduction personified in her head. Nobody is going to buy that."

"You should stop," Siret agreed, watching me with a smile that said *you really shouldn't stop.*

"Seduction," I agreed while pointing at him, my index finger extended and my thumb sticking up: my fingers were arrows and I was shooting Seduction at him.

"It needs to stop," Aros insisted. "She might *look* like me, but I do *not* act like that."

In fairness, I'd never seen Aros make little arrows with his fingers and try to shoot people with Seduction, but *he really should look into it*, I decided.

I was high on the power of looking like the Seduction God. We had decided that the best way to disguise me would be to leave one of the guys behind and have me appear as them. Aros had opted to stay behind, and Siret had given me his form. And his ego.

"Okay fine, I'm finished playing," I lied. "We can go now."

"She's lying. You need to keep an eye on her," Aros warned, as Siret took my arm.

He held me as though he didn't really know how to touch me, just like when I had been disguised as Sienna.

"I'll behave," I promised, as Siret shook his head.

A moment before we disappeared, I made sure to shoot Aros with my Seduction finger-arrow one more time, and I caught his grimace just before the marble cave melted from view. We appeared at the very back of yet another marble platform, with pillars set along each of the square sides to cage us in. The pillars were so high that I had trouble actually seeing where they ended and where the clouds began.

The marble of this platform was shot through with maroon and blue colours, but the platform was otherwise bare of foliage or decoration, barring the display at the other end. It seemed to be a procession of statues, each one almost several stories high, made from the same blue and maroon marbled stone as the platform itself. The statues, I saw, were of eleven faintly-recognisable figures—Staviti in the middle, with a woman on his right, and a man I recognised as Abil on his left. I turned my attention back to the statue of the woman again, realising that it was Pica, looking just as she had when I'd seen her in the walls of the pantera cave that Leden had taken me into. There were eight more figures in total, off to the sides of the statues of Pica and Abil, respectively—three more women and five more men, including Rau, who was on the far left side, facing away from the others.

The Original Gods: all ten of them, with their creator, Staviti.

There was a raised marble dais directly beneath the statue of Staviti, elevating a man over the heads of the gods and goddesses that had gathered on the platform. I assumed that it was Staviti, even though I couldn't see him very clearly. He was wearing white robes that had the same pattern of marbled blue and maroon that I could see everywhere.

He was so important that he got three colours.

"How will we find the others?" I attempted to ask quietly. I wasn't used to my new voice yet, so it came out as a growl instead of a whisper.

Siret turned to look at me with raised eyebrows. "Quit growling at me. Can you feel them nearby?"

I closed my eyes, trying to feel for the connection that bound me to the Abcurses. It flickered there, on and off, muddled—possibly because of Siret's Trickery coating my body, or possibly because of the press of people all around us.

"I think they're over here somewhere," I growled again.

Siret sighed. "Okay, lead the way."

I started to move through the crowd, but I slowed down when I realised that I wasn't jostling anybody. People were moving out of the way for me. People were ... *oh shit, they're staring at me.* I glanced down at my hands, but they were still strong, perfect golden man-hands.

Did Siret give me a girl-head?

"Didn't give you a girl-head," he muttered from behind me. "You still have Aros's head, keep walking, Soldier."

Well then why is everyone—oh. Oh.

"Seduction," I growled, shooting a nearby goddess with my Finger Arrow of Seduction.

She seemed a little unsteady on her feet, having to lean against the woman next to her for support. I thought that was hilarious, so I took aim and shot my Finger Arrow of Seduction again, at the next woman, adding a wink for good measure. She giggled, swaying on her feet.

"Quit that," Siret complained, reaching over me to slap down my weapon.

I didn't get a chance to fight about my right to seduce *whoever I wanted to* because as soon as I opened my mouth, I caught sight of Rome. I motioned to Siret and started walking faster, making my way over to the others, just as the masses of people around us began to quieten—Staviti must have been making some kind of motion up on the dais.

Rome glanced over and caught my eyes as I neared. He moved past me without pause, and then past Siret next, and then beyond us, searching for someone. Me, presumably. Or Sienna.

"Which one is she?" he asked me, as I pulled up at his side. The others—Adeline, Abil, Coen, and Yael—were quiet, waiting for my response. No other person had joined our huddle, and Rome seemed to notice that, because his eyes grew dark, narrowing. "*Where* is she?"

"Right here," I growled out, raising my hand.

"Rocks?" Yael asked, staring at me with slight disgust in his features.

"Seducti—" I began to answer, but Siret cut me off, quickly capturing my finger-arrows before I had a chance to shoot them.

"That's her," he assured the others. "Seduction stayed behind. I'll have to fill you in later."

"No more talking." Adeline's voice was cool, calm, but it held a warning. "He will hear."

I didn't have to ask who *he* was, because she turned to the dais immediately after her warning, and the robed man began to speak.

"My children." His voice projected clearly, his arms splayed out wide in a welcoming posture. He didn't look exactly like I had expected, despite the statues I had seen of him. His forehead was broader, and the statues had given him lines of age and wisdom that didn't exist. His lips were also broad, stern, unsmiling. His hair was dark, kept short enough to tame any wayward curls.

"My fellows!" he boomed. The second greeting suggested a distinction between the collection of immortals, but I couldn't tell where the distinction was, until Staviti bent his head in a nod directed at a specific woman.

She was ethereal, draped in magenta robes, a crimson veil covering her curls. She nodded back to him, her eyes cool. She seemed like a contradiction: both regal and delicate, precious and cold. It was Pica; the Goddess of Love.

"I have called this gathering to announce that the sols able to pass into godhood have become an endangered species. Over the life-cycles, less and less of the mortals have been able to ascend to Topia. They grow strong—strong enough to take their place in this heavenly realm—but fewer and fewer have proven themselves able to pass through. Their strength flees in the immortalisation process. I fear that the overpopulation of Topia has left no room for further ascension. There are no new *lesser* god positions available anymore, which means the god-positions we have now are the only ones we will ever have in Topia." He paused, briefly but dramatically. "There has never been a third—only a God and their Beta, never a third with the same energy. This leads me to believe that the only way for a sol to successfully ascend to Topia now would be for a Beta to die and free up their position—"

He paused as an outbreak of murmuring spread through the platform. The gods and goddesses didn't sound happy about his news. After a click, he raised his hand, cutting off their concerned swell of noise.

"I am not implying that anyone will be killed to allow further ascension. I am only bringing a private observation into the light. On the few occasions that Beta Gods *have* been unburdened from their immortal ties, a mortal has almost immediately taken their place —many of you will know this to be true. I am not suggesting that Betas need to be cleared, I am instead proposing that we create yet another institution on Minatsol, a fourth Academy where only the very best, the very strongest sol in each of the power-groups be invited to study. We must make this process more exclusive, the training more intensive."

"Why don't we simply separate," a voice spoke up, softer than Staviti, but just as clear. A female, though I couldn't see her. "Leave them be and announce that Topia is full."

"The realms are co-dependant," Staviti explained, a frown in his voice. His disapproval was tangible. "As time passes, the relationship between the realms becomes even more tightly interwoven. Minatsol will exist without Topia, but Topia cannot exist without Minatsol, it is where this land draws its energy and magic—"

"It's *what*?" I hissed out, before one of the guys managed to slap a hand over my mouth. Abil glanced at me disapprovingly, and I was sure that even Staviti paused for a moment. I hadn't realised until then, but there was a stillness in his audience that bordered on unnatural, fearful even. I spoke in my mind instead.

I thought Topia was supposed to feed Minatsol. I thought this *place was supposed to be the rich and magical place, giving scraps to our crappy world?*

Four sets of eyes turned my way, but I could tell that they didn't have an answer for me. Coen gave the barest shake of his head and I turned my attention back to whatever Staviti was saying.

"There are pathways between the worlds—faucets, if you will, that can be turned on or off. For centuries, the faucets have been flowing into Topia from the motherworld, Minatsol. When I ascended to this realm after my death in Minatsol, there was nothing for me. I reached for Minatsol and created a bridge. It fed into this place we now call home, and since then I have created many bridges, many faucets. This world grows, prospers, and in time, Minatsol regenerates."

It hasn't regenerated at all, I thought, my eyes narrowing on Staviti.

"If the mortals are told that they no longer have any hope of ascending to Topia, they will no longer reach for us. Though they may not realise it, the bridges I have created can be torn down, the faucets can be turned off. If they no longer rely on us—if they no longer worship us and sacrifice to us—the links between our realms will narrow. It is their constant striving to reach for Topia that allows the connection to be so strong, that allows me to draw the resources from their world."

"So we will attempt to break the natural order?" a man spoke up, sounding dubious. "We will attempt to make them strong enough that Topia will have to accept a second Beta to each god?"

"I have broken the natural order before," Staviti said, his tone condescending. "I am perfectly capable of doing it again. The strongest mortals will be taken from each of the Academies and brought to my newest, greatest institution: Champions Peak. The site of this Academy is sacred, to both the mortals and to me—it is the location of the first bridge I ever created between our world and theirs—"

"A pocket," Coen whispered, his voice so low I almost couldn't catch it.

"I created a temple and told my surviving mortal relatives to worship me there, to bring others and spread the word. In the beginning, my realm, Topia, would not allow me to create others of my kind, and it would not allow me to visit Minatsol for long without weakening me. With the bridge created, and with my family spreading the word of my ascension as a god, things began to change. Minatsol began to give, and Topia to take. Soon, I was able to create a new, powerful family, and they were able to exist in Topia.

Together we have thrived, we have built this world to something which is strong and proud. My family and I have created a platform for further ascension, an opportunity for immortality that *each of you* have been gifted with. I fear that if the connection were severed, those who have ascended since me may be immediately rejected."

I understood what he was saying as far as the theory of it was concerned, but I wasn't sure exactly what to *believe.* I knew he was lying about Minatsol regenerating itself, so what else was he lying about?

Did he really need the magic of Minatsol to fuel Topia?

Did he really want the sols to grow stronger? To make it to Topia?

"The Betas of each differing energy group will be expected to teach at Champions Peak." Staviti's decisive voice cut through my thoughts, forcing my head to turn toward my guys. I knew for certain that Siret was a Beta, but I didn't know about the others. I wanted desperately to ask them then and there, but Staviti was already speaking again, drowning out my question.

"Those Betas will be required to remain in Minatsol for the next life-cycle: a sacrifice you will all be making—" his voice boomed over the voices starting to swell in shocked protest— "for the good of Topia. This afterlife has been a gift from the land itself, but now the land must be repaid. The Betas of Topia will have exactly one sun-cycle to prepare for their relocation, and then they will settle themselves into their new lodgings at Champions Peak. A pocket has been opened directly into the new academy, and it will remain open for one sun-cycle only. Train your sols like your afterlives depend on it, because they do. At the end of this life-cycle, I will host an ascension ceremony in Minatsol. Every single sol will be sacrificed in the old temple, and if any prove themselves too weak to ascend to Topia, their Beta-teacher will be executed by Death."

This information was met with an outcry, but Staviti did not stick around to listen to it. He was gone in the next click, as a sorrowful wail rose up from the crowd. One of the goddesses was crying. Loudly.

"Can he *do* that?" I asked, my borrowed voice choked-up and fearful. I hadn't realised that Staviti held so much power. I'd *heard* that he was the all-powerful, the all-knowing, the all-*everything*, but threatening to kill off half of the immortal population as punishment for being unable to reverse the apparent natural order of the worlds was ...

"He's insane," Coen answered in a terse whisper, finishing my thought for me. "But he's the Creator. He can do anything he wants. We need to get out of here."

"But ..." I stuttered. "But he said that he wasn't implying anyone would have to die, and then he just said everyone was going to DIE!"

Rome wrapped his hand around my—or Aros's—

mouth, cutting me off before I got any louder. He shook his head once. I worked to calm myself. Locking my panic down, I finally noticed the gods around us were starting to stir in a big way. None of us wanted to be caught in the crossfire of a mass-god-tantrum; Yael grabbed a hold of my arm, a little rougher than usual, though I felt no pain inside Aros's body. He tugged me into blackness, and I found myself back in Adeline's room, the others blinking into existence around me. I wanted to ask if I would now have the magical 'pop on and off marble platforms at will' power that the rest of them had, but I was aware that it wasn't exactly a good time for my random questions.

"What happened?" Aros demanded, standing up from one of the couches.

Siret's hand landed on the back of my neck, and I could feel his magic trickling away from me. I knew the moment I was myself again, because his touch changed. It became softer, his palm settling against my skin, curving around the sides of my neck, pulling me backward and into his body. Yael, who must have decided that he wasn't okay with where I was standing, reached out while Coen started to detail Staviti's announcement to Aros.

I was tugged against another hard chest, Yael's arm angling across my front, his hand settling into the dip of my waist, his chin resting against the top of my head. Siret shot him a look before turning to focus on Coen's recounting.

"What does this mean?" Aros asked, his expression shocked.

Adeline appeared then, Abil right beside her.

Family meeting time.

"He's sending all five of you to Minatsol again," Abil announced, a growl riding his words.

"Six," Adeline corrected, her eyes on me.

"We could keep her here," Abil countered.

"No," five deep, angry voices snapped.

A short silence followed that sudden outburst, and then all eyes seemed to settle on me, waiting.

It was almost funny that they didn't know what my answer was.

"Of course we know what your answer is," Rome grunted, turning his eyes back to his parents as he answered my thought. "She's coming with us. She will attend as the strongest Chaos sol."

"You can't decide that." I frowned. "And that will be announcing to Rau that I'm still alive."

"The only person it's going to negatively affect is Cyrus, and Cyrus can look after himself," Aros answered, sounding uncharacteristically hard-hearted. "Rau will think it was all an illusion, that Cyrus betrayed him. Because as far as he knows, you never ascended to Topia."

"Did I actually *ascend* to Topia though?" I asked. "And how are you going to pass me off as the strongest Chaos sol?"

Abil laughed. "Every other Chaos sol is dead.

Staviti saw to that. You're the only candidate in the running."

"Shouldn't I be running *away* then?" I spun on Abil. "Before Staviti kills me too?"

"There is no way in the worlds that you have escaped his notice." Abil sounded condescending, but also a little annoyed that he was having to explain this to me. "He knows more than he lets on. He sees more. Hears more. If he wanted you dead, you would be dead."

"I *am* dead." I threw up my hands. "I mean ... I *am dead*, right?"

I glanced between them all as they stared right back at me, before Abil made a movement for something at his belt.

"Don't even think about it," Adeline snapped, her hand moving rapidly to cover his.

"Think about what?" I asked, when it seemed like nobody else was going to.

"He was going to stab you," Rome replied. "To make sure you're dead."

None of my guys looked particularly angry, but I noticed that they had all moved a few steps closer to me.

"And you *are* dead," Coen added. "We saw you die. We felt it, just as we felt you come back to life."

I wasn't sure if I should be happy or saddened by those words. It was starting to feel like death was a relative term. Everything felt pretty normal about me now. What happened to the other dwellers when they died? The ones who didn't become servers. I already knew what happened to the servers. The banishment cave. That place still gave me a deep-in-my-gut bad feeling, especially the part where I'd promised to free them and never had. It was an unfinished job that would probably haunt me forever.

My head hurt.

"It's going to be fine, Will," Rome told me. "We'll do as Staviti asks, because we need more time to figure out exactly what he's planning. I really don't believe he'll kill off all the Betas. Sometimes he uses big threats to … encourage us."

I glanced between all of the grim faces. "You don't think that he's actually looking for the strongest sols? That maybe this is all just an excuse so he can send the Betas to Minatsol for a life-cycle, because this is where they will grow extremely weak—ready for execution?"

Their expressions didn't change, but I could tell that they were thinking. Probably weighing up their answers so that they didn't scare the undead life out of me.

Adeline was the one to finally answer. "Staviti is about keeping his own power base secure. He is the only one who isn't able to have a Beta—he is accustomed to being the strongest, to having the power of creation at his fingertips, and his fingertips alone."

And that meant what exactly?

Adeline had dodged my actual question, and the

cryptic response was only serving to freak me out more. *What sort of things would Staviti do to ensure he kept that power*? The strongest god in the worlds had a new agenda, and it involved my guys.

We had to figure it out and fast.

It was decided—again, not by me—that I would just show up with the Abcurses at Champions Peak. *Willa Knight, one Chaos Beta at your service.* Cyrus would probably lose his shit when he saw me not hiding in his cave like I had been ordered to do, but it'd be too late for him to do anything about it by then. Personally, I was a big fan of Siret's theory that Rau would be less inclined to attack us at the peak, since the situation was being closely monitored by Staviti. *Okay,* I was the only one actually worried about an attack. The Abcurses were more of the 'bring it on' and 'Rau is a whiny bitch' opinion. Their lack of concern would really worry me ... if I had time to add another worry to my already full load.

When we arrived at the pocket that Staviti had opened, it was like a shimmering, translucent mirror. He had set it up at a central gathering platform that had apparently been used for smaller, less formal meetings. Each Beta was given a time to go across, so that we didn't all crash into the place at once.

At our assigned time, the Abcurses checked to

make sure that it wasn't being monitored—while I hid beneath a cloak that could have wrapped five times around me—and then the six of us stepped through, one-by-one, reappearing on the other side within only a few moments of each other. *My kind of travel.*

"So, this is the new place ..." I trailed off, my eyes running over it one more time. Champions Peak was aptly named for its location. It was a huge residence, spreading out across the top of the cliff it rested upon. The main building was made from a white, shiny stone, square in shape with two towering turrets facing the sea. The building itself was small, though still large enough to hold all of the people called to the Peak.

I turned toward the view, shrugging off my cloak at the same time. Beneath, I was wearing a tight-fitting, blue dress: the top showing sections of plain blue netting, revealing hints of the skin beneath. Small brass tokens had been sewn into the neckline, making this the most elaborately expensive dress that I had ever worn. The skirt had been made up of sections of thin, silk-like material, allowing slits all the way up the legs so that I could easily run or fight in the outfit. As it turned out, Rome had been *really* into the whole fashion-design thing. He had planned the dress with a single-minded determination, stating that it was 'his turn' to put his colour on me.

I smiled as I stared out over the cliff, toward the water. The weather was colder so far up in the sky, but it didn't deter me from wanting to run—okay, probably trip—down all of those hundreds of steps carved into the side of the cliff to meet the crashing water far below.

"Some parts of Minatsol are so beautiful," I murmured again, the guys standing in a line on either side of me. "And others ..." I turned around, to let my gaze rest on the desolation behind us. It was nothing but parched land: desert-red dirt, scraggly vegetation, and bare, cracked rocks.

How could such beauty and life exist side by side with so much desolation? "This is how I see Minatsol and Topia." I voiced my sudden realisation aloud. "One half has too much, the other not enough." The worlds needed to learn to share, and so did the gods watching over them.

"Gods don't share." Coen, as always, brought down the blunt truth.

"We should head inside now, Soldier," Siret interrupted me before I could lecture the lot of them about why sharing was good. *For everyone involved.* "It's time to put our game faces on, because we're about to enter the political arena. And this time there will be a lot of gods to deal with."

I nodded, straightening, mentally preparing myself as best I could. I had a blue dress with tokens on it. I could do this. Maybe it had been the white robes holding me back in Topia. The Abcurses didn't have their robes on anymore either, even though the few other gods we'd spied upon going through the shimmery doorway had been fully robed. I loved that my guys didn't give a fuck about the rules. We all wanted to stick it to Staviti in whatever way we could.

There was also the fact that while robes were extremely comfortable, they couldn't handle any kind of draught, and up on the cliff, the breezes were quite intense. On the other hand, the flowy material gave really easy access ...

"Focus, Willa-toy," Yael warned me, his eyes swirling as they met mine.

Aros's laughter was warm. "Please, for the love of sanity. Keep your focus so we can keep ours."

That was a great plan, I was going to work on that plan immediately. No more naked-under-robes thoughts starting from ... *right now*. Low groans sounded, and then I was being ushered forward toward the gates. The moment that Rome placed a hand on the white structure, it swung open silently. We followed the stone path leading up to the main entrance. The building appeared to be very open-aired, patches of sunlight streaming in around us. There wasn't much else in the first courtyard, so we continued on. There was no sign of any of the other Betas now, but I could hear voices as we moved through to the next room.

It was darker inside the next part, the roof completely closed in, and the room was full. The gods had spread themselves out, taking most of the space while the sols stood in a small huddle on the left side of the room, eyeing off the powerful beings around them.

When the Abcurses entered the room, eyes swung in their direction, and I tried to continue my very causal walking, even though I sort of wanted to hide with the sols.

"She doesn't belong here, she's a dirt-dweller," an aqua-robed male snapped as we passed close to him. "This is for Betas and sols only, and she sure doesn't look like she's serving."

Rome's hand shot out, wrapping around the other's throat, hoisting him up into the air. "I won't catch you saying those words ever again." His words were low and controlled. He could have been discussing the weather ... while killing a god. "If you have a problem with that, I can make the ascension of a new Aviary Beta happen right now."

The Aviary Beta looked like he wanted to talk, but unfortunately the crushing of his throat was preventing words from emerging. Stepping forward, I placed my hand on Rome's biceps. "I think he's got the point," I murmured.

Rome's eyes shot down to mine—they were dark and stormy. He was not happy, and that meant bad things for anyone who pissed him off. I lifted one eyebrow to show him I wasn't scared. *Much.*

With the slightest curling of his lips, he opened his fingers and let the god fall to the ground. The Aviary Beta gasped over and over, hands clutching his throat as he struggled on the floor. This was ignored by the Abcurses, who continued to lead me through the crowd, heading toward the front of the room. I glanced back once to see aqua robes still curled up on the floor, and I hoped Rome hadn't done too much permanent damage.

There was a stage near the front of the large room —it didn't seem to hold much else and was freakily reminding me of the platform we'd gone to the last sun-cycle for Staviti's meeting. At the moment the stage was empty—just a wide, clean, white-marble surface.

Very shiny and clean, which made me think …

My eyes darted across to the side, toward the shadowy wall, and sure enough there were half a dozen dwellers standing at attention. Waiting and watching for their next duty. I scanned their faces, and halfway along the line of males and females my heart stopped beating, just for a click. As it kicked back into rhythm, I started to run.

Muttered curses followed me, but I didn't care, continuing to push my way through gods and sols alike. Nothing was going to stop me right then, not even the wrath of a god. Or my Abcurses.

"Emmy," I cried, throwing myself at her. Warm brown eyes met mine, and I teared up a little. "I have missed you so much," I murmured, my head buried in her shoulder.

So much had happened. I *died* for the love of the

gods. But being here with Emmy, in that moment, was almost like we were back home in our sector. Just two trouble makers—okay, one trouble maker—and a simple life.

"Missed you too, Will." She was choked up. "I haven't even had to save one life since you've been gone."

I pulled back so that I could shoot her a grin. "Well, I'm back now, so you better brush up on your healer skills."

Being back with Emmy—and hearing myself say the word 'healer'—triggered a memory for me. "Have you heard anything about Evie? How are her burns?" It wasn't like I had forgotten that my 'fire' power had burned a dweller almost to death. I hadn't forgotten it at all, just like the wraiths in the caves. It was on my list of things I needed to deal with or do something about. But there were only so many places I could be, especially while hiding from Staviti. I was really hoping Emmy was going to tell me that Evie was almost fully recovered. Just a few little burn marks remaining. Maybe a scab or two ... no oozing sores, though. That sounded like too much.

"She's ..." Emmy hesitated, and my heart sank. "She's doing the best that she can. The burns were extensive and the healers don't believe that the fire was normal in nature. They're a bit stumped on how to heal her."

Nope, the fire was not normal at all. It was from my

stupid powers. I needed to help her, I had to figure out a way. Maybe the Abcurses would know what to do. I was distracted then as Emmy's eyes went very wide; she looked up over my head. Swinging around I found a wall of muscled gods surrounding us.

"Hey, Abcurses," Emmy said, recovering from her shock quickly. "For a click there I thought Willa was here on her own. Guess I should have known better."

She didn't sound resentful, exactly, but there was a slight undertone there. When her gaze came back to meet mine, I raised one eyebrow.

I thought she was going to shrug my questioning look off, but then she let out a long sigh. "I'm just not sure how many more 'god' situations I can handle. I sometimes wish my best friend could just be Willa again. On occasion. Not *Willa and her gods*."

Willa and her gods. I liked the sound of that, though it hurt my heart to hear the sadness in Emmy's tone. I understood: we'd been a team for a long time, and now the dynamics had changed. The new members on my team were certainly not the sort she expected ... or wanted. It was complicated. Emmy had only ever wanted a normal life, to be the best dweller she could be. To serve the gods and make the rest of us look like lazy morons.

I'd gone and screwed that up by dragging her into *this*.

"I'm sorry." I hugged her quickly again. "But at least I can be away from them now, no need for the stone anymore. So ... there's that. We can have some family time, just the two of us."

Emmy was the one now with the raised eyebrow and confused expression. "You can be away from them now? What happened?"

Right ... I had forgotten that she didn't know I was dead. My eyes quickly darted across the Abcurses, hoping that one of them would jump in and tell her what had happened. Emmy was not going to take it well—of that I had no doubt. My pleading expression was met with a range of grins, some lazy, others smirking, but not one of them looked like they were going to save me from Emmy.

I couldn't really blame them. My best friend was scary. Even for powerful gods.

FIVE

J ust as I took a deep breath, preparing myself for what was to come, a god walked across the stage, stopping in the centre and staring out across the masses. His robes were almost the exact colour of the walls behind him, which should have caused him to blend in.

Only Cyrus would never blend in, no matter what he wore.

"What the hell is Cyrus doing here?" Emmy asked. "He's the worst of you all, always in my business, touching my things."

I knew better than anyone how much she hated it when you moved her stuff around. Or lost it. Or traded it to the tavern owner in the hopes that he'd kick your mum out of his establishment for two nights.

"Staviti told him that this was his to oversee," Aros explained. "He wasn't exactly happy about the order."

"ATTENTION!" the Neutral god bellowed, making me jump almost out of my skin. I brought my hands to my ears and glared toward the stage.

It seemed as though half of the other gathered bodies had displayed a similar reaction to me, because one of the dwellers was being helped from the floor, and Cyrus was wearing the smallest hint of a smirk.

"You're all here because you were chosen," he announced, a sharpness to his tone that hinted at impatience. He was still projecting his voice far too loudly. "And I'm here because I'm clearly being punished for something. As you were told when you received the invitation to attend Champions Peak, each sol here is decidedly the most powerful of their particular ability, and they are being given an opportunity to train with a god sharing that same ability. WHAT THIS MEANS—" his voice broke out into a shout again because some of the sols had started excitedly murmuring. "What this means," he repeated impatiently, clearing his throat, "is that each sol will be working with a god. Every sun-cycle. For the remainder of this life cycle. At the end of the life cycle, every single sol at Champions Peak will be sacrificed to the will of the gods—those who have proven themselves worthy will ascend to Topia. Those remaining ..." he glanced around as the unease began to stir through the gathered bodies again. "Well, they'll just be dead."

Someone started freaking out then, and I glanced

over the heads to what seemed to be a small crowd pushing in on a female. She was flailing about, as though trying to escape, and she kept shouting something about not wanting to die. Cyrus audibly sighed, the sound carrying over the platform through whatever means he had been using to amplify his voice. He raised his hand, an exasperated look on his face that was clear even from where I was standing. The crowd suddenly sprang away from the girl and she lifted into the air. Her freak-out got even worse then. She started screaming—not in a pained way, but in an *I'm floating and I don't know why* kind of way—until Cyrus flicked his hand to the side and her body jerked rapidly over the heads of the other sols, flying right off the side of the platform as though she'd been a bug crawling on his robes.

I blinked in horror at the spot where she had disappeared, hearing the sound of her screams getting further and further away until they suddenly stopped. Cut-off. Because Cyrus had *thrown her off the gods-dammed mountain*.

"And you can consider that an early sacrifice. She could have been a god, but instead, she's going to wash away, unclaimed, a useless waste just because she couldn't keep her shit together." His voice boomed over the platform again, setting my teeth on edge. "My name is Cyrus, and I'll be running this Academy. Don't annoy me. Don't get in my way, and *don't throw any tantrums unless you want your blood to paint the rocks at the base of this mountain.* Any questions?"

"Maybe you should tell them where they will be sleeping," a dry voice answered, projected as strongly as Cyrus's voice had been. I wondered if all gods had that ability, or just the bossy ones.

The speaker was a woman, red hair cascading over one shoulder, braided along the other side. She was wearing shimmery silver robes and her mouth was hooked up into an amused grin.

"Right." Cyrus was downright scowling now. "You'll be sleeping in special rooms set into the sides of the mountain. You will have a single dweller assigned to your needs for the life-cycle—they will be kept in your lodgings unless you push them out. Be warned, however, that if you kill your dweller, it will not be replaced. *Any other questions?*"

He enunciated that last part almost as a dare, and I was pretty sure that nobody was brave enough to ask any more questions, until the silver-robed woman spoke up again.

"Maybe you should tell them how to get there," she suggested, crossing her arms over her chest, her smile growing. She clearly wanted to die.

Cyrus seemed to agree. His eyes narrowed on her for a click, like he was committing her face to memory, and then he turned to the sols—who were now all too frightened to move, speak, or breathe.

"Figure it out for yourselves," he snapped. "As soon

as the sun rises, your training will begin. You will return to this platform to meet with your trainer—it is up to them to punish you if you are late, and believe me, they will. This is as much a waste of their time as it is mine." And with those words, he turned and stalked away.

"Come on," Emmy muttered, her temper clearly rising, if her tight grip on my arm was any indication. "I already know where they're putting everyone, they had us set up the bed-mats earlier."

I didn't argue, and surprisingly, neither did the Abcurses. We followed her as she led us from the platform; we were the first to leave the marble hall— the other sols were too busy freaking out. Thankfully, the exit was on the opposite side to where the screaming girl had been tossed off. We passed down several sets of stone staircases that had been built into the mountain, curving around the outside and leading to different platforms and structures built into the rock. Eventually, we came to a much larger opening, almost like a cave, though I could see light at the other end. It was a gigantic tunnel through the heart of the mountain, with lanterns swinging from the rock ceiling. There was a wooden sign also swinging from the ceiling, chains dropping it down so that it hung above the entrance to the tunnel.

The Falling Caves, it read.

"Please, gods, no," I muttered, looking from the sign to Emmy's grim face, and back again.

"Figures," Rome grunted. "He wants to make the sols stronger, not pamper them."

"I think I should just go tell everyone I'm not a sol," I decided, spinning on one foot.

"Not so fast," Aros chuckled, catching me before I could escape, his arm wrapping around my waist and pulling me back. "You're really going to tell Cyrus that you're not a sol? The god who *killed* you?"

"Wait …" Emmy's voice was hoarse, barely above a breath. "Wait …" now she seemed to be struggling to breathe at all. "*What?*"

"Oh, right," I started casually. No more avoiding this conversation. "I'm dead. Cyrus killed me." *Still a bastard.* Just ask the girl who sailed off a cliff.

Emmy staggered back, her hands reaching out to press against the nearest wall. "I don't … understand."

That made two of us.

With a sigh, I took a step closer to her. Just in case she collapsed. I owed her for the last million or so times she'd caught me. "It's a long story, and right now I don't think we have time to go into all the details. Let's just say that Rau was trying to make me into his Beta, and Cyrus was trying to stop that from happening, and the only way he could think to do that was to stab me and let me die in his arms. Then he smuggled me into Topia—to the Abcurses."

Yael made that angry noise which usually meant that someone was about to get Persuaded to do something really bad. Emmy didn't look away from me, her eyes wide and glassy. Shock had a hold of her.

"Are you a god now?" she whispered. In a fraction of a click she had run through all the logical explanations and reached the only possible conclusion. Except we had no idea if that was the only conclusion.

Reaching out, I wrapped my hand around her forearm, giving it a little squeeze. "We don't know. Usually to become a god, Staviti would have to anoint me or something, but that didn't happen. So right now, I'm *other,* and we're working to figure out what that is, while trying to escape Rau and Staviti's attention."

I'd never seen her so pale, and considering everything I'd put her through over the life-cycles, I considered this a personal achievement.

She shook her head, tears sprinkling her eyelashes. "All of these life-cycles I've been trying to keep you alive. You were in so many scrapes, so many accidents that should have been your last, but you always pulled through."

She straightened then, anger flashing across her face. Her right index finger jabbed in the direction of the Abcurses, who were waiting behind me. "You five!" Her voice and finger shook. "You were all supposed to keep her safe. I trusted each of you. I let Willa go into your world, into your care—into the care of *five* gods— and somehow she still managed to get *LITERALLY MURDERED!*"

I waited for one of them to defend themselves, to explain that it wasn't their fault. We had all trusted Cyrus, and I had been the one to go off without them —one of those stupid things that I often did. I waited, but no one spoke. They just stood there, their expressions shuttered, their eyes blazing while Emmy ripped them a new one.

Holy father of the gods. They were still blaming themselves for what had happened to me.

"Stop!" My word had some bite, and while it pained me to talk to Emmy with anger, I would not let the Abcurses take the fall for this. "This is not their fault," I told her before I turned to look at them.

"This. Is. Not. Your. Fault," I repeated with more force. Five sets of eyes held mine. I looked between all of them, wordlessly reiterating my point. When some of the tension relaxed from their broad shoulders, I took a deep breath and faced Emmy again.

Working some calm into my voice, I said, "I was cursed long before I met them. My life has never been one of safety or longevity. I think we all knew that. The reality is that it's probably because of the Abcurses that I am standing here right now. They saved me, more than once. I'm soul-bound to them—we're linked in a way that goes beyond life and death. It's forever."

This fact no longer had my insides squirming. I wanted them forever. I took a step back, until I was pressing into one of them. I couldn't turn to see who it was, but multiple arms wrapped around me as we pressed closer. "I would choose the same path over and over again, Emmy. I love you so much, you are my sister and that will never change. But the Abcurses are part of my very soul, and I choose this life with them."

My feet left the ground then as one of them picked me up, and in a dizzyingly quick movement, we were out of the tunnel, moving too fast for me to track our path as we ended up in a dark, cold room. Emmy wasn't with us: it was just me and my five guys. I blinked stupidly up at them, trying to figure out what had gone wrong.

"Is Rau here?" I murmured, my eyes darting around as I tried to make sense of what was going on. "Why did you leave Emmy behind? We have to go back for her."

It was difficult to see everything properly, with the only light streaming in from the stone hallway. Aros captured my hand, threading his fingers through mine.

"Rau isn't here. Emmy is fine, Persuasion *asked* her to go back up to the main building."

"So what was with the rapid race through the tunnels?" I asked, still confused. The expressions on their perfect faces were not helping me figure it out.

Aros was still holding my hand. Siret stepped in on the other side and took my other hand. The low level of energy that had always been between me and the guys thrummed to life, like I'd just touched a live wire and the current was spreading through my body. I was starting to feel very hot again, and I said the first thing that came to mind. "We should go swimming!"

Rome and Yael chuckled, and then all I could think about was the way they had touched me that night. The sensations of being with them like that.

"You chose us, dweller baby," Coen said, moving closer so that his body was almost touching mine. "Whatever force brought you into our lives, did so for a reason. You could not have formed a soul-bond with the five of us if it wasn't meant to be."

"You belong with us," Siret added, drawing my gaze to his glittering green eyes. The gold slashing through them in bright arcs drew me closer. He lowered his head so that our lips could touch, and I felt Aros tighten his grip on my hand. But he didn't do anything else to stop the kiss.

I lost all thought then. When we finally pulled apart, I struggled to catch my breath. The pure sweetness of that kiss had been like nothing I'd ever felt before. Looking down, I blinked at my hand, which was clearly no longer being held by Aros. A quick look around the main room of the cave told me that Siret and I were now alone. It was considerably darker, but my eyes were quick to adjust. Someone had closed the door.

Turning back to him, the raw emotion on his face had my heart thudding hard and fast. "Where did they go?" I whispered, already pushing closer to him, moving up onto my toes and trying to fit myself snugly against his body.

One of his arms wrapped around my back and his movements were rougher as he swept me in. "They're giving us some privacy. If that's what you want?"

Holy shit. I'd never thought they would share so well, but if 'keeping it even' meant that I got Siret all to myself in this moment, I was all for it.

To answer his previous question, I pressed my lips against his, grateful that he was holding me high enough that I could reach them with ease. This time there was nothing sweet about the kiss—it was hot, hard, and delicious. My body was already aching to be touched. I needed more than what we had right now. I needed everything.

Pulling my mouth from his, I inhaled deeply and wiggled back so that I could try to pull his shirt up. I'd dreamed about touching Siret's chest like this and I couldn't wait another moment. Siret moved to set me down, but I didn't let go of him, keeping my legs locked around his waist. "You're not going anywhere," I muttered.

His only response was a rumble of his chest and then his lips were on my neck, trailing down my throat. My body tensed and relaxed in the same instance, my legs sliding down to the floor. Siret straightened then, towering above me as both of his hands went out to brace against the stone wall behind me, framing my face. His right hand slid across my dress and I felt his

Trickery energy follow that path. When I looked down, my blue dress was melting away. It was hard to see in the dim light, but the colour also seemed to be shifting, growing a deeper, darker shade of ... purple. The material shrunk away until it was a set of underwear: a silky purple bra and panties.

"Your turn now," I said breathlessly, my hands already scrambling to get his shirt off. Siret moved back just enough so that he could reach over his shoulder and grab the back of his shirt, pulling it up and over his head. Every single cell in my body was happy that he did the undressing the dweller way. His power, while convenient, took some of the fun out of it. I was pretty much panting by the time he was done. Siret's body was a work of art. Golden, cut muscles— long lines for my eyes to trace over and over.

"Pants now, too," I ordered, leaning back against the stone like I was the powerful god and he was only there to serve me.

Green eyes twinkled at me, a smirk in place, and he reached for the button on his pants. "Are you sure about this, Soldier? There's no other layer to take off once these go."

Holy gods yes. I nodded, smiling. "Pretty sure."

He kicked his boots off, one at a time, drawing out my pleasure—and torture—as he slid his black combat pants down his body. I didn't know where to look, mostly because I wanted to look everywhere. And touch everywhere. I moved forward until there was only a fraction of a breath separating us. He raised a hand to cup the side of my face and I let out a shuddering groan.

His head ducked down, his lips inches from mine again, but just before I was lost in another heated, dizzying kiss, a flash of silver caught my eye from over the top of his right shoulder. I pulled back an inch, my gaze flicking to the side. It was entirely dark, except for the sprinkling of silver dots scattered about a single wall.

No ... not dots.

Stars.

I was looking at the night sky. But *how*?

Siret began to pull away, but my hands found their way to his shoulders, hanging onto him, keeping him close. I needed the warmth of his body. I was confused at the vision of the sky, and there was a coolness to the air that also battered at my mind. Something wasn't right and it was begging for my attention, but Siret was right there, and he was hot enough to banish the cold. He was perfect enough to pull my attention away from the stars.

"There's something wrong with this room," he muttered distractedly, his lips brushing over mine. He'd noticed as well, but just like me, it wasn't quite enough to pull our attention from each other.

I went up on my toes, allowing my hands to travel into his thick, slightly wavy hair, threading my fingers through the strands, before grabbing two handfuls to force his mouth harder against mine. He laughed, but the sound ended on a groan as I opened my mouth to him, his leg pushing between my thighs, his hand at the small of my back, arching me into him.

"I need you," I gasped, releasing his hair so that my hand could slip between us. I didn't have a whole lot of sexual experience, but I was more than willing to bow down to my instinct. I wanted to touch him, I needed to experience his reaction to me.

His breath grew heavy as my fingers gripped his hard length, his palms once again pressed to the stone wall behind me, on either side of my body. When he seemed close to reaching his limit, he encircled my wrists, pulling them away and moving them behind my back, trapping them there and pressing me flush against him. His other hand brushed slowly down my front, a glittery intention in his eyes, visible in the dim light. I should have paused to figure out where exactly the light was coming from, since it had a flickering quality to it, indicating a bare flame nearby. I *should* have been asking many questions, but I was done with thinking.

It was time to forget about everything else. The urge to gather my Abcurses around me and forge us into a tighter, closer link was almost overwhelming. I had no idea why it was happening, but I was past the point of questioning it.

The further down Siret's hand travelled, the more I could sense his magic slowly rolling over me—not that

I needed to actually feel his magic to know that I was now naked, because his fingers didn't pause in their downward motion, travelling over my belly, my hip, before pushing between my legs. I lifted up onto my toes, my arms stretched behind me, held at the base of my spine. I dropped my face against his chest, my sounds of pleasure caught against his bare skin as my legs went immediately weak. He was taking away my ability to stand while keeping me upright with his grip on my wrists. It was bordering on painful, but I didn't want to break free or stop him, because his fingers were driving me insane, sending liquid heat through my body.

There was nothing that I could do to take control of the situation, to drive our encounter in the direction I wanted it to go. If it hadn't felt so amazing, I would have fought him; I would have tried to gain the upper hand somehow, but I had no strength to fight. I gave in, letting him drive me closer and closer to the edge, before he pushed me mercilessly over.

I slumped against him as I cried out, emotion welling up inside me, and he immediately released my wrists, cradling me gently in his arms. I didn't know why, but tears were gathering at the corners of my eyes, a strange elation filling my chest. Undead sex was different to ... swimming.

"Don't say undead sex," Siret muttered, laughter in his voice, though it had a roughness to it that only served to remind me that we hadn't actually *had* sex, yet. I let my body ride the heavy wave of emotion as I pushed into him. I could feel every inch of his skin beneath me as we sank down to the cold stone floor. I wanted to wonder why the room wasn't furnished, as the rooms had been at Blesswood—why there weren't rugs and blankets, couches and beds—but as soon as the questions jumped into my mind, they were pushed out again at the feel of Siret's smooth skin beneath my fingertips. I straddled him, my knees settling on either side of his.

"Put it in," I demanded, still struggling a little to breathe.

"That's ... really not how this goes," he replied, and I could hear the laughing grimace in his words.

"You don't put it in?"

"No, you *do* put it in ... I meant that you don't say things like 'put it in'."

"Well *I* do, because I just did."

"I can't believe we're having this conversation."

I reached down, my hand wrapping around his hardness again. He groaned heavily.

"Put it in," I repeated.

This time there was no laughter from Siret, but his eyes burned. Branding me. Claiming me.

His hands clenched and unclenched at my waist, until he eventually pulled my hand away from him and grabbed my hips, pulling me onto him. He entered me, our bodies immediately finding a shared rhythm as though we were starved, and maybe we were. I felt deprived of them—all five of my Abcurses. In a way, there was an emptiness between us now, one which had been there since my death. Like we needed to secure the soul-bond between us. It wanted us to acknowledge it—to give ourselves to each other.

Siret was losing his grip on control, his touch becoming more demanding, his god-strength leaking through his caresses. It wasn't painful to me the way it might have been before Rau's curse had hit me—now, I revelled in it. I returned it twofold, until we were finishing together, a pile of limbs and laboured breathing. He never stopped touching me, the entire time his hands gliding, rubbing, soothing. His lips feathered out over my temple before finding mine, and it was the most natural thing in the world to tell him how I felt. I opened my mouth to say the words, but he was already saying them, his voice a husky whisper against my hair.

"I love you, Soldier."

I really had to die more often if this was the reward.

SIX

Siret was cradling most of my body, his hands gliding across my skin, but still the cold crept inside of me. It was so cold, and I could feel a draught ... which shouldn't have been possible inside a cave.

"What's wrong with this room?" I murmured, shivering against Siret.

Before he could answer, there was a burst of light from across the room. I was on my feet in a flash, hidden behind over six foot of angry god.

Angry *naked* god.

"Oh shit," a nervous voice exclaimed.

I peeked around Siret to find a sol standing there. A male, with shoulder-length dirty blond hair pulled back at the nape of his neck, held there by a piece of leather. He had in his hands a single throw, thin, not at all warm looking, and a small pile of clothing.

"You have less than a click to tell me what the hell

you're doing in here." Siret's voice sounded all drawly and calm, but I was touching his rigid back. He was anything but calm.

"Uh, I'm ... this ... what."

This sol was definitely going to have a heart attack if he didn't calm down. He also seemed to be spending an awful lot of time staring at the ceiling, and since it was dark and a single-toned stone up there, I couldn't figure out what was so fascinating.

"He's trying not to look at you naked, Soldier," Siret informed me. "Because then he knows I'll throw him off this cliff."

Right, I had forgotten we were both naked. "They're just boobs," I told the sol, still trying to get around Siret, who was still shuffling me back. "We all have them, mine are just bigger than yours."

The sol made a choked noise. His face was very red, reflected in the beam of light from the door he'd opened to come into the room.

"Why are you in here?" Siret barked, having had enough.

"*Thisismyroom,*" the sol rushed out. "I didn't know anyone was in here."

Noticing Siret's pants a few feet away, I quickly leaned over and snatched them up, handing them to him. He pulled them on, turning to still block me, before he ran his hand across my front. My insides tightened, but this time it wasn't *fun* touching. He was dressing me again.

It was then that I finally took the time to absorb my surroundings.

"There's no furniture in here." I squinted at the twinkling lights. "And there's a huge hole in the side of this room! Someone could just roll out of it during the night."

Half of the wall was missing. That had to be a hazard of some kind—namely the *falling to your death* kind.

The sol shuffled his feet, looking miserable. "Staviti wants only the strongest to survive. We will be living with less comforts than usual."

"Hell no," I declared, crossing my arms over my chest. "I will not be sleeping with a hole in the wall of my room. On a mountain. That's tempting fate way too much for me."

The sol spoke up again. "Gods are not in this section, it's sols and dwellers only. The Abcurses will be … somewhere else."

Siret, still shirtless and wearing that dark look he only pulled out when he was seriously annoyed, wrapped an arm around me. We started toward the open door.

"Uh, nice to meet you," I said over my shoulder. "Thanks for the room." I really should have been more embarrassed by our situation, but I wasn't. I'd lived through worse, that was for sure.

Siret led me down a dark tunnel and then we were in what looked like a central mingling area. It was well lit; there were sols everywhere trying to figure out which death-trap of a cell they were in. Dwellers were scurrying about, directing the sols. The moment Siret stepped into their midst, his beautiful bronze skin on display, absolute silence filled the cave. Wide eyes followed our movements, and I would guess they both feared and craved the god who walked among them. Craving was definitely an emotion Siret brought out in me as well.

My body already wanted more. From all of my Abcurses. Undead sex was definitely the best. The corner of Siret's lips quirked up, and when he lowered his gaze to meet mine, my toes pretty much curled in my new Trickery boots.

"How are we supposed to find your rooms?" I asked to distract us both. "We need Emmy. She'll know."

Before he could reply, a deep voice drifted in from a dark archway. "Here's my little trouble maker." White robes swished into view as he stepped forward, looking all dangerous and beautiful.

"You're an asshole, I hope you know that," I snarled at Cyrus. "You threw that girl off a cliff. She's dead now!"

He shrugged, like it was no big deal, and I fought against my urge to punch him. Would I actually be able to hurt him now that I was some sort of undead *thing*?

"If you don't hurt him, Soldier, I could try," Siret drawled casually.

Cyrus let out an exasperated sound. "This is not the fucking sun-cycle to *try* me. I'm not supposed to be babysitting all of these pathetic wormers. I have a life. I have duties. I don't just laze around all sun-cycle doing nothing."

I shrugged, mimicking him from before. "Kinda looks like you do to me." I still wasn't sure exactly what Cyrus did with his Neutral powers.

Before he could make whatever disparaging remark was about to come out of his mouth, I interrupted. "We need to go to our rooms, so we can't really hang about and chat."

I *might* have still been a little cranky about the killing thing.

Cyrus's eyes shone, and he looked to be on the edge of doing that really scary thing he did. I had no idea what usually followed after the really scary thing, though, because at that point, I usually ran.

"Your room is back there." He pointed toward the round cave.

"No."

He blinked at my blunt reply.

"I stay with the Abcurses. You know that. And Emmy stays with me." I took another step closer to him, my finger coming up to jab him in the chest. Siret grabbed my arm before I could, edging himself between me and Cyrus.

I ducked my head out to the side to shoot another glare at him.

"You and your brothers are in the god-residences a level above," I heard Cyrus mutter. "If Staviti comes down to check on everything, I will not be covering for Willa being in your rooms."

Then, in a swish of white robes, he was walking away.

Siret reached out and captured my hand, threading our fingers together. We walked hand in hand the rest of the way back to the edge of the mountain, and up several winding steps to a higher level of stone hallways, connecting rooms and meeting areas carved into the mountain.

"Are you worried about Staviti finding me in your rooms?" I asked when we were almost there. I couldn't get Cyrus's warning out of my head.

Siret snorted, low and with real humour. "Don't worry about it. You just leave Staviti, and whatever he has planned, for us to deal with. Our family isn't easily threatened, especially now that we have our parents back in this realm together. We have something other gods lack: a true family. We back each other up, no matter what. Staviti has allies and enemies. Both of which are interchangeable depending on the life-cycle."

That made me feel ... better. I'd always thought—after hearing the fables of Staviti—that he was a lonely sort of god, always trying to create a family. Trying to control everything. Most of the time failing. I was more than a little lucky to be bonded to the only true god family.

Leaning in close, because the hallway had begun to narrow, leading off into the separate residences, I whispered, "Do you think Staviti has been deliberately draining Minatsol?" Siret slowed, turning to face me. "He said there are channels, pathways ... does that explain why more than half of this world is dead, and Topia is thriving and beautiful?"

The flaming torches set into little stone nooks high above us were washing warm light over his face. I got lost staring at him for a moment, almost missing his words. "I'm not sure exactly what Staviti did to the worlds, but it's clear that the balance is off. There is no reason for Topia to be unable to take more gods—we populate a very small percentage of it. Something bigger is going on here."

Laughter rang out close-by, then, and we cut our conversation off. Siret kept me close as we moved into yet another common area. Long tables were spread out everywhere and gods were sprawled in high-backed, padded chairs. They were eating, drinking, making merry. There were sols scattered about the place, serving the gods. Either they had already found their rooms on the level below, or else they had a nice little surprise in store for themselves later. It was almost funny to see, since the sols were tripping over each other to wait on their appointed 'god-trainers', though they didn't appear to want to do any of the actual *chores*. The majority of them were standing to the sides of their gods, waiting for any sort of command, or any way to make themselves useful. Occasionally, a god would turn to their sol in an annoyed sort of way, remembering that they were there, and would bark an order. The sol would then turn to their dweller attendant and bark the exact same order.

It didn't take me long to spot the Abcurses; they were against the far wall, claiming the warmest spot in the room and stealing all of the attention. There was a raging fireplace between Rome and Yael, flickering light over their small gathering. The girl standing behind Rome looked uncomfortable and angry. She had her dark hair pulled into a sharp bun, and was dressed more like a male sol. There was also a girl behind Yael, though she was much more feminine. She leaned against the wall in the same way that Yael was leaning, a knowing smirk on her lips. Whenever Yael shifted, she shifted to match him.

I was starting to get a sick feeling in my stomach.

I glanced at the armchair Coen was sitting in, turning my eyes on the girl standing behind his chair. She was tiny, her eyes dark and her fringe falling over her face. Her skin was fair, her shoulders a little hunched. *She* was the most powerful pain sol in all of Minatsol? There was something utterly terrifying about that fact.

Aros was in the other armchair—I cringed before turning my eyes to the Seduction sol behind him.

Another girl. *Of course it was.* She had red hair that bordered on pink, and her skin was the colour of a moonless night sky. Dark, rich, almost shimmering as she moved. Her lips were also the brightest pink that I had ever seen. I almost expected her to be wearing pink clothing and carrying a little packet of pink candies, but she was dressed in a tight, black leather corset-dress, the material of the skirt turning to silk as it reached her thighs.

She turned, locking eyes with me, and I immediately wanted to throw up.

There was a loveseat between Aros and Coen, with a single girl sitting directly in the middle. She had purple hair, and when she turned to glance over the back of the chair—because the whole group had turned to look at us by this time—I noticed that her irises were also purple.

That was Siret's colour.

The colour of Trickery.

I gagged silently, and Siret had to steady me, his deep voice floating down to my ears.

"Soldier? What's happening?"

"You all have sols," I muttered, the bitterness on my tongue refusing to go away. "They're all women. Beautiful women. Staviti, or Cyrus, or someone, is trying to break up our group."

The truth of that hit me harder than it ever had before. None of the gods liked that the Abcurses were a unit, and many of the gods were annoyed that I had become integrated into that unit. It seemed too coincidental that each of the sols tasked to the Abcurses had been female, and that they would now be forced to spend every sun-cycle with those females for the entire life cycle.

"I see." Siret didn't sound happy. We had stopped moving altogether, both standing in the middle of the hall, staring over toward the fireplace.

Aros and Coen stood, but they seemed to be waiting for us to come over to them. They looked unsure. After a click, I realised why. They had given us privacy, allowing Siret and me to have our time, but now they were unsure. The balance was uneven. Pushing away the panic that wanted to take over my thoughts, I forced my feet to move, carrying me the rest of the way over. I reached out as I got there, taking hold of Coen's hand, and then Aros's. They both pressed in against my sides, comforting heat flooding into me once more.

"Everything okay, Will?" Coen rumbled, his free hand pressing somewhere just beneath my ribs, while Aros's hand slipped around my back.

"You've been assigned your sols." I nodded my head toward the girl beside Rome. She had stepped forward as I approached, her fists clenched.

"Shouldn't you be somewhere else, dwell—" she began, but was cut off as Rome's hand shot out, colliding with her shoulder and sending her flying several feet across the room.

We all turned to watch as she slammed into a group of gods and sols, knocking them all to the ground, and then we turned back to Rome. I was sure that my mouth wasn't the only mouth hanging open.

"You shouldn't shove girls," I stuttered out, though I was less upset about the girl being shoved than I was about the fact that he'd beaten me to it.

He shrugged.

"You really shouldn't," I repeated, sounding even less convincing.

Siret started laughing then, the sound causing even more silence to descend through the hall. We were beginning to cause a scene.

"Why not?" Rome grunted. "Nobody gets to speak to you. I don't care if it's a man or a woman, I will use my Strength against any of them."

"You can't ban people from *speaking* to me." I rolled my eyes, but only a little bit, because I didn't want to miss even a micro-click of the girl's embarrassment as she apologised profusely to one of the gods, her fists still clenched and her face still pinched in anger as her gaze flicked back to me.

What the hell is her problem?

"Other than being shoved halfway across the room?" Aros answered my thought, laughter clear in his voice.

"I just did what we all wanted to do." Rome apparently felt completely justified in shoving a girl across the room for daring to speak to me.

"People are going to speak to me," I cautioned him. "They're going to call me dirt-dweller, they're going to threaten me, they're going to try to get between us—" I was just about to get to the rousing and inspiring part of my speech where I declared that I wasn't going to let any of those things get to me, but Yael cut me off.

"That won't happen," he growled, stalking forward and wrestling me from the other two, before walking me out into the centre of the room.

He released me and jumped up onto one of the tables.

"ATTENTION!" he shouted. Whatever conversations we hadn't already cut off with our previous display, now ended. All heads turned in Yael's direction. "There's something you all need to see," he announced, once everyone was silently waiting for him to continue.

I was standing there, waiting right along with everyone else. I wanted to know what he was going to say or do, but apparently his demonstration was done. He jumped down, his hands wrapped around my waist, and suddenly I found myself being lifted to the table.

"Show them," he demanded. "Show them exactly what a dweller can do."

I melted, my eyes on his. He hadn't said *show them that you're not a dweller*, but *show them what a dweller can do*. I wanted to jump down off the table and kiss him, and by the smirk on his lips, he knew that, but he shook his head, indicating the waiting people.

People. Ah, shit. I wasn't ready for this. I hadn't even attempted to use or unlock any new abilities since dying. My eyes darted toward Yael and he gave me a decisive nod. He believed I could do it, so I had to try.

Taking a deep breath, I turned so that I was facing the majority of those gathered about the room. I tried to widen my legs, for a more secure stance, but there were little grooves between the wooden planks of the table, and the edge of one of my boots got caught. My arms waved as I stumbled and I would have gone head-first into the marble below if Yael—no doubt anticipating my clumsiness—hadn't caught and straightened me before any blood could be shed.

That didn't mean the damage hadn't been done, though. The crowd around us erupted into scornful laughter, the sound seeping deep into my soul. In that moment, I felt like I was a million life-cycles old, and so utterly tired. I'd been laughed at a lot in my life; so many times that I'd basically turned my every thought and movement into a joke. If you pretend for long enough that you don't give a shit, and that it's all fun and games, eventually some of it sinks in. Right in that moment, though, the raucous, biting nature of the laughter was too much.

I saw the flash of dark green in Yael's eyes; his anger had my own flaring brighter. Just like Emmy, and so many others: I was no longer content to dwell in the dirt. I was Willa freaking Knight. Undead. With zero fucks left to give.

Flames shot up around my table with an almost deafening roar. I hadn't been planning on doing anything quite that spectacular; they were a little wilder, and more out of control than I had expected. With a gasp, I yanked Yael into me, because he had almost been taken out by my wall of flames.

When he was up on the table with me, my breathing started to slow down. "Did I get you?" I asked, eyes frantically darting across him. I thought it looked like one of his sleeves was smoking a little, but he just shook his head.

"I'm fine. You did good, Willa-toy."

In that moment, I realised that there wasn't a single sound in the hall, other than the roar of my fire. I shifted from facing Yael to staring out over the top of the flickering flames, meeting the eyes of as many gods as I could. I needed to do this for dwellers, everywhere.

"You did that, Trickery," a voice rang out. "She's a damn dweller, they don't have gifts."

It came from a god I didn't know. "Chalice, the Beta of suspicion," Yael murmured to me.

Well, it did make sense that he'd be the one to question it. I lifted both of my hands then, letting that whirl of energy free, pushing it out further inside of me. The panteras had tried to teach me about harnessing my energy. I hadn't quite understood what they meant. But I did now. The moment those flames roared around me, I knew the reason my power had been locked away since I awoke *undead*. It was fear. Ever since my fire started hurting people, like Evie, I had feared it. And it seemed that now I had the strength to keep it locked down if I wanted to.

Which I no longer did.

I was going to show them who they were messing with.

As I shifted forward, my boot got caught in the groove again, sending me catapulting forwards off the table.

"Willa!" Yael roared.

He had reached for me, but my clothing slipped through his grip. My back slammed into the cool marble, and I let out a deep groan.

Yael got to me in a heartbeat. "Kill the flames," he growled.

What? My head was fuzzy from the hit, and I couldn't figure out what flames he meant. The marble was cool, nothing was burning me. As my head cleared, the flickering reds, oranges, and blues around me came into clear focus. I jerked upright, finding myself half-sprawled across the flame circle I'd created.

Yael attempted to grab me again—his arm looked to be burning as he reached into the fire.

"No!" I shouted, stumbling to my feet, shaking off the disorientation. I tried to push him back, only he wouldn't move an inch. Instead he wrapped a hand around my wrist and pulled me with such force that I smashed into his chest.

He held me for a beat before he started to run his hands across me, patting every part of my body like I was on fire, even though not a single inch of me burned.

"I'm fine!" I yelled, still disorientated. I scrambled for Yael's hand, tears already pooling in my eyes at the sight of the red, weeping skin across his forearm and palm. "I am so sorry," I cried.

"It's fine, Will." His voice was nothing more than a gravelled rasp. He was upset. That was very clear. Still gently holding his hand, I lifted my eyes to his.

"How did you do that?" he asked, the look on his face like none I'd ever seen before. "I've never felt flames like that."

I shrugged, trying to clear my throat enough to talk. "I ... I don't know. It didn't feel like anything to me. Maybe because I created it ..."

He shook his head, but before he could answer, a shout had me spinning around.

"Willa!"

The other Abcurses were standing at the edge of the fire, their expressions very much like Yael's. The flames were still strong and high, separating us. Concentrating through my emotional breakdown, I tried to will the fire away, to suck the energy back inside. It took me more than a few clicks, the effort almost draining me. Apparently, I was better at starting the destruction than I was at ending it.

The moment the circle faded away, they were surrounding me, hands pulling me close. I closed my eyes and buried my face in someone's chest.

"Yael," I half-sobbed. "He needs a healer."

I didn't look up as whoever held me started to walk, but the silence around us was deafening. I didn't hear a single whisper, or even any evidence of breathing. Maybe everyone had gone.

Shifting my head to the side, I peeked out through blurry, tear-filled eyes. Dozens of faces stared back. No one had moved. But they sure were staring hard as we strode past. I could see Rome and Aros on my right, and I was thinking it was Coen that held me, judging by the way we towered over everyone else.

By the time I managed to get myself together enough to want to walk on my own, we were in another expansive common area: I was carried through a kitchen, several small, intimate dining rooms, and huge marble-lined pool. Eventually, we ended up in a sprawling area of comfortable chairs and small, contained firepits, covered in ornate, carved metalwork.

"Out!" I heard Siret shout. "If we see your faces again tonight, you won't have to worry about ever becoming gods!"

I was on my feet now, Coen keeping one hand on my back. I tilted my head around him in time to catch sight of the Abcurses' five female students—all shooting me death glares as they scurried toward the main door. Siret closed it forcefully after them.

Now that the interlopers were gone, I hurried over to Yael. His bronze skin had a worrying pallor about it, and I sucked in a few ragged breaths. "Where is the healer?" I asked, my attention locked on those beautiful green eyes of his. His face was relaxed despite the paleness—he didn't seem worried. But I could tell he was in a lot of pain.

"They'll be here shortly, but there is no point," Siret told me. "No mortal could heal a burn like that."

I was already shaking my head. "That can't be right. What about an immortal then? You guys must have healers. You get hurt, right?"

There was a knock on the door then, and before anyone could call out, it swung open and a god strolled casually in. He wore bright yellow robes.

"Thought you might need a healer," the man drawled. "I waylaid the sol who was hurrying here, mostly because sols are useless little creatures when it comes to healing."

Definitely a god. Attitude and all.

"Lancaster. Thanks for stopping by." Coen gave him a nod.

Lancaster wasted no more time, striding over to Yael. His eyes met mine as he passed and it almost looked like he flinched back slightly from me. I didn't blame him: what I lacked in finesse and skill, I more than made up for in accidental destruction. He took Yael's hand in his and I felt a burst of energy. It lifted the hairs on my arms and sent goosebumps over my skin. I held my breath, waiting to see the red angry burns subside. At that stage, I'd have taken any improvement to his damaged skin.

Come on!

"It's going to be okay," Aros said, wrapping his arm around me. "This wasn't your fault."

It was completely my fault, but I appreciated him trying to make me feel better.

After about three clicks, Lancaster released Yael. "I can't help him. This is god fire. The strongest I've ever encountered. He will have to wait for his body to repair the damage, and there will be extensive scar tissue."

"No!" I cried out, hurrying to Yael.

Lancaster jumped out of my way, and I shot him a confused look, which he turned away from immediately. He couldn't even bear to make eye-contact with me. As he moved toward the door, Rome shifted in front of it, crossing his arms.

"You didn't see this," he grunted. "If anyone asks, Persuasion was brought here, where he promptly healed. Nothing else happened. Is that understood?"

"You can't threaten me, god-child," Lancaster muttered, disdain marking his tone. "I'm just as powerful as you are, just as old as you are. You're not that special."

"No," Rome agreed, sounding bored. "I was just

born in the world you worked your whole mortal life to get to."

"Exactly," Lancaster sneered. "I *worked* for it. I'm stronger than you. All of you. You think the Beta of Healing wouldn't have allies in Topia? I have so many people on my side that not even Abil's family can make a dent in my existence."

"Maybe." Yael spoke up, his voice a rasp. "But guess who *can* threaten you?"

Lancaster spun around, glancing at Yael, before his eyes slid involuntarily to me.

"That's right." Yael let out a hacking laugh. "So keep your mouth shut about this, or we set Willa on you. Ashes don't tell tales, do they?"

I expected Lancaster to sneer again, to shower me in his disdain, to tell me that he had all the god friends and that I didn't stand a chance ... but he didn't. He shuttered his expression and gave a short, sharp nod. Rome moved out of the way and he escaped the room without looking back.

SEVEN

The room was silent for only a click before the door burst open again. This time, it was Cyrus. He appeared in a flurry of white robes and flashing eyes as his attention snapped straight to Yael.

He snorted. "I knew Lancaster was lying. You don't *look* like you healed yourself. What the fuck happened?" That last part he had aimed at me, his attention shifting from me and back to Yael's burns.

"I did my fire thing." I shrugged, helpless. "Just the same as always."

"Except this time you tried to turn the mountain into a volcano, and you burned one of Abil's sons. Not that I'm complaining, by the way, this is much more entertaining than babysitting a bunch of dweller-bugs and sol-princesses."

"I need to heal Yael," I said, ignoring him. I placed my hands over Yael's blistered forearm.

"Oh you can heal things now?" Cyrus sounded amused. "Why not, I guess. Let's see it."

I could feel the colour rising to my cheeks, humiliation sinking into me. "I can't," I countered. "I just meant that I should do *something*."

I was embarrassed because it seemed that the only thing my power was capable of, so far, was devastation. Maybe I was the new God of Devastation.

"There's already a God of Devastation," Siret said, answering my thought. "And a Beta. Are they still alive, Neutral?"

"They are," Cyrus replied, watching me.

"So according to Staviti's *rules of the universes*, you can't ascend to Topia when there's already an established God and Beta with your particular energy."

"Also according to Staviti's *rules of the universe*," I countered, "Topia is full. *Every* energy has a God and a Beta. I'm guessing this would have been the case when I died ... so why did I ascend?"

"Maybe you didn't ascend," Cyrus answered. "Maybe you snuck into the afterlife. Maybe you were reborn. Maybe you were *already* dead. The panteras wanted to help you, so I'm guessing they know the answers. We need to ask for an audience with them."

"We?" Yael croaked out, wincing in pain. "Since when are you part of this group, Neutral?"

"I don't want to be part of your six-way sex group." Cyrus rolled his eyes. "I want to know what Willa is and what that means for the rest of us. I don't trust you lot to keep me informed, and without my protection, Rau will tear that girl's soul from her skin and send it straight to the *imprisonment realm*. Also, I saved her life."

"You killed me," I spat.

"It was the only way to save your life."

"*What the hell are we going to do about Yael!*" I was on the verge of a meltdown. I couldn't stand around talking about it anymore. I needed to do something.

"We're going to stand around talking about it some more," Coen answered, his voice low and smooth, as though he was trying to calm a wild bullsen. "Look at me, Willa, nowhere but me."

Confused, I turned my head to the left, meeting Coen's eyes.

"That's it," he encouraged, his calming voice rolling over me. "Just keep your attention here. Do not look at Yael. Do not look at anyone else. Focus here."

"I'm focusing," I answered. "But I don't know why. What the hell is going on?"

A small laugh escaped from one of them, but I wasn't sure who, because I was being a good Willa and keeping my eyes on Coen.

"Is there a bug on me?" I eventually asked, feeling my skin start to crawl.

"No." Coen's lips twitched. "Keep your focus here. Tell me, do you want Yael to get better?"

"Yes, of course I do." My brow was furrowing in confusion, my hands twitching against Yael's forearm.

"Good. Do you want him to get better?"

"Uh, still yes." It wasn't like any of the gods to repeat themselves, which made this even odder.

Coen smiled, his stare finally breaking as he glanced down at Yael, and then back to me. "You can look now, Willa, it's finished."

Frowning, I flicked my eyes to Yael. *Why the hell was everyone suddenly so quiet?* Yael shifted as my eyes met his. He moved to sit up. I started to panic, leaning forward to push him back down again, but then I caught sight of his skin.

His *unmarked* skin.

"You h-healed," I spluttered out, relief flooding through me. I tossed my arms around his neck, half climbing onto his lap in my enthusiasm.

He laughed, pulling me the rest of the way onto his lap before his hands found my face, tilting it up to his. "No." He shook his head, his eyes glinting with wonder. "You healed me. We could all see the colour leaking from your hands. Coen didn't want to distract you by pointing it out, so he guided your focus."

I froze, my eyes wide. "What?"

"You healed him," Cyrus reiterated. "The colour wasn't clear, but it was there; a brief light emanating from your palms."

"I did something good?" I felt stupid asking these questions, but I could barely believe it.

"Yeah, Rocks, you did something good," Yael

murmured, his hands tightening on my face, drawing my lips up to his.

The kiss was strong, completely capturing my attention. Within a fraction of a click, I had forgotten that there were other people in the room. My legs had found their way around his waist, my hands threading into his hair. Yael groaned, pulling his mouth back from mine.

Somewhere in the room, there was an awkward cough. It sounded like Cyrus. This was followed by a few barked commands, and then the room was blissfully silent. Yael stood then, bringing me with him, my legs still around his waist. Our lips clashed again, our tongues tangling together. "I'm so sorry I hurt you," I said against his mouth. "I feel terrible."

His rumble of laughter sent intense vibrations down my body. "It was nothing, Willa-toy."

Sparkling water came into view then, and just as I was about to ask what he was doing, he walked us into the pool, warm water washing across my legs.

"We're going swimming?" I blinked up at him, excitement wrapping around my emotions.

He laughed again. It felt like both of us were a little too euphoric in that moment. The healing had clearly done more than just repair his skin.

"This is the bathing area, the water has healing minerals and properties, and it's cleaned and filtered constantly."

He was holding me in waist-deep water; I struggled

to get down. When I was standing—the water almost to my shoulders—I took a proper look around.

"This is a bathing area?" I asked drily. "It's twenty times the size of those baths you have in your marble god box on Topia."

Yael just nodded, his eyes mesmerising in the low light of the room. On top of the huge mineral bath, there were statues in all four corners. They looked almost like baby gods, with wings, and musical instruments. The water was aqua in colour, the dimly illuminated lanterns mixing with the steam rising from the surface gave it a very ethereal look.

"It's so pretty in here," I mused, turning in a circle, my hands gliding across the surface of the water.

Yael looked around as well. "I figured we could both use some healing properties right about now."

My focus was immediately back on him, my hands already reaching for his arm. "Are you not healed properly?" I asked in a rush.

He twisted his arm so that he could take my hand in his. "I'm fine. I was worried that you might be feeling the aftereffects of healing. It takes a lot of energy."

Weird. I didn't feel tired at all. If anything, I was amped up. Swishing my arms in the water again, I grimaced as my sodden shirt caught on Yael. Both of us were fully dressed, and wet clothes were the most annoying thing ever.

"Do you mind?" I asked Yael, half joking as I

struggled to get Siret's Trickery clothes off. Asshole always tricked me into the tightest outfits.

The right corner of Yael's lips quirked up and it took every ounce of my self control not to kiss him. He didn't answer me: he just reached forward and untangled my arms, helping me out of my shirt and pants. His hands were wrapped around my back, holding me up, and when my shirt was finally off, I realised how close we were pressed. Tilting my head back, I parted my lips and breathed him in. Yael and I had been together, but ... also not really. I ached at how beautiful he was, his hair darkened by the water. His eyes locked on me with intensity.

I reached for his shirt, which was plastered across his hard body, and slowly lifted it. He was so much taller than me that I only had to bend a little to press my lips to the sliver of stomach that I had revealed. As I pushed his shirt further up, I followed the movement with more kisses. My lips pressing to every rigid line of his abs and chest.

"Willa." There was a rough quality to his voice. He threaded his hands through my hair, holding me close to him.

I responded by opening my mouth a little wider and using my tongue to explore him. The water which beaded across his skin had an odd taste to it, almost like there were herbs in it, but it wasn't unpleasant.

By the time his shirt was pulled up and over his shoulders and head, I could barely keep my legs from collapsing under me. My body thrummed with need. It was stronger than ever. Undead sex was the freaking best.

Yael groaned above me, and I pulled my lips away from his body to meet his gaze. "Don't say undead sex."

"Sorry, it's hard to remember all the rules when I start undressing you."

His hand cupped my chin, tilting my head back even further. His hold was firm, almost rough, and I was getting the feeling that Yael liked to be in control. My body twitched at the thought. At his firm hand. His lips came down on mine with force, his hands spanning across my breasts. His palms covered my bra completely. As his thumbs brushed across my nipples, I almost lost it. My body was wound up tight. The sex with Siret had only started the need. I was starting to think it wouldn't be sated until I was with all five of them.

"Stop. Thinking."

His command had my mind going completely blank, as though my body had been designed to obey him. At least during moments like this. I pressed myself closer, needing to feel more of him. In response, he ran his hands down my sides, stroking my skin before sliding them under me and lifting me out of the water. My legs went around his waist, and he moved so that he could lay me back on the angled entrance to the bath. As Yael settled between my legs, water covering our lower halves, my body arched up to meet his. I wanted to cry at the fact that he was still wearing pants.

"Take them off," I ordered.

He silenced me with a single finger over my lips. "I make the rules here, Willa-toy."

My centre clenched, my legs moving involuntarily.

He lifted himself up, his powerful arms holding his body above mine, his eyes running across the length of me. "You need to get naked. Right now."

At his command, my hands started moving. "Are you Persuading me?" My voice was so breathless it would have almost been embarrassing. Except I was too turned on to really care.

Yael shook his head once. "No powers, this is just you and me."

A low heady sensation was already building deep in my body. My hands scrambled to remove my underwear, and I revelled in the feel of the water across my naked skin. Clothes were stupid. It was a fact. Yael, who was still between my legs, shifted his weight back so that he was resting on his knees. That freed up his hands, so he could run them along my body. Heat followed his every movement, as though his touch shot sparks through me.

"Don't move, Willa. If you move, I will stop," he warned me, and then he put his hands under my butt and lifted me up so that most of my body was out of the water. He leaned over and pressed his lips to my chest.

"How come you were so compliant when I was with Rome?" I gasped out, not sure who this guy was. Yael had always been competitive, and really, I should have expected this side of him to come out—but I hadn't experienced it before now.

His voice was low and muffled. "You needed gentle and healing that night, and that wasn't just about you and me. This, here, now ... this is just us."

I gasped again as his tongue and lips worked their magic across my skin. He teased and drew out every ounce of pleasure from my body. Whenever I wiggled against him, unable to help myself, he drew away. Eventually I learned that if I wanted the pleasure to continue, I needed to stay very still. The control was driving me crazier than I ever expected.

When his tongue reached my centre, I knew there was no way I could stop myself from moving, and as Yael slid one finger inside of me, followed by another, his gaze lifted to meet mine. I begged him with my eyes to release me from his order.

"You can move now," he told me, staring up along my body. Watching me while I fell apart under his command.

Holyfreakinggods.

I was on the edge of release. It was building like a cyclone inside of me. Just when I was about to tip over the edge, Yael lifted his head and pulled his hand back. I was panting when he slid higher and settled between my legs, ridding himself of his pants.

"Good girl, Willa-toy."

I wanted to yell at him, because he had deprived me of the pleasure that was supposed to be mine. Then he shifted forward, sliding his length inside of me. I shattered around him, unable to stop when I was already so close.

Yael grinned down at me. "That's one."

Of course the competitive bastard would want to keep track. Already, my body was tightening in anticipation of 'two'.

He started to move, slowly at first, drawing out my first release, and then with more speed. After a few clicks, he shifted his position, placing his hands under me again, lifting me up for a better angle. He was so much deeper this way, and I let out a low moan as the strong sensations built within me again. A slow, steady, deep build. I could feel tingles from the top of my head, all the way to my toes. My nails bit into his shoulders as I held on, Yael's eyes as green as I'd ever seen them as they captured me in their glow.

"Come for me, Willa," he ordered, his lips moving to mine.

Unable to deny his command, I exploded, my body moving with his, and he let out a low groan, his tongue tangling with mine, my mouth absorbing the way he called my name.

"Two," he murmured against my mouth.

I was starting to wonder if I would survive three. My breathing was harsh and I couldn't feel my legs, but

I was certainly willing to give it a shot. Yael's smile was wicked as he pulled back, clearly having read my thoughts. His pace picked up, and I tightened my legs around him. My body was tender from the last orgasm, but soon need built within me again. He shifted back a little, before he reached down between our bodies and pressed a finger against the sensitive part of my centre.

"Three, Willa-toy," he ordered again.

I was helpless to deny him. The force of my next orgasm had my head spinning, and dizziness pressing in on me. Yael stole my focus then with those gem-like eyes of his, whispering my name as he too found release.

I struggled to bring air into my lungs as we lay together, our bodies tangled, until our breathing had slowed. Yael's touch turned gentle, running along my body soothingly. When he finally pulled from me, we drifted back into the water, staying very close together. There was a satisfied glint in Yael's green eyes, and I was starting to suspect I might be addicted to swimming. The same way he was addicted to winning. He grinned, picking up on that thought, before a loud pounding on the door broke through our moment.

"Time's up!" a muffled voice shouted.

"Shit," Yael muttered, quickly moving to the ledge and pulling himself out. He reached for me, tugging me to the side of the pool, and then he started pulling his wet clothes back on. "I think Trickery got everyone to leave before, somehow, but the illusion must have worn off by now."

"Three clicks!" the voice shouted again. This time, I recognised it as Siret's.

My eyes went wide, flying to the door, and then I was scrambling out of the water and looking for my clothes. Obviously, I didn't care about the Abcurses seeing me naked, but Cyrus was another story. I managed to wrangle my way into the sodding material just as the door flew open. The other Abcurses strode through. Siret glanced at me, the right corner of his lip twitching. His eyes were laughing, but the others all appeared serious. Cyrus followed them, looking mad as hell.

"Why the fuck are you two wet?" he snapped. "Tell me that whole illusion trick wasn't just so that you two fools could go swimming?"

"What's wrong with swimming?" I asked.

"We were in the middle of something." Cyrus threw his hands up, beginning to pace on the spot, his eyes flicking between Yael and me. "You almost incinerated the entire mountain. You burnt a god and overpowered his natural healing reflexes. Those are the reasons we were all in this room. And you use Trickery to send me out of the room so that you can go *swimming*? This is ..." he was shaking his head, his hand flying out with a sharp, frustrated motion. A long, deep crack fissured through the entire length of the stone wall. I stumbled back a step. I might have had some kind of crazy ability with god-fire, but I couldn't go up against Cyrus.

I took another step back as the Abcurses all tensed, closing in around me. I was stepping backwards, sure, but that didn't mean I was *backing down*. I would never back down, not even against a Neutral. Mostly because I didn't really understand what the Neutral power could do, and there was a lot of bravery to be found in stupidity. I was happily ignorant of all the ways that Cyrus would be able to successfully torture me.

"You don't understand *this*," I finally said, indicating the five bodies now forming a solid wall between us. "You don't understand what it's like to be going about your life and then suddenly you're not yourself anymore. You're one part of a whole and nothing makes sense unless you're with the other parts of your whole. So I'm *sorry* that we had to kick you out of the room, but I hurt one of them. I hurt a part of myself. I needed to fix it."

"And," Yael added, his voice a little darker than mine, "if you try to come between us and Willa one more time, this little alliance we have going on is broken. Finished. You might be the Neutral, but she belongs to us and we belong to her—no amount of power is going to stop us from protecting that."

"I think we're done here," Coen declared, apparently not willing to wait for Cyrus's response.

He turned, holding his hand out to me. I linked my

fingers through his and we walked to the door, all six of us spilling into the corridor beyond.

"Wait." Cyrus moved after us, filling up the doorway, his eyes on me. "I have no interest in breaking up your group. There's something about this stubborn loyalty you all have for each other that I respect, even though the rest of it makes me want to shove one of Death's knives into my eyeball. I'm sorry I overreacted. Even so, you need to be punished for what you did. If I don't punish you, it will only draw the attention of the other gods. That is not something you want. You will report back to me at first light *without* Abil's sons. Am I understood?"

I didn't wait for the Abcurses to start another fight, I just nodded quickly and drew Coen away, knowing that the others would follow.

"We need to find Emmy," I muttered, as soon as we were out of hearing range.

"Ten disks she's waiting in your room," Rome grunted.

"Twenty disks she's around the corner," Aros countered.

"Thirty she's—" Siret started, but he was cut off as we rounded the corner and a flurry of blond hair attacked my face, arms wrenching me away from Coen.

"*Stop. Doing. Things. That. Give. Me. Chest-pains*," Emmy ordered, each word punctuated by a too-painful squeeze.

I thought she was hugging me, but when she drew

back, there was a coat wrapped around my shoulders. Apparently, *I* had been hugging *her* and she had only been trying to give me a coat. She must have been squeezing me to let me know that she wanted to be released. For some reason, I found that funny. A giggle slipped past my lips, and Emmy cut herself off mid-chastisement, her eyes narrowing dangerously on my face.

"I've decided that we need new sister rules," she told me, folding her arms over her chest.

"Uh..." Rome shifted nervously behind me. "Should we maybe ... go ... somewhere else?"

"No," four other voices all argued, before Aros added: "That's up to Willa."

"What rules?" I asked Emmy cautiously, ignoring the boys completely. I knew I had made her angry again, but as my exhaustion levels crept up, I lost my will to defend myself.

"Rule Number One," she began immediately, also ignoring the others. "All perilous ideas must be cleared with your best friend *first*. Especially if they involve almost dying."

"I could probably do that." I scratched my head. I was getting nervous now. She sounded like she had a lot of rules to get through.

"Number Two." She was beginning to calm down, but there was a suspicious glint in her eyes. She had expected me to put up a fight. "I was brought here to assist Cyrus, but I will ask to be assigned to you, instead, since you weren't given a dweller. Technically, you weren't even given a spot on the Peak, but there's no reason *not* to give you a spot ..."

"I get the point," I cut across her before she could launch into a list of reasons I deserved to be where all the best sols were. "But what's Number Two exactly?"

"We stick together. Like sap on a tree. No more leaving me behind."

"That one might be a problem," I admitted, thinking back to the way Yael had taken control of me in the pool. Behind me, a low chuckle sounded.

Emmy rolled her eyes. "I've been given quarters with Cyrus, since I'm supposed to be attending him for the next life-cycle. I can sleep there, and you can do all your freaky sex stuff at night time. Deal?"

"Was that one of the rules? I can only do freaky sex stuff at night time? Does that mean you can only do freaky sex stuff at night time as well? Does that mean you're going to do freaky sex stuff with Cyrus?"

Emmy's face turned the colour of a ripe berry, and when I saw that red spread down to her hands, I knew that I needed to back away fast. Between Cyrus and Emmy, I was starting to think that I was the least scary person on the mountain. I backed up and she levelled a stare on me that said *what the hell are you doing?*

"You're scary," I answered her look. "Your hands are red." I pointed to the clenched fists in front of her.

She let out a sigh before flexing her fingers and shaking off the tension in her shoulders. "Cyrus and me … there … never. I will never touch that arrogant god."

"Famous last words," Siret added lazily. "Now that you've put it out into the universe …"

"Bring. It. On!" Emmy tilted her head up, giving us the most stubborn of her looks. Then she spun around and stormed off. "I'll see you in the morning, Willa," she called over her shoulder. "Don't forget the rules."

I was seriously hoping that there was absolutely no reason for me to break the rules that night. And that there weren't any additional rules that she hadn't gotten around to telling me about.

"I'm going to need some dry clothes and a bed," I said to the Abcurses. "And sleep. Lots of sleep."

Looks were exchanged, and I realised that we had reached the dilemma of where to sleep. Since I'd died, we had all been sleeping in our howler pile, and I wondered if they would want to continue that now. Or if we were going to start separating.

The thought of that sent a feeling of unease through me.

"Let's check out the arrangements," Coen suggested, breaking through whatever tension held us.

I wasn't moving one more step in my wet clothes, and Siret must have realised that because he moved close enough to run his hands across my body. The sodden mess disappeared and when I looked down, I was in a robe. Not a god robe though, this style was more like a coat, which crossed over the front and tied with a long cord. It was the colour of cream, softer than clouds, and so warm that my entire body relaxed and I almost fell asleep right there on the spot.

Yael didn't bother changing—wet clothes didn't bother him apparently. Actually, on closer inspection, it looked like they were almost dry. *Really?* I mean, he did throw off a lot of body heat ...

I really had to stop thinking about swimming.

"Yeah, that would be great," Rome grumbled.

I hurried ahead of them, opening the door that Coen pointed at, stepping into what I hoped was a bedroom. The last thing I wanted to deal with was a quintet of fighting gods. I felt like I had to be extra careful until I managed to keep it even. Right now, things weren't balanced, and if I didn't fix that soon, we were going to end up in all-out war.

Ah, the things I have to do for balance.

I focused on the room, realising that it pretty much just contained a bed. The most perfect bed in all of existence, possibly. Huge and decadent, with more pillows than twenty people could use and thick blankets that begged me to crawl under them. Before I could think it through, I was moving, the softness cushioning my knees as I scurried up to the end with the pillows. "Looks like Willa found her bed," Coen drawled with a laugh.

I would have responded except I was too busy snuggling my way under the covers.

"Does anyone know who was next on the

schedule?" I heard Coen ask. Always the responsible one, my Coen. He was falling back on the scheduling that had made our lives easier in the past. Things had changed so much since then, though.

"I think it was Aros's turn next," Yael said, crossing his arms. I could feel his eyes on me, and I tried not to think too hard about the swimming incident. Mostly because I was way too tired to swim at the moment, despite my new-found love for it.

"Aros and Coen," I said sleepily. "We need some balance."

I thought they were going to argue, but outside of some murmuring and shuffling of bodies, no one said anything. A warm hand brushed my hair back, and I snuggled into it, my eyes already closed.

"We'll just clean up and be right back, dweller baby," Coen murmured

"Mmkay," I mumbled.

Darkness dragged me under, then, and I drifted off to sleep feeling safe, content, and very satisfied.

EIGHT

"Willa Knight! You were supposed to be up twenty clicks ago!"

The annoying voice was familiar, buzzing through the heavy sleep that was still attempting to hold me under. I was so warm and comfortable, heat pressing in on either side of me. I wiggled a little and tried to open my eyes, only to slam them shut again because it was too bright. A large hand rested against the bare skin just below my ribcage, beneath my sleep shirt. Another hand gripped my thigh, the hold somehow both sleepy and possessive.

"How attached are you to Dweller-Emmy?" Coen rumbled in my ear.

I pulled one of the pillows out from behind my head and blindly threw it in the general direction of Emmy's voice. "I'm considering answering that unfavourably."

The blankets over us started to shift, as though a bossy hand had grabbed them in preparation for something horrible. "I will rip them right off," a bossy voice warned—undoubtedly the accompaniment to the hand. "I don't even care how naked the three of you are under there."

Before I could stop myself, my hands went out to either side to feel along Coen and Aros's bodies. Disappointment hit me when I realised that both of them were wearing underwear, and the low chuckles that sounded in response to my thoughts had my body clenching.

"One," Emmy started. "Two ... *I'm going to rip it off*. Thre—"

"Wait!" I shouted, finally managing to peel my eyes open. I pulled myself up, squinting at my best friend. She looked the same as always, her clothing conservative, modest, and muted. Everything was the same, dull *dweller* black; I couldn't even tell where her shirt ended and her pants began. Her hair was pulled up into a perfect braid. Not a thing out of place, except for the slight look of panic on her face.

"You're supposed to meet Cyrus at dawn, Willa."

Oh, right. The thing that I had to do as punishment so that Staviti didn't hop down to Minatsol and smite us all. Coen and Aros were sitting now as well, the blankets pooling around their laps, leaving all of that bronze, muscled skin bare. I looked between both of them, my mouth and throat going dry.

"Unless you want an audience," Emmy brought my attention back to her, "I'd suggest getting your butt out of bed, getting dressed, and getting to Cyrus. Don't make him increase your punishment. He's not one you should mess with."

"When did you become a Cyrus expert?" I asked, managing to get out of bed with a little help from Coen.

Emmy shot me a withering stare as I attempted to wrangle my sleep shirt back into place. "Ugh, please don't say it like that. I'm not an expert, but gods are arrogant and demanding ... he just happens to be the worst of the lot."

Coen and Aros shot me those half-smiles that did nothing but make me want to crawl back into bed between them.

"We can get you out of the Cyrus thing," Coen told me. "Just say the word."

I shook my head immediately. "I'm not causing any more trouble for you five—I know it wouldn't be as simple as that. I don't trust Cyrus. He has his own agenda, but he's not going to hurt me."

"He stabbed you," Emmy reminded me dryly. "Only you would think that he was still okay after that."

A sudden crashing sound to my right had us all whipping our gaze around to the wall as it started to crack apart, sprinklings of dust fluttering down to the floor.

"What in the worlds was that?" I squeaked, pulling my fists up, ready for a fight.

"This is *not* the time for a distraction," Emmy complained.

"Sorry," Coen smirked. "Willa, maybe you should ask the distraction to come back another time?" Since he was making a joke out of the fact that something was about to come crashing through the wall, I assumed it wasn't a threat after all, and lowered my fists a little.

"I'll try," I replied, glancing at Emmy out of the corner of my eye to see just how far I would be allowed to push her before she exploded. "But I'm not sure how the collapsing wall is going to respond to our scheduling conflict."

Coen and Aros were laughing, but Emmy was reaching for me—either to strangle me or to drag me out of the room, I wasn't sure—when the wall suddenly collapsed inwards and a giant form passed through the rubble, forcing more of the wall to break off and tumble to the ground.

"Morning," Rome muttered, passing through the destruction and strolling nonchalantly past us to the other wall, raising his fists.

"Um ..." I struggled to form a coherent thought.

Emmy's mouth dropped open and she turned to watch him. He smashed his fists into the wall, forcing it to collapse inwards. He had to do it in several places to get the whole wall down, and then he was passing through that one, as well.

"You know I have a door, right?" I heard Yael's sardonic voice from within.

"You know what," Emmy was shaking her head, reaching for me again, "I don't even want to know. We don't have time. Let's go."

"Meet you guys back here!" I yelled out, as she pulled me to the door. "Don't crush anything I wouldn't crush!"

Emmy almost pulled my arm out of its socket as she forced me down several stone hallways and out to the edge of the mountain. We hurried down several sets of natural stone steps curved to the shape of the mountain, and then through another hallway—this one several levels below the sol bedrooms. Finally, we reached a doorway. It was huge and circular, set into a hollow in the rock. She knocked once, and it swung open a moment later.

Cyrus was sitting at his desk, but his hand was raised, as though he had used some kind of Neutral power to open the door.

He glanced up from the scroll he had been writing on, a frown taking over his face. "Sit down," he ordered, motioning to a chair in front of his desk.

I started to walk over to it, but before I had even taken my second step, the chair itself was moving. It slid backwards and then past me before reversing directions and swooping forward to catch me. I found myself seated right where he had indicated, my eyes wide.

He made another hand motion and the door slammed closed.

"What are you doing here?" he snapped at Emmy, who had moved to stand beside my chair.

"I'm Willa's serving dweller," she explained.

"Says who?" his eyebrows shot up. "You do realise that I'm the person in charge of this, don't you, bug?"

"Bug?" I broke into their conversation, forcing Cyrus to falter in the intense stare-off he had going with Emmy.

"She's an insect," he told me, his lip curling up in disgust. "Annoying. She's always there, always buzzing. She's a bug."

"You can't talk about her like that," I shot back, but apparently Emmy didn't need me to defend her. She was already stepping up to Cyrus's desk, her fists clenched again.

"And you are a ... a ... *addicted to wine*!" she shouted, apparently having trouble deciding on what she wanted to accuse him of.

"I feel like that was a poor choice of retorts," I told her helpfully. She turned to glare at me.

"That's ridiculous," Cyrus sounded like he was laughing, but he was managing to keep the expression of amusement from his face by some miracle.

We both turned to him just in time to witness him

pulling a small wine-skin from beneath his desk. He was in the process of raising it to his lips, the laughter finally creeping into his eyes, when he paused, realising what he was doing. He scowled, taking a quick swig before stashing it away again.

"I'm drinking because I'm *bored*," he snarled at us. "And I'm bored because I'm babysitting *insects*."

"Don't want to be rude or anything," I rushed out before the two of them could get into an all-out fighting match, with fists and magic and weird sexual chemistry. "But can we move on to the punishment portion of the meeting? I have to get back to the Abcurses before Rome tunnels right through the side of the mountain."

"What?" Cyrus asked, apparently ignoring the practical part of my request and jumping straight to the unimportant part about Rome.

"The punishment," I reminded him. "That's why I'm here. Last night I made an accidental little fire and you seemed to be in a bad mood about it so you said I had to come here—"

"No, Willa." He sighed dramatically. "Obviously I know why you're here. I was asking about Rome tunnelling—*ugh*, you know what, never mind. Yes, let's get on with the punishment." He leaned back in his chair before continuing. "I'm going to need you to periodically return to Topia *without getting caught*, in order to carry out a few things that I am no longer able to do, since I'm stuck in this gods-forsaken hellhole. Understood?"

"Nope, not really," I admitted easily. "That doesn't so much sound like a punishment as it does you using me to do illegal things in Topia while you sit here at your desk, drinking and writing scrolls."

"I wasn't writing scrolls." His lips curled in disgust again. He shoved the paper toward me. It had one word scrawled across it in cursive writing.

Bored.

I snorted. "Right."

"And I can't do illegal things," he added, ignoring my sarcasm. "I'm the one who punishes others for doing illegal things. I'm above the rules. I *am* the rules."

"But I'm not." I stood from the chair, planting my hands on my hips. "So when I go to carry out your rule-breaky tasks, I might get caught. When I'm caught, I can't be like 'I'm above the rules. I *am* the rules'," I mimicked, putting on a deep, moody baritone. "They'll laugh me right into the imprisonment realm."

"The what?" Emmy spoke up, her voice holding that little hint of mania that I had grown accustomed to hearing.

"Tell you later," I whispered out of the side of my mouth, before returning my attention back to Cyrus.

"It's my decision," he said dismissively, his gaze

flicking to Emmy for a moment. "And that's final. Now leave me alone, I have important things to do."

Emmy and I both stared at the single word on the parchment, before raising our eyes to his face.

"Get. Out!" he shouted.

"That's a great idea," I said as I jumped to my feet and started shuffling back toward the door. "You should take your own advice. Get out, get some air. You're going mountain crazy; it's a thing, trust me—I was trapped in a cave, once. See, I wandered off from a school group and ended up having an unfortunate meeting with a mountain cat, so I ran into a nearby cave to get away from it ... or her ... or him. It didn't exactly expose its underside to me, so I'm not sure on the gender, but you don't look like you care about that particular detail."

Cyrus looked like he wanted to gouge his eyes out. He was rubbing his temples in a shaky, agitated way.

"Don't mountain cats live in caves?" he finally asked.

I nodded. "Oh, yeah. Apparently there was a reason it was standing right there, so close to the cave. It lived there! Fancy that. A few other cats also lived there. What a memorable sun-cycle. I almost lost my innards."

"*What the hell does this have to do with mountain sickness!*" Cyrus was on his feet now as well, his white robes askew.

I stopped moving toward the doorway. "Right, well,

I ended up crawling up into a small ledge. It had an opening that the cats couldn't fit into, though they kept sticking their paws in and attempting to skewer me with their claws. They trapped me there for two full sun-cycles."

Cyrus turned pleading eyes on Emmy. "Summarise, please. I just can't speak Willa this morning."

Emmy's face grew tight with an approaching lecture, and I was starting to feel sorry for Cyrus. The poor guy: he seriously didn't know what he was getting himself into.

"Firstly," she began sharply, "if you stopped drinking so much, your brain wouldn't hurt."

Cyrus's eyes narrowed and he opened his mouth, but she cut him off with a wave of her hand.

"Secondly, Willa is just saying that by the time we managed to find her, lure away the beasts and get her down from the ledge, she was delirious. They called it mountain sickness because she wasn't the first dweller to get cornered by a mountain cat."

"How could you tell the difference between mountain sickness and her usual sickness?" Cyrus asked dryly. "Was she talking crazy? Tripping over things? Or did she have a completely normal conversation with you while keeping her clothes on the entire time?"

I crossed my arms over my chest, choosing to be the bigger person and not acknowledge his words. Mostly because they were ... well, *accurate*.

Emmy's lips twitched, but she held in her laugh like a loyal friend. "It doesn't matter how we knew. The part you need to worry about is the delirium she caught. Being trapped with stone surrounding her for many sun-cycles was enough to make her a little loopy. We all get sick from being inside too much, we need the sunlight and fresh air."

"I'm not in a cave right now," Cyrus stated, his tone far less snide than I had come to expect from him.

Emmy's face softened. "Marble is still a stone, even if it's smooth and shiny. You're still always inside, secluded away, plotting to kill the rest of us."

"It's making you cranky," I added.

Cyrus frowned. "Gods don't get cranky."

I could have rounded up half a dozen protesters to contest that—just by walking down the hallway, but whatever he wanted to believe.

"We should go splash in the ocean," I suggested, excited at the prospect. Growing up, it had been something we couldn't even dream of, but the vast water was suddenly surrounding us, trembling in wait at the base of the mountain.

For a click, I almost thought that he was going to agree, but as darkness flashed across his eyes, he dropped back into his chair. "You have duties, Willa. You're a sol trying to be a Beta now, right?"

Wrinkling my nose at him, I grabbed Emmy and together we backed away. "You know that's bullsen shit. Think about the splashing thing, it's probably better that I'm not right in the midst of things anyway."

"Especially after last night," Emmy piped up, sounding less than pleased.

I swung my head in her direction. "What do you know about last night?"

She lifted one eyebrow, giving me her *are you serious* look. "Everyone is talking about the dweller who has the power of a sol. The dweller who has somehow leeched power off the five gods she attached herself to. All of the sols are trying to figure out how you did it so that they can do the same. By their calculations, if a dweller can be as powerful as you, then a sol can be as powerful as a god."

Naturally, that's how the arrogant sols assumed I'd managed to draw my power. It couldn't possibly have been mine by nature ... and well, they were probably right about that, but they could have believed in me anyway.

"It's probably better that they think I'm leeching from the Abcurses rather than I was stabbed to de—" My words were cut off by Cyrus as he moved at super-speed, coming around from behind his desk and wrapping his hand around my mouth.

"Staviti and Rau have ears everywhere," he warned me quietly.

Wrenching my face out of his grip, I took a step back, before pointing a finger at him. "Didn't you just order me to hop, skip, and sneak my way into Topia for you? If there are ears everywhere, shouldn't you have … written the order down or something?" His face was turning an interesting shade of red. "Look, Emmy," I pointed at the rising colour, "he does the same thing you do when you're mad."

"Just get out," Cyrus ordered for the third time.

I decided we'd pushed him enough for one sun-cycle and hightailed it out of there, Emmy following closely behind me.

"You can't go to Topia for him, Willa," she murmured as soon as we were clear of his little den. "You shouldn't be drawing any attention to yourself. Don't give Staviti any reason to send you to the imprisonment realm …"

I smiled. She was bringing up the imprisonment realm in the hopes that I would explain it to her—I knew her well enough to recognise the way her statement trailed off, waiting for something from me. If there was one thing Emmy hated, it was not knowing things. Usually she had all the knowledge.

"It's getting really hard to navigate the politics of this world," I admitted to her as we walked back toward the level housing the god-residences. "I'm not good at walking a fine line."

"Your guys aren't going to let him do this. All you have to do is tell them."

I hesitated, slowing my steps. "I'm not sure if that's the right thing to do. Telling them feels like it might just create a huge drama."

"How do you think they'll react if you get yourself thrown into this *imprisonment realm!*" she whisper-yelled the last part.

I waved a hand at her. "I'll explain the imprisonment realm later. Suffice to say, it's not a place you want to go. It's worse than death—pretty much the god alternative *to* death."

That explanation did not satisfy her at all, but it was too late for further protesting, as we had reached the room we had left the Abcurses in. Sure enough, we were greeted by five, pissed-off looking gods waiting in the entrance.

"Um, hi," I squeaked, stepping closer to them. They closed around me in a circle, their shoulders blocking Emmy from view, making it feel like it was only the six of us.

"You went to Cyrus without us?" Yael sounded somewhat calm, but his eyes were telling a different story.

"Do you know how dangerous he is, Willa?" This was from Rome, who reached out for me like he was going to shake me. Only his hands stopped just before touching me.

"He could have snatched you up for Staviti this time," Siret added, his features pulled into hard, angry lines. "We're a team, Willa. Don't leave us behind."

"You were all mostly here when I walked out," I hedged. "You knew I was leaving, and in case you forgot, Cyrus's condition was that I turn up *without* you all."

Rome grunted, reaching out and hauling me up and into his chest, holding me tightly against him. "We almost lost you to Cyrus once before," he muttered against my cheek. "We know you had to go alone, it was just hard to wait behind."

I snuggled closer to him. "I don't trust him either, but I also don't think he's going to try to kill me again. Whatever his motivation is, it seems to line up with ours for the moment. I'm more useful to him in my current state ... whatever that is. He was the one who put me in this state, after all."

Rome set me back on my feet, and Yael quickly snatched me up. I settled myself against him, letting him take my weight as I faced the others.

"So, what did he say?" Siret asked. "What's your punishment?"

"I have to run a few errands," I blurted, without really thinking. *Damn*. I should have taken more time to formulate a plan.

"What kind of plan could you possibly think through?" Aros rolled his golden eyes. "We would have heard you trying to think about what to tell us and what to not tell us, and then we'd know everything anyway."

"Out with the truth, Rocks." This came from Siret.

I sighed, pulling away from Yael to cross my arms

over my chest. I wanted to appear tough, just in case one of them flipped out.

"I have to go back to Topia to do some possibly bad things that will possibly also be dangerous because they involve Cyrus, who has issues with rage and drinking."

"He does?" Rome was blinking, getting a little side-tracked by my assessment of Cyrus.

"He does now." I shrugged. "So, we're cool then? No big deal? No *Willa, what are you doing?* Or *Willa, you're in trouble.*" I said the last part with a deep grumble in my voice—a poor imitation of any of them.

"Why would you be in trouble for something Cyrus is forcing you to do?" Siret asked, a smile stretching across his face.

"But yes, you're in trouble," Rome added, toneless.

I threw my hands up with a groan, spinning around just in time to catch Emmy's smirk.

"Not okay," I told her, wagging my finger in her face. "Not. Okay. You're supposed to be on my team."

"I think you have enough people on your team." She arched her brows, grinning at me. It was good to see her loosening up a little, even if it was at my expense.

"*Why* am I in trouble?" I asked Rome, pushing past them to get into the room. The walls were still destroyed. "And *why* did you smash your way through everybody's bedrooms?" I paused, a few steps into the room. Something was missing. I frowned, turning to face them all again. "And where the hell is the bed?"

To my complete and utter astonishment, colour seemed to rise in Rome's face. He glanced down at the ground, grumbling something in a moody voice. I just blinked at him, before turning my eyes to the others. Aros moved toward me slowly, as though afraid I would jump away from them again. When I didn't move, his fingers quickly threaded through mine. His golden eyes glimmered at me, holding some kind of delicious secret.

"Come, look." His voice was low, sending a reaction through my body and rendering me momentarily unable to walk. He had to tug me into motion.

He brought me to the wall and then helped me through the rubble, into the next bedroom. The bed was also missing from that room and the next wall had been similarly demolished. The only difference in this room was that the demolished wall had a set of sheets strung up to the ceiling, hiding the next room from view. Aros led me to the makeshift curtain, pausing before drawing it back. Instinctively, I glanced over my shoulder. The other four guys were following us, but Emmy wasn't, which made me want to laugh. Even Emmy knew better than to follow the six of us into a bedroom. We weren't exactly afraid of showing our affection for each other. If anything, we seemed afraid of *not* showing our affection for each other. There was an urgency between us, a fierce need to claim each other, as though something would try to rip us apart at any moment.

When the curtain fluttered back into place, sealing us in there together, I walked towards the beds. It was a little hard to tell how many had been pushed up against each other, because the snowy, fluffy blankets covering them were strewn about in all directions, as were the pillows.

"Is it okay?" one of them asked from behind me.

I was tearing up and I wasn't sure why. I was happy, almost ecstatic, and there was a warmth inside my chest growing hot enough to burn all the way through my body. *Oh, that's why I was tearing up.* It was because there was a fire in my chest, not because I was a complete wuss. I was reacting to the chest pains, not weeping over a romantic gesture. I was Willa Knight, badass extraordinaire, Undead Soldier. I didn't weep at romantic gestures.

"Thank you," I choked out—choked, because of the chest pain, not because of any kind of wussy emotions.

"She's obsessing," Siret remarked, folding his arms over his chest.

"Keeps calling herself a wuss," Yael added, shaking his head.

"Would a wuss do this?" I snapped, striding up to him and grabbing his face.

His eyes flashed and he leaned in, as though to kiss

me, but I grinned and let go of his face, sending my fist into his stomach.

He laughed, while I hopped around in pain.

Like a wuss.

"So you *do* like it?" Coen asked, appearing just a little bit concerned. "The new room?"

"I love it." I grabbed Yael again, pulling him into a hug. He was still chuckling, but he hoisted me up and plastered me against his chest, ceasing his laughter as he nuzzled his face into my neck. When he set me down, I went to Coen, raising my arms for a hug. A smile broke through his worried expression and he pulled me in against his body, his thick arms surrounding me. I hugged the rest of them in turn, but had barely wrapped myself around Aros before there was a knock on the wall between this room and the next bedroom. Not that any of the other rooms were really *bed*rooms anymore.

"Willa?" It was Emmy. She sounded apprehensive. "There are some ... um ... people waiting outside. For the Abcurses. Some sols. *Their* sols. For the training ... you know, the whole reason we're all here and everything. They said the guys weren't in the breakfast room this morning to give them their assignments so they came up here."

Aros let out a frustrated, growling sound before releasing me. The five of them strode to the curtain, Coen jerking it aside. Emmy jumped away from it and then scurried back into the other room without

JANE WASHINGTON & JAYMIN EVE

another word. I heard the door slam as she escaped to the corridor beyond. I didn't blame her—she already had to deal with Cyrus on a regular basis now, she was learning to pick her battles. Coen was stalking after her. Rome, Yael and Siret followed. Aros took my hand again as we trailed behind, but I paused at the curtain, turning to take in the room one more time.

Our room.

I smiled, but quickly ducked my head so that none of them would look back and see the expression of stupid, dopey happiness that was plastered all over my features. We exited into the hallway and I set my eyes on the girls from the night before, a frown taking over the previous happiness. I was going to have to split up from the Abcurses. I couldn't follow them around while they trained champion sols. I had no place in that scenario—I was just an unnecessary addition.

"Come on," Aros murmured, his hand tightening around mine as he drew me past the others. "Let's go back to the top of the mountain again. Cyrus didn't give very elaborate instructions, but I assume people will have returned to the same platform that he made his announcement on. From there, we will decide on the schedule for the sun-cycle."

Nobody argued, and we formed an awkward, single-file line through the corridor housing the sleeping quarters of the gods. When we passed out to the paths winding around the outside of the mountain, Siret moved behind me, his hand brushing along my spine. Immediately, I was shielded against the bite of the mountain air as a heavy black cloak folded about me.

I glanced back to thank him, but instead found my eyes searching for the sols. They were trailing behind, struggling to keep up with us. That made me smile.

NINE

We made our way up the winding stone steps, my cloak brushing against the frost that was forming on the surface. It was a dangerous path, slippery with ice, so I was glad that I had a hold of Aros. I wondered if the path was part of Staviti's test of survival: if any of the sols slipped and fell from the mountain, they were unfit to be gods. Or ... he wanted them dead anyway. I shivered, pressing closer to Aros. I doubted that Staviti would care if he took down an Abcurse along with me, but it was easy to convince myself that I wouldn't be swept from the side of the mountain if I held on to one of them tightly enough.

When we reached the top platform, we discovered that the space had drastically changed overnight. Marble trees rose from the platform itself, their shapes flattened and stretched out, so that they only appeared to be trees when you were standing in front of them or behind them. From the side, they just looked like odd, carved marble walls.

"Cyrus has been busy," I noted.

"Not Cyrus," Emmy muttered, brushing past me. "He got a *friend* to come in here and do it." Emmy made a face when she said the word 'friend'. "And then after she was done, he thanked her by taking her back to his room and fucking her right there in the bed with me sleeping on the floor beside him."

I jolted to a stop, my wide eyes staring after Emmy. She wasn't even waiting for a response—she was just charging on, through the raised marble trees, toward something I couldn't see.

"Emmy just said a bad word," I told the others, as I felt bodies shifting restlessly behind me. "And she's sleeping on the floor beside Cyrus? And Cyrus is having sex with mysterious decorator-gods?"

"She said more than a single bad word," one of the student sols muttered, her tone somehow both snide and satisfied. "She said a whole lot of bad words, and all of them about the Neutral God. That little dweller is going to die." Now her tone had turned to glee, and I was half a click away from turning and shoving my fist into her throat, but Aros started pulling me forward again.

"You know Emmy isn't going to die," he whispered to me. "Just ignore her. Cyrus would never have allowed a person to stay in the room with him while he had sex—much less a dweller—*unless* he wanted to get a reaction from that person. If he really took someone back to his room, he did it more for dweller-Emmy than whoever was in his bed."

I nodded, knowing the sense of what he was saying —even though Cyrus's logic wasn't the best. My temper stayed with me, however, as we walked toward the marble sculptures, heading toward a gap in the first line of marble trees—the same gap that Emmy had passed through. It turned out to be a hallway or passageway of some kind, and I realised that the flat-sided trees were acting as sectionals. We walked a few steps and came across another gap in the marble, forming a small doorway. I glanced inside, ignoring the current occupants of the space. The marble sectionals had formed a little alcove, just large enough to fit three plush, red couches along the back and side walls of the room. There was a crystal lamp dropping from a marble branch that was extending from the sectional in the shape of a real tree branch, reaching far above the room.

It was a marble forest of tiny rooms. The adventurous spirit inside me wanted to release the others and take off, to explore every secret hiding room that the forest could be concealing, but Aros must have heard the thought, because he chuckled, releasing my hand, his arm wrapping tightly around my shoulders.

"Let's just find a room that will fit us all, and we can figure out how to survive the rest of this life-cycle."

"*You* five will survive the rest of this life-cycle just

STRENGTH

fine. You're all *immortal*," I shot back, purposefully leaving myself out of that equation, just in case the sols were listening.

"I didn't mean Staviti's champion game." Aros glanced at me, and then shot a look over his shoulder. "I meant teaching. As an occupation. I don't know how long we're going to survive that."

"And by *we*," I interjected, "you mean—"

"*Them*, yes. Obviously. Whenever I say that 'we' can't survive something, you can assume I mean every other person who is in the same situation but isn't one of us."

"So, you really mean 'they' every time you say 'we'?"

"Yes, but I try to be sensitive about it."

I laughed, snuggling closer to him. It was a sad time when your asshole gods became endearing by way of their massive, all-consuming egos.

"Here!" Aros called over his shoulder, slipping off down another narrow passageway. He brought us into a large room with a central meeting place and several half-concealed alcoves branching off from it.

"I think this one is taken," I whispered, my eyes riveted to one of the alcoves.

I couldn't see anything more than a female figure plastered up against a much taller, male figure, but I could see one of the male's hands on the female's ass, while the other was tangled in her wild blond hair ...

wild blond hair that had been neatly braided only five clicks ago.

The male made a sound, somewhere between a growl and a groan, and the female stepped back from him. His hands dropped as his face was revealed, and then his eyes flicked over to us in realisation.

Cyrus.

Emmy, on the other hand, hadn't noticed us at all. She was re-braiding her hair with cool efficiency, her hands steady. "Don't even bother telling me you don't want me," she remarked. "You just gave up your game, Neutral."

She turned on her heel, and then paused, noticing us. I raised my hand in an awkward wave, but she barely even skipped a beat.

"Oh hey, Will," she said, smiling calmly as she moved to the centre of the room.

There was a circular table set up there, with an open stack of scrolls and two stools pushed back. A lamp was burning near the scrolls, illuminating her face just enough for me to make out the red that was creeping up her cheeks.

"Did you have an appointment with the Neutral?" she asked, checking her scrolls and then looking back up again.

"She takes this fucking job too seriously," Cyrus growled, stalking angrily to the table.

"Uh," I managed. The others remained silent. "We were just, uh, looking for somewhere to have a meeting. All of us. This is the biggest room in the forest."

"In the forest?" He grinned, but his eyes were avoiding mine. "Well, it's the biggest room because it's mine. And you need an appointment to see me."

I scowled, turning to Emmy. "Can I have an appointment to see the Neutral?"

She glanced down at her scroll again. "He has made it clear that the majority of the rotations in the sun-cycle are to be reserved for his silent contemplation of wine. However, I think I can shuffle a few things around."

The darker Cyrus's expression got, the wider my smile grew.

"Excellent." I rocked back onto the heels of my feet. "I'll just wait here while you shuffle."

"Ah!" Emmy fake-exclaimed. "I spot an opening in his schedule, seeing as everyone is too afraid of him to make any appointments. How does right now sound?"

"Right now sounds perfect!" I fake-exclaimed in return. "Thank you so much for your assistance."

"Any time." She smiled at me in a very professional way. "That's what I'm here for. I'm here to assist. Now please make yourself comfortable. I will notify the Neutral that you have arrived for your appointment."

She turned to face Cyrus as we filtered in, moving toward the furthest set of alcoves. They all opened into the common area of Cyrus's room, and there were only partial walls separating them, raising up as far as the backs of the couches.

"Your appointment has arrived," I could hear Emmy telling Cyrus.

"I am going to have you sentenced to eternal damnation," Cyrus growled back. "Make them go away!"

"Is that really a thing?" Emmy asked, and I turned to watch as she pulled out another sheaf of parchment, running her finger down a list that only she could see. "Nope, it's not a thing. It's right here on the list of things you assured me weren't real, right along with gods who have sex with dwellers—as I recall, it was impossible because they find dwellers repulsive—oh wait," she paused dramatically, and then started scribbling on the list, "we can cross that one out, can't we?"

Cyrus was digging into the pockets of his robes. He pulled out a flask, took a deep pull, and then strode toward us.

"Willa, come with me," he barked. "I have your first assignment."

"I can't right now," I quickly replied, before one of the guys could start a fight about it. "I have lessons this sun-cycle. For the whole champion thing? Remember?"

"You don't have lessons." He shook his head, taking another frustrated swig. "You don't have a teacher. There's no Chaos Beta."

"Yeah, well, I'm going to teach myself. I mean there's no harm, right? Staviti said the strongest sol in each power group, he didn't say the strongest sol in each power group, minus the Chaos sols."

"How do you know you're the strongest Chaos sol at all?" he countered, as I felt one of the guys step up behind me protectively, another at my side.

Cyrus was smiling, but it was humourless. He knew that I wasn't a Chaos *anything*, and he was calling me on my bluff ... but why? *So that I didn't make his life complicated by insisting that I train at Champions Peak*? Or ... understanding suddenly dawned on me. He was worried that word of a Chaos sol would get out to the gods, and then Rau would realise that he had been betrayed. That Cyrus had lied to him. I hadn't ascended to Topia as a Chaos Beta, I had ascended as myself, but Rau didn't know that. All he knew was that I hadn't ascended as his Beta, and that I was supposed to be dead.

The most logical explanation for him to draw would be that Cyrus had lied to him, and that I hadn't really died.

Would that mean Rau would start trying to kill me again?

Did I really care, if I couldn't die?

Did I really trust that I couldn't die?

"Let's just focus on the important question for right now," Siret whispered behind me. "Do you care if Rau finds out about you being here?"

"No," I answered Siret loud enough that Cyrus thought I was talking to him.

His brows crinkled, his eyes glimmering. "No what?" he asked.

"No, I'm not going to let you take this opportunity away from me," I told Cyrus. "This is what happens when gods try to plan everyone's futures as though it's their right. If there is a stronger Chaos sol out there, they're welcome to come and take my place, but until then, you have a Chaos dweller, and I'm going to teach myself."

"I supposed it would be an impossible task, keeping this hidden forever," Cyrus muttered. I knew what he was talking about, but the sols in the room would possibly assume that he was talking about there being a dweller with Chaos powers. "Very well, Willa. You can have your place here, I just hope you're ready for the kind of attention that will bring you. See me after you have finished *teaching* yourself. I will have your assignment ready."

I nodded, turning my back on him as we all spread out through the alcoves. I noticed that the girls all took seats, while the Abcurses stood, lingering by the entrance to the alcove. I glanced around, trying to figure out what to do with myself. Rome dove into his teaching session without much of a pause. I watched as he reached over and broke off the arm of one of the couches, tossing it at his student.

"Do that," he told her.

She reached over and did the same thing on the other end.

Rome shrugged. "Can you crush someone in a hug?"

"Not yet," she answered, brushing at the blunt line of her fringe. She was scuffing the toe of her boot against the ground, glancing from Rome to the other sols and back. "Should I be able to do that?"

"Yeah, probably."

I turned away from them, mostly so that I wouldn't start laughing. Rome was *not* the teacher type. He was definitely more the *crush things into pieces while grunting incoherently* type, and he was trying his best to utilise those exact skills in his task.

Beside Rome, Coen sighed very loudly. "I'm not going to teach you shit," he told the small, dark-featured girl sitting before him.

"Why?" she shot back, colour rising to her cheeks. She shot to her feet, shifting her eyes over to me, and then back to him. "You have to. That's your job."

"I don't need to," he sneered. "You want to cause pain, but there's nobody here you can experiment on. I don't believe it's a skill you should practise at all, unless you really need to, so fuck off. Find something else to do."

She stalked away from him, shoving her shoulder into mine as she passed. Pain shot through me, from my arm to my centre, sharp and fiery. I bit down on my lip, turning to watch her so that the guys wouldn't see the look of pain on my face. When I had myself under control, I tried to shake it off, turning back around again.

Coen was now sitting on the couch that the girl had vacated, his feet kicked up on the other couch, his muscled arms folded behind his head, his eyes closed in respite.

Beside him, Yael and Aros were huddled together, whispering. Their students were sitting beside each other on the couch opposite them, talking to each other in a very surface kind of way, as their attention was almost entirely still on the two brothers. I shook my head, turning to find Siret, except that he wasn't there. I blinked, striding forward. Gone.

"Where'd he go?" I asked the sol he was supposed to be teaching.

She was sitting on the couch, still awaiting instruction. "He's right in front of you." Her voice was laced with irritation, her words spoken hurriedly. She quickly flicked her eyes back to a spot in front of her.

"Yeah, Rocks." Yael was beside me now, a smirk on his face. "He's right there, teaching and instructing like an obedient god. Why do you have to be so dismissive of him like that?"

My mouth was dropping open, but I was distracted by a thunderous, grating sound from the other side of the room. I peeked around Yael to discover that Rome had pulled a marble tree branch clear from the divider wall behind him, leaving a gaping hole that looked into another room beyond them. A sol boy appeared in the opening, staring through at us. He opened his mouth, seemingly forming words, but I couldn't hear anything.

"An enchantment," Yael answered my unasked question. "Each of the alcoves is sound-proof. You shouldn't be able to see between the marble branches, either, but I think Strength just poked a hole in that enchantment."

I shook my head as Rome tried to fit the branch back into place, before giving up and throwing that at his student, too. She managed to catch it in time, turning and placing it on the couch beside her. The seat cushions were flattened under its weight.

"Was that supposed to be a lesson?" I asked Yael beneath my breath.

"I can still hear you," Rome answered in a raised voice, "you're not that damn far away, Rocks."

"Oh, right." I shoved my thumbs up. "You're doing a great job! Mind if we all just sit here and watch?"

"Go ahead." He kicked one of the couches aside and then picked it up, leaning it against the wall to cover the hole that he had made. "I know I'm doing a great job. I do a great job at everything."

"Can we maybe do training somewhere other than here?" his student finally asked. Her voice was rough, short, and lacking refinement. Her eyes were also sharp, and she couldn't seem to decide where to put her hands.

"What's wrong with here?" Rome gestured at the space by spreading his hands out. "It's lovely in here."

I snorted. Yael was trying to hold back his laugh. Aros was shaking his head. Everyone seemed to have turned to watch Rome, except for Coen, who was possibly taking a nap, and Siret's sol, who was still listening intently to a Siret that the rest of us couldn't see.

"There aren't that many things to demonstrate my Strength on," the girl replied.

"Strength is more than the physical damage you can cause," Yael spoke up, stepping toward the girl with a very familiar look on his face.

He was being 'persuasive'.

"Oh?" She turned fully to face him, as did Rome.

"Yes." Yael nodded wisely, coming to a stop in front of her. "Strength is of the mind, also. The best exercise to demonstrate strength of the mind is to stand without movement or sound, for extended periods of time."

"Really?" She sounded half-convinced already.

In reply, Yael simply walked her to the wall, and then stood back, looking proud. "You're doing so well already. Mind you don't move a muscle or make a sound, though. Blink three times if you understand."

I was impressed that Yael had managed to trick her so easily. She was trapped in the experiment now, as questioning it further would break the experiment that he had sneakily started right under her nose.

She blinked three times.

"Can we throw things at her?" Aros asked, suddenly interested in the experiment.

"Don't see why not." Rome glanced from the chunk of marble on the couch, to his student, and back again. "It would certainly build strength."

"Oooo-kay," I interjected, jumping forward and standing in front of the weapon that would probably do more decapitating than strength-building. "Why don't we all just let the girl do her experiment without torturing her?" I tugged on the sleeve of Rome's shirt, pulling his attention to me. "Two? Want to take a nap? Look how much fun One is having."

Rome glanced over at Coen, who miraculously still had his eyes closed.

"It does look fun," he admitted.

"Okay, that's settled then. You're going to nap and the sol will still have a head for you to throw things at tomorrow."

His hands found my hips, lifting me up and away. He then tossed the marble off the couch, causing another horrible cracking sound as the chunk of stone hit the ground. He slumped heavily down onto the couch, but too much abuse in such a short period of time caused it to splinter and collapse beneath him. He jumped up, scowling at it, before stalking into Aros's alcove.

"Switch," he demanded, staring at the Seduction

student and the Persuasion student, and pointing at the broken couch.

The Seduction student got up from her seat gracefully, flicking a silky mass of red-pink hair over her leather-clad shoulder, before brushing past Rome. I fought the urge to pluck each gorgeous red-pink strand of hair from her dumb, gorgeous head. I couldn't watch her as she sauntered seductively over to the broken couch, so I turned my attention to the Persuasion student instead. She had soft blond hair, left in waves about her shoulders, and a childishly beautiful face. She didn't exactly have commanding features like Yael's, but I could see how her suggestions would be taken easily. There was something about her that I just wanted to *trust* even though I kept trying to tell myself that the only thing I could trust about her was how much I wanted to lock her in a closet so that I could have my Abcurses back.

Was that unreasonable?

"A little bit," Yael answered my thoughts, "but we're not complaining."

Rome sank down onto the vacated couch, propping his feet onto the other couch in that alcove and tipping his head back just like Coen's. I watched as he shifted around uncomfortably, constantly re-adjusting his position. *How the hell was Coen remaining so still?*

"What did we miss?" a familiar voice asked from behind us.

Rome jumped up again, his eyes shooting open. "I

knew there was no way you could sleep comfortably on those things!" he announced, sounding victorious.

Coen and Siret were striding into the room, and the apparent illusions of them had flickered out of view. Coen was no longer sleeping on the couch, and Siret's student was no longer fixated on the spot where he was supposed to be standing. She had jumped up in alarm and was now staring at the real him, stuttering in confusion.

"You *are* a sol of Trickery, *aren't* you?" Siret bated her, stopping at Cyrus's circular table and dropping an assortment of wooden food containers onto the surface.

Emmy must have followed Cyrus out of the room earlier, because I didn't hear an outraged scream when her scrolls were crushed.

The Trickery student looked appropriately chastised, her purple eyes downcast, her hands shoved moodily into the pockets of her pants.

"Not to be a dick or anything—" Siret began, before Rome cut him off.

"He definitely means to be a dick."

"*But*," Siret continued, "you should really be able to tell when you're being conned by an illusion. It's part of the power, being able to see through other people's tricks. I guess it was slim pickings for Trickery sols this life-cycle." He shrugged, taking the lids off the food containers.

He definitely meant to be a dick.

The Abcurses all grinned then, amused by my thought.

The Trickery student snarled, stalking past me for the door. "I'm just going to go, since you five clearly aren't going to teach us anything."

"We'll stay," the Seduction student piped up in her honeyed voice.

"Oh joy." I rolled my eyes. "Did you hear that, guys? The sexy one is staying. That'll calm things down."

"The sexy one isn't allowed to go anywhere," Coen muttered, pulling me against his chest. His hands slipped down over the curve of my back, finding their way into the folds of my cloak and down over the curve of my ass. He pulled me harder against him, making a deep, rumbly sound in the back of his throat. "You belong with us. Always."

I was having trouble finding a response that didn't involve me winding my legs around him and pushing my lips against his, so I only nodded and threw my arms around his neck. My face ended up pressed against his collarbone, so I dropped a soft kiss there. He shifted me up higher against the growing hardness that pushed into my belly. He was having that reaction over me. *Me.* Not some perfect, pink-haired, honey-voiced seduction sol. *Just me.* I pressed another kiss to his skin, and then another, and his hands tightened before reluctantly releasing me. His eyes found mine as my feet hit the floor, and I could see the promise in them. The heat of what might happen later.

TEN

I didn't have the energy to do anything other than slump down at the circular table and start pulling food toward my face. Rome came along behind me soon after and looped an arm around my middle, lifting me up from the stool. In response, I just leaned further over the table so that I could continue shovelling noodles into my mouth.

Shifting his position slightly, he took my place on the stool and sat me down so that I was now on his right leg. Then, without a word, he began pointing to the various foods arrayed before us. With one hand, I fed myself, while my other followed his indication, picking up the foods he was interested in and handing them back to him. The others watched our process with slightly astonished looks on their faces.

"That's actually impressive." Siret saluted me with his bread roll.

I tried to swallow most of the food in my mouth before I thanked him, because multitasking was only good up until the point where you were talking and eating, and then multitasking suddenly wasn't something to be that proud of.

We didn't say anything more as we ate, mostly because the two remaining sols were still in the room, but also because we were all starving. I wasn't sure how many meals we had skipped, but it was too many. After eating, Rome gently set me down again, and we started to file out of the room. I was sure that the guys had forgotten all about the two sols by that point, but they all seemed to be in a good mood so I didn't want to ruin it by pointing out that the two girls had slipped out after them and were now following us.

"So, how did we do on our first sun-cycle of being godly instructors?" Siret asked me, throwing his arm around me and pulling me into his side.

I was grateful for the embrace, because I still didn't want to slip on the frost-covered stone stairs leading down the mountain. I clutched at his shirt as we stepped down, wondering why the five of them didn't seem to need any further protection against the cold, whereas I did.

"You did great," I told him. "Your student really seemed to be ... learning ... so much. What was your illusion teaching her?"

"He was running through a list of all the

punishments given to gods who make eye-contact on Topia."

I arched a brow at him. "That doesn't happen."

"Hi." He held out his free hand to me. "My name is Siret, I'm the god of *Trickery*. Of course it doesn't happen, but she learnt something at least."

"She learnt something that isn't even true."

"Better than nothing."

I wasn't sure whether I wanted to argue with that logic or not, so I dropped it. "Where are we going?"

"We're going to find Cyrus, obviously. We have our assignment, remember?"

"I have *my* assignment," I corrected him. "And I don't really think that the last rotation and a half counts as the required amount of teaching."

"We're coming with you." Rome was the one to answer. "No arguments."

I stopped walking suddenly, causing one of them to almost run into me from behind.

"Oh my gods, we left your student in there," I realised aloud, spinning to face Rome.

"Who?" he grunted.

"Your student!" I reached out and swatted his arm. "She must still be standing against the wall."

"Oh." He scratched his head. "Well if she's still there tomorrow I won't throw her off the mountain. Happy?"

I glanced behind him to the two sols loitering on the path.

"You can go and tell your friend that she's free to move," I said, pointing back the way they had come. I might have disliked the sols because they were working far too closely with the Abcurses—therefore impinging on my Abcurse time—But that didn't mean I could stand by while they were tortured, no matter how mild the torture. I'd faced too much bullying in my own life. It wasn't in my nature to be okay with it, even for Abcurse-stealing sols.

The girls didn't budge, instead choosing to look down at me with varying amounts of disgust and disdain.

"Go," I repeated, putting a little bit of steel into my voice. My softer emotions toward them were going to disappear really quickly. Especially if they kept up this superior attitude.

"Or what?" The Persuasion sol folded her arms over her chest, looking down at me.

I could tell that she was holding herself back from what she really wanted to say and do, on account of the Abcurses. Unfortunately for her, I didn't have that same problem.

I pushed through the male bodies attempting to surround me, until I was facing her alone, my guys backed up behind me. The temper was bubbling up inside me again, feeling like some kind of dangerous force. For just a moment, it distracted me from the girls in front of me. Usually, when my emotions flared out of my control, it manifested in flame, but after what had happened with Yael the night before, I felt panic at the thought of causing another fire.

Instead, I directed my energy toward the ground beneath me. I had thought that it would help to focus me, but when the rocks along the side of the path began to shiver, I knew that I had made a mistake.

"Or. What?" the sol repeated, leaning forward to poke a finger into my chest.

Nearby, a large boulder splintered, sending tiny little rock pieces everywhere. One of them flew past my cheek fast enough to cut me. I felt the sting of it, and the sensation of blood running down my jawline. The sol didn't look so confident anymore, and I knew that it was probably because I was looking at her like some sort of crazy person in my attempts to focus my power. I hadn't even flinched when the rock had cut me. The ground beneath us was beginning to shake with small tremors.

"Let's go," the Seduction sol muttered, pulling on the arm of the other.

They both cast one final look in my direction before turning and hurrying back up the stone stairs. I watched, just in case I might have the pleasure of seeing one of them slip on the ice, but it wasn't meant to be.

"Soldier?" Siret was behind me, his hands on my arms, spinning me around. "You're doing great, just focus on my voice, look at me ... that's it, good girl."

His hands slipped up to my neck, warming my skin

as he pulled me forward, his lips pressing to the side of my mouth.

"Just focus here," he whispered, brushing his lips across my mouth.

My fingers were in his hair suddenly, pulling his mouth fully onto mine. I wasn't sure who had deepened the kiss, but his tongue was against mine, and the heat of his body was all the way along my front.

"Hate to break up the party..." Emmy's hesitant voice spoke up from further down the path, "...but I came to see how the lessons were going."

Siret set me down with a frustrated groan. "If that dweller interrupts us one more time, I don't care how attached to her you are, I'll—"

I slapped a hand over Siret's mouth, glancing through the guys to Emmy's pale face. *Shit*, she didn't even have a cloak. Cyrus was such an asshole.

"He didn't mean that," I told Emmy. "And it's lucky you showed up, because we need to find Cyrus."

Emmy sighed, and I released Siret to make my way to her.

"I was using checking up on you guys as an excuse to get away from him. Now I have to go back. Worst timing ever."

"I thought you would love this job, considering, you know ..." I shrugged off my cloak, handing it to her. "You love rules and gods and organising things."

"My problem isn't with the job, it's with the asshole

who's making me sleep in his room and eat all my meals with him. I can't get a break."

I tried to hold back my smile. "Oh? Why is he making you do that?"

"Because he says I'm a bug and it's fun to torture bugs?" Her answer was more of a question. She threw up her hands, sending the cloak billowing out around her. "How do I know? He's just an asshole."

"Sounds like he wants you around but he doesn't want to admit it." I tried to say the words innocently and casually and—

"Ow." I rubbed my arm, where Emmy had hit me. "So can you take us to him? I want to get this assignment out of the way before dark, not that sunlight will make a huge difference, but I can hope, right?"

"I wouldn't have any kind of hope for anything when it comes to *him*," Emmy said.

She turned and began to stomp back down the stairs. Siret was at my side again, fashioning another cloak for me before I could take even a single step.

"Thank you." I turned to him, reaching out for his hand. As soon as our skin touched, my thoughts immediately returned to the kiss that had just been interrupted. How his lips had pressed insistently against mine, how his tongue had driven into my mouth with enough purpose that we should have ended up naked and swimming.

"Please stop," Yael groaned, appearing at my other

side. "You're going to cause an embarrassing situation out here for everyone to see."

I bit down on my lip, turning to head after Emmy.

Either Emmy was deliberately taking us the longest way possible to find Cyrus, or else Cyrus was using all of his godly talents to avoid her, because it took us thirty clicks to finally track him down.

"What are you doing?" I asked, as soon as I saw him.

My words seemed to startle him, but that was only his fault, because he had startled me. He was *floating*. Or, more accurately, hovering. He skimmed across a small pond, west of the main platform at the top of the mountain. His feet didn't touch the water, even though small ripples spread out from where he floated, as though he was actually wading through the water. As he turned in the direction of our group, Emmy crossed her arms and let out a huff.

"I thought we had scheduled in a break from drinking for the next four rotations."

Cyrus arched his left eyebrow at her. "The schedule said to take a 'drink break', not a 'break from drinking'."

His foot slipped on the last word and I watched as an arc of water shot across the pond in our direction. I was pulled out of the way just before it splashed me, but no one helped Emmy. She ended up drenched, dripping wet from head to toe.

My body was so tense that my muscles were

starting to ache from the force of being held so tightly. Emmy was already on a knife's edge when it came to the Neutral God. She seemed to be one incident away from murdering him in his sleep. The water-drenching might have snapped her final thread of control. She didn't speak or move, other than the slight twitch in the corner of her eye. Not that she would succeed if she *did* try to murder him—seeing as he was immortal. Might have been fun to see her try, though.

Cyrus, who had finally recovered from his alcohol-induced stumble, actually looked slightly apprehensive. I'd never seen him show an ounce of unease, even when in the presence of other gods, but something in Emmy's expression was throwing him off.

"Uh ... sorry," he muttered, moving closer to us, while still remaining out of reach, hovering over the water. "It was an accident."

Emmy lifted a hand. I flinched.

Run, Cyrus.

I was mentally urging him on because I'd only seen Emmy this angry a few times in my life, and there was nothing that could make me stick around when she snapped like that. Your only chance was to hide until she cooled down.

"I. Quit."

She said those words without emotion. No inflection at all. Every one of us gasped. *Okay*, that was a lie—I was the only one who gasped. But dwellers couldn't quit. It wasn't a thing. They didn't get to just decide not to do their jobs anymore. That was like deciding not to live anymore. There weren't any other options. Life or death, dweller or death. It was the same thing.

"Emmy!" I rushed forward, reaching her in a moment. "What are you saying?"

She wiped her face, shaking off the excess water. "You heard me, Will, I refuse to take any more orders from him." She stomped to the water's edge. "You no longer control me, Cyrus. I will take my punishment, but I'm done with you."

Then with a huff, she spun around and stormed off.

Anger rose in me again. I swung myself toward Cyrus. My hands were shaking as I waved them at him. "You will fix this, Cyrus. So help me. Otherwise I am going to ... uh ... I'm going to do something really bad and annoying. Every single time you close your eyes you'll fear that this is the night I strike."

He wasn't looking at me, despite my threat. His eyes were directed along the path Emmy had just taken, even though she was no longer visible.

When he finally turned back to me, his expression was one of pure astonishment. "No one quits me."

I let out a derisive laugh. "Cyrus, you're a real asshole most of the time. Don't try and tell me that this is the first time someone has told you to go fuck yourself."

He glided across the water, his feet finally standing

firm on dry land. He was beside me now, towering over me. Heat washed down my spine. The Abcurses moved closer, clearly uncomfortable with Cyrus's sudden proximity.

Cyrus leaned down to me. "I've never let anyone get close enough to 'quit' me before. The dweller does not know who she is messing with. There is no way she's leaving."

I reached out and grabbed a fist full of his shirt, yanking his face even closer to mine, since I assumed the intense eye-contact he had going on was supposed to be some kind of intimidation tactic. "If you don't go and apologise to her right now, I'm going to make you wish you'd never been born ... created ... whatever the hell you are. That's my sister. I don't care if she's a dweller, or a bug. I don't care if she just quit you. If you mess with her, you mess with me. If you mess with me, you mess with the Abcurses. She might be a dweller, but I think you understand just how annoying *all* of us can be, when we want to be."

I heard a few rumbles of laughter from behind, but there was also a lot of tension riding the group. Everyone was wondering if I'd just pushed Cyrus too far. We were about to find out if the leverage I'd had over him since he killed me was gone.

We remained close together, silence growing between us. His eyes were raging, swirling in the scariest way. But I didn't break the stare-off. *Dweller or death.* Emmy was remaining a dweller, that was the only option.

"Fix it, please." I tried to give him something, so that he could feel like he had the upper hand. The *please* was my offer.

His jaw tightened, but the icy rage in his gaze lessened minutely.

"Fine," he snapped, pulling away from me. He tilted his head up, squeezing his eyes tightly closed for a moment, before letting out a breath.

"Your punishment still stands," he told me. "Go to Topia, to the panteras. They have something of mine. I find myself in need of it."

I tried not to let my excitement show. Cyrus had given me exactly what I needed: a reason to go to the panteras.

"Is that all?" I asked, almost bouncing on the spot.

He nodded. "For now. Let's see how you go with one assignment before I give you the next one."

He brushed past me then, striding back toward the main platform in a rush of white robes and icy energy.

Tension had been holding me rigid for so long that my leg muscles actually ached when I finally relaxed. I found myself leaning back against Aros as he draped an arm around me, his warm heat seeping through my clothing and into my skin.

"You shouldn't antagonise Cyrus," Rome told me. "Let his wrath be directed at us. We can handle it."

I shrugged, straightening a little so that I could

clear my head. Aros was very distracting.

"Everyone knows that taking me on means taking you all on. I might as well use that to my advantage."

He shook his head at me, but the half-smile on his face told me that he wasn't as upset as he was acting.

"Do you think Cyrus will hurt Emmy?" I asked them. If they thought there was even the smallest chance, I wouldn't be leaving Champions Peak that sun-cycle.

Siret flashed me his trademark, wide grin. "She has you and you have us, not to mention she's always been mouthy as hell when it comes to Neutral. I'm pretty sure that if Cyrus hasn't thrown her off a cliff already, he's probably not going to start this sun-cycle."

"She'll be fine." Coen sounded confident. "Cyrus has a soft spot for her, otherwise he'd have killed her already."

"He has a soft spot for Willa, you mean." Yael didn't sound particularly happy about that fact.

"For both of them, then," Coen revised.

None of them seemed particularly worried about Cyrus killing Emmy, and I figured they were probably right. My friend hadn't ever tried to hide how much the god pissed her off—not from us, and not from him either—but still, he hadn't killed her yet. He also said he'd fix it. So ... I had to believe she'd be fine.

"Okay, I guess we're off to Topia. Anyone know the best way to sneak in?" The pocket that Staviti had opened was gone now.

Five almost identical grins broke out, all aimed at me—though Coen's had a hint of a grimace to it.

"Staviti is going to be watching this mountain closer than Topia right now," he told me. "So, the pathways back to Topia should be safer than usual. As long as we get in and out as quickly as possible."

"That's right," Rome chimed in. "They're going to notice if we're not here to train our champions tomorrow, but we can get this done in a night."

"Maybe Cyrus will have thrown them all off the cliff by the time we get back?" I suggested hopefully. I was pleased to see that my comment widened their smiles, but the good mood quickly drained from our group as we travelled down the mountain.

As it turned out, there were a lot of 'back ways' into Topia, but they weren't so common that you could just turn a corner and slip into the other realm. You had to travel a short distance to one of the known pockets, or else traverse harsh terrain for some of the lesser known —for good reason—pathways. The Abcurses were of the opinion that since I was undead, I wouldn't have the same problem crossing through the energy as I'd had on my first trip through a back door into Topia.

So, getting *through* the pocket wasn't going to be a problem, but getting *to* the pocket was a whole other issue. We made it down the mountain and began walking.

I tried to listen as Siret explained how we were going to get there, but the moment he started using words like "east" and "miles" my attention began to drift to the scraggly bushes lining the valley.

"Are you even listening, Soldier?" Siret asked with a chuckle, the brush of his hand across my shoulder returning my focus to him.

"You lost her at east," Aros told him. "Her eyes glazed right over."

I narrowed my eyes on them. "I was listening." I jerked my head up and pointed forward. "We have to go in ... that direction."

Siret laughed at me again. "That leads to the outback stockyards, where the bullsen are herded between breeding seasons. You should probably leave the direction thing to us."

"Freaking east," I muttered, stomping harder as I followed them.

Our conversations were brief then as we picked up the pace. We travelled down the mountain, up another mountain and around a small river that fed back into the ocean. We were now approaching a dense forest, and I was hoping the pocket would be *before* the treeline.

"Are we there yet?" I huffed out.

"Not yet," several voices grunted out in reply.

"I was really hoping it wouldn't be in the forest," I added conversationally. "I was killed in a forest just like this. Do you remember?"

"That's not something we're ever likely to forget, dweller-baby," Coen told me, brushing aside some low hanging branches that would have smacked me in the face. "And we're getting closer."

Sucking in another deep breath, I pushed on, trying to enjoy the moment alone with my Abcurses. The trees really were bothering me, though. The forest was so much like the last one we'd been in.

"Think about the swimming instead," Yael suggested.

Aros groaned before Yael had even finished his suggestion. "Gods, please don't. I only have so much control. Willa's thoughts drive me crazy."

Think unsexy thoughts. Think unsexy thoughts.

Everyone laughed, except Aros, who groaned again. "The mantra is even worse than if you just tortured us with the thoughts."

"New plan!" Yael declared. "Think about ... your new energy."

My feet were swept out from under me as Rome scooped me up and somehow managed to navigate a jagged boulder the size of a small hill. No doubt he knew that it would have taken me twenty rotations to climb it on my own. I relaxed in his arms, enjoying the brief respite from walking.

"It's strange, my energy," I told them. "It feels more controlled, and yet at the same time, I don't really know what to expect from it. It's almost like ... I have no rules."

Saying the words out loud made me realise how true it was. My energy didn't seem to want to subscribe to a particular category of power. It was swirling so strongly—no part of it felt like 'fire' or 'earthquake' or 'chaos'.

"Is that possible?" I asked. "For me to have multiple god-powers?"

There was a moment of silence before I continued. "Do you all feel your power? Are you able to tell that it's Pain or Trickery? Will I ever know what I'm capable of?"

"You don't just wake up one sun-cycle a god and know instinctively what your power is," Rome told me. "Generally, you use the power and learn from it. There are cases of some gods who thought they had a particular power, only for it to end up another, closely connected power."

"Exactly," Aros chimed in. "Love and Seduction are closely-related powers, but ultimately different. For the most part, though, the moment you use your power, it's pretty clear."

Coen nodded. "Yep, like mine could have been electrical forces. There's a god who can harness the energy of a storm, and my Pain mimics lightning energy. But I have no control over the weather."

I felt the zap of his power run across my skin, and it was exactly how I imagined an electrical current would feel ... right before it killed you.

"Chaos fits me," I mused. "It encompasses so many different things. Anything that disrupts the normal way of existence, right?"

They didn't have an answer for me, and I wasn't even sure myself. It still didn't quite feel right, and Cyrus seemed so sure that I wasn't the Chaos Beta. So ... *what the hell was I?*

Rome had set me back on my feet now, but he was still close enough to wrap his giant arm around me. The warmth he exuded—along with his intoxicating scent—was enough to make me lightheaded.

"The panteras might have some answers for us," he said. "Try not to stress about it until we talk with them."

By the time we made it to the pocket, I was exhausted enough that I could have fallen asleep right there in the woods, but Coen encouraged me through the lightly misting waterfall and pulled me through the magical energy without so much as a warning. Arriving in Topia didn't curb my need to rest, however. I wanted to curl up with the Abcurses: the six of us together, safe, where nothing could ever tear us apart. This, of course, was pure fantasy, because I was pretty sure we'd never been so unsafe in our lives. Staviti was keeping a close eye on everything now. No one was safe.

We emerged in a part of Topia that I had never seen before. It was still lush, overflowing with life and colour, but the plants and trees were so dense that they seemed to be closing in on me somehow. I could barely even move through all the foliage.

"This is the Garden of Everlasting," Coen

explained, as we pushed our way through. "The plants here are resistant to magic and energy. They do not die. Every life-cycle they merge closer and closer. We believe that one sun-cycle, no one will walk through this land unless the garden allows them to."

Huge, purple flowers hung from vines above our heads, intertwined with the large trunks and branches of the nearby trees. Instead of feeling claustrophobic, as might have been expected, I actually felt safe. I was overwhelmed by the feeling that not even Staviti would be able to see through the magical garden.

Tension I hadn't even realised I was carrying eased from my body. My shoulders relaxed, and I started to move with more carefree abandon than I'd felt in a long time.

"You're right at home here, Willa-toy." Yael wore a lazy grin, his eyes following the movement of my hands as I brushed them across a very bright, green leaf. "Most people wouldn't be brave enough to touch a *canterpode*. They'd be worried about getting spiked."

The moment he said its name, the canterpode I'd been touching became visible. It was the same colour as the leaf it was spread out across, it's body segmented, almost furry. I jerked my hand back in a rush, flinching as I brushed something thorny.

Spinning around, I threw my hands in the air. "Why didn't you tell me earlier?" I asked Yael. "I thought it was a plant!"

He blinked at me like I was an idiot, before shaking his head. "It looked right at you, I figured you saw it."

"Well, I didn't," I shot back, wiping my hands on my pants to try and dispel the sensation of furry bug. After that, I kept my hands to myself, and my eyes on the constant lookout for creatures. I had never imagined that Topia would be filled with so many animals. Before I had visited the realm, I had mostly pictured it as a world of gods. Nothing else, really. Just gods, standing around looking at each other. Maybe throwing some balls of fire.

"Balls of fire," Siret snorted.

"Stop listening to my thoughts," I told him firmly.

"Stop shouting them so loudly," he countered. His words were softened by his actions. He was holding a really large plant—probably filled with canterpodes—back for me, keeping me from accidentally befriending more wildlife.

"We're almost free from the Garden of Everlasting," Rome said, using his height to peer above the landscape. "Just a few more clicks and we'll be out."

"How do we find the panteras then?" I asked, slightly breathless from all the hiking.

Siret was the one to answer. "We'll call for them."

That made me think of Leden, and the bond I'd felt with her. I wondered if she would know if I called for her. *Had she felt it when I died? Would she have any answers for me?*

ELEVEN

When we emerged into the open countryside, I fought against the urge to return to the garden. It might have been overrun by creepy, camouflaged bugs, but it held a note of safety and protection. Once free of the garden, I felt exposed and vulnerable.

The Abcurses must have picked up on my nerves, because they closed in around me. When the five of them were towering over me, some of my panic finally eased. They were better than a garden.

"Knowing Staviti is out there makes me nervous," I admitted.

"He'll never touch you," Yael vowed. "Not while we're here to protect you."

The thought of them *not* being with me was enough to have the panic rushing back again. They were already immortal—I just needed them to stay that way. They had to live forever, for my sanity.

Heat brushed across the backs of both of my hands, and I ended up intertwining my fingers with Siret and Aros, who were the closest to me. Their touch instantly calmed my frazzled nerves and I felt my step grow lighter. I had no idea how they managed to soothe me the way that they did, but I wasn't going to complain.

"I'm going to call for the panteras now," Coen announced.

The others slowed their steps, bringing me to a halt as well.

Leden. Her name sprang to mind and I felt an almost giddy anticipation at seeing her again. She was smart and funny, more personable than most of the dwellers, sols, and gods combined. Plus, she had a sense of humour. Who didn't like a beast with a sense of humour?

I had no idea how Coen was going to call for the panteras, so I just stood back and watched him. He had tilted his head back and was focussing his attention toward the sky. I mimicked the posture, calling out to Leden in my mind. She had been the fastest pantera, which surely meant that she would beat the others here.

Coen let out a low chuckle. "You want our panteras to race?" He directed his full attention to me, the sky forgotten.

I shrugged. "I don't think there'll be much of a race. Leden is superfast."

Coen's tolerant amusement melted into a smirk, which I ignored. I knew Leden would arrive first. A flash of white cut through the blue of the sky, then. I directed my attention upward again and the brightness blinded me for a click, until the figure loomed closer.

Leden. Most of the panteras had similar markings or features, with common shades of fur, but I knew that it was her. The brilliant, snowy white of her coat seemed unique, at least to me.

Hello, sacred one.

"Leden!" I shouted, before quickly shutting up. I had forgotten that this was supposed to be a stealth mission.

I've been waiting for your return. We have much to discuss.

"Can any of you hear her when she talks in my head?" I asked.

"No." Aros briefly pulled my attention from the sky. "The panteras choose who will receive their words. Even with our bond, she can block us."

"They're so powerful," I mused. "How did the gods manage to exile them from the populated areas of Topia?"

Maybe we chose to leave. Leden's voice filled my head. *To protect the main sources of this world's power.*

Usually, cryptic comments like that would have had me confused, but this time I knew exactly what she was talking about. Along with guarding a stream of water that somehow unlocked a person's magical ability, the panteras were also the protectors of the mortal glass—whose depths of knowledge I could put no measure on. The water, the glass, and whatever else they guarded were all special. It made sense that they would prize those sources of power above all others.

It's time for you to learn more of the truth. Leden landed softly, about ten feet from us. *It's time you righted the wrongs of Topia.*

The wrongs of Topia? Was she talking about the fact that the gods seemed to be draining Minatsol to sustain their world? Or was this specifically about Staviti and his actions? The servers, for example. The only thing I did know was that *righting the wrongs of Topia* was not a suitable job for me. Pushing through Siret and Coen, I rushed across to her. My hands lifting to brush across her soft coat.

"I missed you," I said, only realising in that moment how true it was. I might not have spent much time with her, but I already knew—and had experienced—that bonds could form quickly, and strongly.

I have missed you also. It is not easy to be bonded to one so far away.

Her tone held only sadness, no blame, but I still felt terrible.

When a familiar heat brushed across the right side of my body, I wrapped an arm around Siret's waist.

"Are you going to introduce us, Soldier?" he asked.

He dropped a kiss on my head then, and for a click, I forgot what he'd asked. Leden nudged me, bringing my focus back.

"Abcurses—meet Leden, she's the fastest pantera." I felt her satisfaction at my words. "We're bonded. I don't know if it has an official name, but I definitely feel the connection."

"Nice to meet you, Leden," Aros said, finding my other side. "Panteras are loyal and wise," he added, whispering to me. "They won't bond with just anyone."

Willa is unique. I knew that Leden had directed those words to the others as well, evident by the way they turned to her.

"We know," Yael said bluntly. "She's special."

I'd been called special before, but usually the tone indicated that my kind of special was a physical hazard to others. Yael and Leden weren't talking about *that* kind of special, though. Their words made my heart a little light and my knees a little weak.

I really needed to start thanking someone for how my life had turned out. Not Staviti, of course—he was an asshole. And not Cyrus, because you should never thank the people that stab you in the chest. And not Rau, either, because the only thanks he deserved was the thanks I'd give him after he let me douse him in my crazy-fire. So ... someone else. I needed to thank a completely unrelated third party for how my life had turned out.

The beating of wings drew our attention as five additional panteras appeared on the horizon, sweeping across the sky toward us. I assumed they were the panteras that the Abcurses had bonded with, the same way I had with Leden.

It is time to go, Willa. Staviti stalks these lands, we must not linger.

Leden's words had barely brushed my mind before hands were on my waist. Aros lifted me onto her back, letting his touch linger on me. I found myself leaning down and pressing my lips to his. Just like every other time he'd kissed me, the desire his touch evoked just about knocked me over, and I almost toppled straight off Leden.

"Looks like you might still have the power to roll her, Seduction," Coen noted, from where he stood with his pantera.

The pair exchanged a look, and my body tightened.

"It's stronger than I expected, since Willa is no longer a dweller," Aros admitted, his eyes meeting mine again. "I thought she'd be able to resist at least a little bit more now."

Siret took a step closer. "I think our emotions heighten the powers. Willa can definitely handle our abilities now, we all know that. I'd say your love for her, and hers for you, is elevating the draw of Seduction."

"So, I'm going to need Coen and you together," I blurted out, before slamming my mouth closed.

Something shimmered almost visibly in the air

between Aros and me. Coen was too far away, but I could see the way his eyes darkened. It was like energy, lightning, electricity ... and I was about half a click from getting off Leden's back. Siret quirked a brow at me, but he didn't seem upset.

This is not the time. Leden's voice was tinged with amused impatience.

"Are you sure?" I murmured back.

"She's sure, Soldier." Siret winked at me and then moved to his own beast.

With a snort and shake of her head, Leden thrust her wings out to the side, before leaping high into the air and taking off across the sky like we were being chased. I could sense that her mind was now focused on the task at hand, so I tried not to think or speak.

At first, I watched the world below, riveted to the beauty of Topia, but after a few clicks of staring down at the scenery unfolding below us, my stomach started to roll with nausea. I mainly focussed ahead after that, only peeking over my shoulder on occasion to make sure that the Abcurses were there.

They're still there, Leden assured me.

"Are you going to tell me more about this *truth* I need to learn?" If she was talking, it must be okay for me to talk as well.

There is only so much we can share with you. Some of it you have to learn for yourself. All I can do is send you on the right path.

One sun-cycle, I decided, I would find a friend who was less cryptic.

Amusement from Leden flittered across my mind.

By the time we landed in the fields where the pantera lived, my butt was numb. When I slid off Leden, my legs almost collapsed for a moment, before I was able to straighten again. I wandered closer to the creek that Leden had landed beside, feeling an insane urge to touch the water again.

It will always draw you.

I didn't acknowledge Leden's statement, even though I really wanted to know what she meant by that. *Why did it draw me*? How could I possibly have had this water before, if there was none of it in Minatsol?

"Heavy thoughts?" Yael's face appeared next to mine in the reflection of the water, followed by the others. The six of us stood there for a click as I admired their perfect reflections.

"I'm just trying to figure out my connection to all of this," I told them. "The panteras ... this water. The answers are here, I just need to dig deeper. I know we came here for Cyrus, but I feel like there's something here for me, too."

The mortal glass.

I wasn't sure which one of the winged creatures had whispered that in my head—we were now surrounded by them. It really didn't matter, though, because the end result was the same. I needed to stare into the glass again. I needed to uncover the answers it held. Last time had been a history lesson ... maybe this time the history would be more personal.

Leden was right behind me, and I turned to her. "Can you please take me to the mortal glass?"

I thought you'd never ask.

We walked to the mountain, and then paused at the entrance. Coen took my right side, Rome on my left, and I realised that I was rarely between the twins like that. They were both so huge that it made me feel extra small, but also safe. I was protected between them. Having been alone so much of my life, always on the outside, it was an odd concept to be the centre of something. To feel like I was important. And because I could, I reached out and captured their hands.

We all moved together into the cave, the other boys close behind. The panteras didn't follow us this time, and I briefly wondered why, before deciding that it didn't matter. I had the Abcurses with me. The cave felt different this time. Familiar, like it was a piece of my history now, and stepping back inside brought old memories to the surface of my mind, memories that I couldn't properly grasp, memories that didn't even seem to belong to me. On my last visit, I had struggled to see through the darkness of the cave, but everything was much clearer this time.

"Wow," I said, blinking as I stared. "Undead eyesight is so much better than dweller eyesight."

"I really wish she'd stop saying undead," Aros groaned.

Siret snorted. "You haven't suffered until she starts talking about it while you're naked."

Aros was silent for half a click, before shrugging. "Still worth it."

No doubt I was blushing, but thankfully we were now at the mortal glass, so the focus shifted from my sex life to the glittery surface. Just like last time, the scars and gashes from whatever asshole had hacked at the wall were visible, but as we stared into the glass, the bleeding stone disappeared, replaced by an image of a kingdom, slowly settling into view.

The castle was perched high on a hill. Very similar, actually, to the cliff at Champions Peak. The ocean behind it had rolling green hills on every other side, and a small village of stone houses scattered all the way down the cliff into the valley below. The only difference was that there were no dead zones around this land. Everything was green and thriving.

"Do any of you recognise this place?" Yael asked, his voice low.

"I think it's Minatsol," Coen replied.

Our view, at that point, was from above, stretching all the way along the countryside. Then, in a swirl, the scene zoomed in closer. My head spun as we sped through the gates of the castle and into the stone building. Once inside, I was able to focus again. The interior was decadent: tapestries covered the stone walls, rugs were piled onto the stone floors, and greenery climbed through every open window, sunlight streaming after it. Not even the richest of sols —the most talented of beings—had homes like that.

We reached a set of closed, ornately carved double doors. The carving depicted a scene of what appeared to be a crowd surrounding a couple who were elevated on a low dais, their arms in the air—

The doors slammed open. On the other side was a bedroom the size of most sol houses or at least five dweller houses put together.

"This is just getting weird now," Siret grumbled. "If someone is having sex in here, I'm out."

I didn't answer, too fascinated by what we were about to see. The scene continued to zoom closer until we were beside the huge bed, piled high with furs and blankets. There was a woman right in the centre of the bed, propped up on a mound of pillows. She was pale and sweaty, her long dark hair a tangled mass. Her beauty was apparent, even with her face screwed up in pain. She let out some low gasps and then the man at her side came into view. He was handsome, tall, and broad-chested. He also wore a look of complete and total devastation.

"My love, please hold on." His voice echoed from far away. "The healer is almost here."

She gasped in and out, her words hoarse. "I fear they will be too late. The babes are not patient."

It was then that I noticed her stomach, mostly

hidden beneath the furs, but clearly round and swollen. She had said *babes* ... twins. I glanced toward Rome and Coen. It was still impossible for me to believe their mother had twins *and* triplets. Lucky she was a god.

Unfortunately, the woman on this bed—despite her beauty—was not.

She arched up then, screaming. Her wail had the man at her side jumping, before he reached out and captured her hand in his. "They're coming now," she cried. "But there is something wrong."

A few women rushed in then, holding towelling and wooden bowls of water. They started to strip the top layer of bedding away. "Do not push yet, my Queen," one woman warned her. "Let me check your readiness first."

Queen. I knew this looked like a kingdom, only ... there had not been a king or queen of Minatsol for many life-cycles. This had to be a royal family from the past.

The woman who was stripping the bed went very white, and I was guessing it was because the bed was soaked in blood. Red spread out under the queen, far too much to be part of the natural birthing process.

The king let out a strangled sound of pain before he began to shout for healers. I realised that I was holding my breath as I waited to see what would happen. My heart pounded hard in my chest, my body unable to understand that this wasn't happening now.

That there was nothing that I could do to change the fate of this woman.

There was a loud crash in the background—another door opening as a man wearing a guard's uniform rushed into view.

"Your Majesty, the healer has not arrived. I fear he will not get here in time."

The king looked like he wanted to rip the guard's head off. "Fetch me Elliot," he ordered, his voice hard.

The guard hesitated, blinking. "That crazy preacher? You think he can help the queen?"

"Do as I tell you!" The king dismissed him, turning back to his wife.

When she came into view again, I let out a low gasp. Someone wrapped an arm around me and I sank into the warmth of one of my guys, needing the comfort.

"She doesn't look good," I cried, pressing a hand to my mouth.

The woman was as pale as parchment. Her ladies were piling towelling beneath her in an attempt to stem the bleeding. The king was shouting again, and just as I took a step closer, my eyes glued to the scene, everything went dark.

The mortal glass seemed to die for a brief click, and then suddenly they were back again. Only this time, the royal couple were no longer in Minatsol.

They were in Topia.

I knew that because I recognised the stream from

my first visit. There were only three in this scene: the king, the still-very-pregnant queen, and a ragged looking man with wispy white hair. "Are you sure this will work?" the king asked. He was carrying his wife, who appeared to be unconscious. "No one has ever stepped foot in the untouched world. I didn't believe it was possible."

The ragged man—Elliot, I was guessing—just shrugged. "The pathways are there, Majesty, one simply needs to know the way. The water is pure on this side, the original source of power. This is your only chance."

They stopped before a waterfall, which trickled into a small stream.

"Place her there," Elliot said, pointing toward a shallow section.

The king didn't waste another moment, wading out into the water to lay his wife down. The water rose up around her body but wasn't deep enough to cover her completely. The king never let her go and—not that I would admit it to anyone—I was starting to get a little weepy over their love. The possibility of losing his wife and children was obviously destroying him, but he hadn't stopped fighting for her. Not for a single moment.

"This better have a happy ending," I murmured.

The Abcurses pressed in closer to me, the six of us locked together, invested in this scene.

At first there was a lot of blood in the water, but

then it slowly drifted away, and no more replaced it. "Drip the water into her mouth," Elliot told the king.

The king again obeyed, without hesitation, parting the queen's lips and letting the water slowly trickle inside. With each drop, more colour returned to her face. I was about an inch from the glass now; if I got any close I'd be in the actual scene, but I didn't want to miss a moment.

As a healthy pink flush returned to her face, her eyes fluttered open. She stared up at the man cradling her in his lap. "What ... happened, Leon?"

The broadest of smiles pushed his cheeks up. "You almost broke your promise to me, my love. You're not allowed to die, remember?"

She smiled tenderly, lifting her hands to touch his face. Just as she did, her eyes got wide, and then her face screwed up in pain. She arched in his lap, her legs drawing up. "The babies are coming," she cried out. "You need to deliver our children."

This spurred him into action. His focus, now that his wife was no longer dying, was to save his children. He pulled her further back in the water, resting her head against a smooth stone surface, which stopped her from slipping under the water. He then slid across the wet rocks to pause before her legs. The stress that had been marking his face was now replaced with determination.

"I can see something," he said, as he pushed her

long dress higher. "I think you need to push now, whenever the next wave of pain hits you."

She gritted her teeth, closed her eyes, and with a deep breath she pushed. Her hands slid across rocks until she found her grip on something. The moment she had a hold of some rocks, she pushed again. Her breathing was heavy between each scream of pain.

The first tiny cry that hit the air brought an actual tear to my eye. That tear slipped down my cheek, followed by another. The king lifted the child higher, giving us the perfect view of his chubby body.

"It's a boy." Rome sounded proud. Like he'd somehow had something to do with it. "Strong and healthy."

I almost suggested someone get him a drink to go with that pride, but ... who was I kidding? We all felt it. Leon handed the child over to his wife, and she cradled the young boy against her chest, holding him like he was the most precious thing in the world. Her eyes drank the baby in, her fingers tracing across his cheeks. "Welcome to the world, Jakan, you are truly loved."

"Are you ready, Madeline?" The king used her name for the first time, distracting her from her child. "I think you're going to have to push again."

The queen was tired, anyone could see that. Despite the healing waters, she had lost a lot of blood. She'd almost died, but strength and determination to bring her children into the world was enough to have her leaning up, one hand holding her son close, while she pushed again.

It was quicker the second time, and soon another boy was placed on her chest, right next to his brother.

Her arms shook as she held her children, tears streaming across her cheeks and into the waters of Topia. When her husband moved to her side, they both stared at the boys. Madeline brushed her hand across the second child's head and said, "Welcome to the world, Staviti, you are truly loved."

Then the mortal glass went blank.

TWELVE

I was staring at the glassy rock-face, my eyes wide and unblinking.

"Staviti?" I was asking for a confirmation of some kind as I reached out to touch the smooth surface. "That was Staviti. Why did it show me Staviti?" I spun, directing my question to Leden. She must have entered the cave at some point.

The mortal glass holds the secrets of the land. Leden's calming voice washed through me, soothing some of the confusion that was clouding up my mind. *It will show you the lives of those connected to the land: their truths, their histories, their realities.*

"Show me my sister," I requested, turning back to the glass, my heart beginning to thump against my ribs. "Emmy. Emmanuelle."

The glass remained blank, the surface glittering darkly. It seemed infinite, even though I could reach

220

out and touch it. It was dizzying, staring into that endless blackness.

The dweller you call your sister is not one of the land. She is born of people, not of magic. This had been spoken in the voice of another pantera, one with a deep, dusky tone. I turned and found myself surrounded by unblinking, luminous eyes, filling the cave behind us. The panteras shifted soundlessly, waiting. None of them stepped forward as the speaker.

"Show me ... my mother." I revised my request. Surely my mother would be part of the land. She had been made a Jeffrey by Staviti's magic, after all.

I waited, my heart pounding harder and faster with every passing moment, and sure enough, the colours inside the glass began to emerge.

My mother was in Cyrus's cave, right where we had left her. She was sitting on the bed that I had slept on, her eyes focussed blankly on the wall ahead. I knew that it couldn't mean anything, but I still found myself clinging to the hope that she had chosen my bed to sit on for a reason. She missed me, maybe. She wondered where I was. I scoffed, shaking my head. My mother would never have missed me or wondered where I was. Even before she became a Jeffrey.

"Show me Staviti again," I asked next, my mind wandering back to the image of a tiny baby boy in Madeline's arms.

I wanted to know why the glass had shown me that particular piece of history. *Why Staviti's birth*? Was it because it marked the beginning of the gods? Topia had been a land free of gods, once. Staviti's birth must have marked a significant turning point for the land itself. The water had saved his mother's life. Had it changed him as well?

The scene before me slowly filtered into view, as though filled by slow tendrils of coloured smoke, gradually gaining substance.

There was a little boy before us. He was standing in a field, staring up at a mountain. I recognised the landscape after only a click, though the coastline had changed, and so had the surrounding vegetation. It was Champions Peak—the craggy rocks formed the same shape: a rough stone wall to guard against the violent waves of the sea.

Everything else was different, though. *I was seeing into the past again.*

"Stav!" a boy's voice called out, and the child we had been looking at turned around. Another boy ran into view, holding a stick almost as tall as he was.

"What do you want, Jakan?" Staviti seemed agitated, his small brow furrowed, his eyes squinting at the other.

"You know you can't go there," Jakan replied, throwing down the stick, his voice losing some of the playfulness it had held only a moment ago. "Father said you can't go back to Topia. If you go there again it won't want to let you return. It might keep you."

The boy version of Staviti rolled his eyes, picking

up the stick that Jakan had dropped. "We belong there, both of us. We aren't like mother, or father, or the other children. We're special, can't you feel it? Can't you tell?"

"Don't go back there …" Jakan's voice began to fade, and the scene trembled before me, beginning to dissolve into something else.

"Stav! Stop!" the other boy was crying out, frantically scrambling over the unforgiving stone that lay at the base of the mountain.

Staviti didn't look back, and the scene fell away completely, leaving the mortal glass black, once again.

"Show me Jakan!" I cried out, my hands flattening to the stone, as though I could climb through it and deliver myself to the base of the mountain with the two boys.

The glass remained blank, cloaked in darkness. I waited, and then I repeated myself, my words softer this time: a request rather than an order.

"Show me Jakan, please."

The glass glimmered back, refusing to shift into another scene.

"Why won't it work?" I asked.

"Jakan must not be connected to the land," Aros replied, sounding just as confused as I was.

"He has to be." I shook my head. "He was Staviti's brother. He should be connected just like Staviti is."

"He *was* Staviti's brother," Rome corrected me. "He must no longer be alive. What you're seeing is the world as it was hundreds of life-cycles ago. Perhaps Staviti was the only brother to survive."

"Was he a god, even back then? Was he born a god?" I stepped away from the glass, towards Leden.

I can answer many of your questions, she replied, *but the others have forbidden me. It is not for us to choose a side in the battle between mortals and immortals.*

"I didn't even know we were in a battle." I glanced from Leden to the glowing eyes behind her. There was a humming sound emanating from them. It sounded like some kind of warning, a resonance of disapproval.

We have allowed you to speak to the mortal glass. A deep pantera voice skimmed across my mind, seeming to echo all around me. The Abcurses stirred, as though wary of the sudden change in the atmosphere. *It is time, now, for you to carry our gift to the Neutral God.*

I was almost surprised that they actually had something for me to bring to Cyrus. I had been more of the opinion that I would have to figure out what Cyrus's object was, before stealing it and sneaking it back to Minatsol. I had been agonising over how to ask the panteras what the object might be without alerting them to the fact that I was going to 'borrow' it. So far, the best I had come up with was: 'if there was a god with silver-white hair, a drinking problem, and rage issues … what might he want to steal from you?' followed by, 'can I hold it for a click?'

"What is the gift?" I asked, as the panteras inside

the cave began to stir, moving toward the entrance at a slow and languorous pace.

It will be arriving very soon. Leden had been the one to answer me, her flank brushing against my upper arm as we followed the others.

We moved out of the cave and I turned to glance behind me to make sure that I hadn't accidentally lost an Abcurse. Siret's smile hiked up at the corners and Yael's eyes flicked down my front, as though taking stock of me the same way I was taking stock of them. Coen nodded at me, his eyes shuttered, his expression guarded—*we're fine*, he seemed to be saying. Aros held my gaze a little too long—causing me to stumble sideways into Leden, who paused until I had managed to steady myself again. Rome nudged his chin forward, indicating that I should start watching where I was walking.

I was about to do just that when the shifting of colour caught my eye. I could have sworn that one of the trees had moved. I stopped walking altogether, squinting at the entrance of the cave—except that it was no longer there. There was a forest there, right where the dark opening should have been. The branches interlocked thickly, time-worn roots threading through the ground, making it look like they had been there for an eternity.

"Where did the cave go?" I whispered to Leden, my hand on her silky mane.

Just as the mortal glass does not see the secrets of those unconnected to the land, it does not want to be seen by such people, Leden replied, her voice in my head almost a whisper now. *The glass is selective—it will only appear for those who are connected, and the cave's purpose is to protect the glass. By that logic, the cave will hide itself from any person who is not connected to the land.*

"You mean ... a dweller is here? In Topia? That's your gift to Cyrus? A dweller?"

Leden snorted out a gentle sound, possibly amused. *There are many ways to be disconnected. For a god, it is the soul that connects to the land, not the body— the body is only a receptacle. If the soul is taken away, the person is no longer connected.*

I opened my mouth to ask exactly *how* a soul could be disconnected from a person's body, but the answer came to me before I had managed to voice the question. *The imprisonment realm.* I had seen it with my own eyes: Sienna tied to the chair, her dark hair falling about her, her wrists and ankles bound in chains. I thought back to Jakan, and how the glass had refused to show him. Maybe he wasn't dead after all—maybe there really was a reason the glass had chosen to show me Staviti's brother. Jakan was the key to figuring this out—I wasn't sure *how* I knew, but I was somehow sure of it. *My intuition is never wrong.*

"Your intuition is wrong all the time," Siret muttered, suddenly behind me.

"I can't recall it ever being right," Rome agreed.

"It was right about you five all being assholes," I

shot back, before glancing over at Leden. "Excuse the language."

"They can read your thoughts, Rocks," Coen informed me. "I'm sure they've heard worse."

I turned and kicked a rock with the toe of my shoe, watching as it sailed toward his face. It had been a small rock, but I still found myself frowning at how he flicked it out of the way so easily. It wasn't until I caught up to Leden again that I realised I had *kicked* a *rock*. With my own foot. As in, I had managed to do something slightly athletic without tripping and falling on my face. Kicking rocks was a *very* dangerous athletic activity, since it was so easy to misread the position of the rock and allow it to roll beneath your shoe instead of launching from the toe of your shoe— therefore throwing off your momentum and sending you falling backwards. That had been my previous experience with all rock-kicking attempts.

"Come to think of it," Aros mused, apparently joining in on my thoughts, "you *have* been less clumsy since your ... recent change. There has been less falling, tripping, and crowd-toppling."

"More fires though," Siret countered.

"Less fires actually," I shot back, liking the idea that I might have left some of my clumsiness behind, in my other life.

"Well, *bigger* fires then." Siret was smiling, raising his brows at me.

The panteras had stopped moving, coming to rest

by the stream that they had made me drink out of before showing me the mortal glass for the first time. I allowed Siret's smile to draw me over to him, and then I allowed him to draw me to the bank. We all took seats along the side of the bank, claiming large rocks that were nestled into the reeds. Whoever we were waiting for clearly hadn't arrived yet, because the panteras were just milling around in preparation.

I dropped my voice, leaning toward Coen, who sat on the boulder beside me.

"Whoever we're waiting for doesn't have a soul," I whispered.

His head snapped toward me, his eyes darkening in some kind of warning. "What? How do you know that?"

"Leden told me."

"She told you we're meeting someone with no soul?" Yael hissed out, jumping from his rock and moving in front of me. Very quickly, I was surrounded by Abcurses.

"Sort of." I shrugged a little. "She implied it. That's why the cave disappeared. It won't show itself to a person unless they're connected to this land. Whoever is coming isn't connected."

"Is it a dweller?" Siret asked, his brow furrowing, his green-gold eyes flicking to the nearest grouping of panteras.

I shook my head. "I don't think so. Maybe, but she

seemed to imply that it was a god. A god without a soul."

"It's not possible." Rome sounded angry, or maybe it was a hint of fear. Neither option was good news for me.

"It is though!" I paused, working my tone back to a whisper. "The imprisonment realm, remember?"

"That's my point." Coen seemed to be agreeing with Rome. "If they're locked in the imprisonment realm, they can no longer access their body. They're locked away, removed from themselves. They can never return and they can never truly die. That's the whole point of the imprisonment realm—you may never return to your body, and it's the only way to separate the soul from the body."

My mind flashed back to Jakan again, and I briefly entertained the thought that *Jakan* himself was the person we were waiting for. He was Staviti's brother, after all. If anyone could escape the imprisonment realm and find a way to access their body again, it would be the brother of Staviti.

Rome was shaking his head, listening to my thoughts. "Cyrus would have told you if he expected you to smuggle Staviti's long-lost brother into Minatsol, and you saw the glass when you asked to see him: that man is long gone, or long lost. Cyrus specifically asked you to fetch an item, not a person."

"What kind of item could a soulless person possibly have for Cyrus, though?" I wondered out loud, even as the panteras began to display signs of agitation, knocking their hooved feet into the ground and flexing their giant wings.

I stood, the others pressing in close about me. Our guest had arrived.

The man didn't have to push through the panteras —they got out of his way on their own, practically repelled. The air around him crackled with energy, and whatever inbuilt system I had to warn me of danger was currently going haywire.

Run!

"Abcurses don't run, Soldier," Siret murmured close to my ear.

"Are you sure?" I fired back, watching as the tall stranger moved closer. "This no-soul-guy is kind of scaring me."

Aros, looking far more relaxed than he should have, casually crossed his arms. "It's just Crowe, nothing to panic about."

Crowe. As in ... *the freaking God of Death?* That sounded like the *definition* of a great time to panic. No wonder the cave didn't want to show him the glass. Crowe was the only Original God capable of killing other gods—unless Staviti could *un-create* gods as easily as he created them. Crowe was still a god, though, so the only explanation for the cave hiding was that Crowe had somehow lost part of his soul.

He stopped about ten feet from us, his black robes swinging gently in the breeze. I found myself examining him closely, imprinting his face in my mind. Crowe wasn't at all like I had imagined him … though I really had no idea what I had expected. He was taller than Rome by at least a foot; he towered over almost everything around him. His hair was like burnt gold, brushing across the top of his shoulders, thick and straight. His features were slashed together in angry, hard lines, but this didn't make him unattractive.

His eyes met mine and I managed not to gasp, even though I wanted to. His entire pupil and iris were black, swirling mesmerizingly. For a moment I wondered if he was blind.

"I can see you."

His voice was deep, and it felt like it infiltrated into my brain, tendrils digging deeper with each word.

"You can also read my mind, apparently," I said.

At this stage I was on the verge of just assuming that every god could read my mind and that I'd have to adjust my thoughts accordingly from now on.

"She won't adjust her thoughts," Yael warned Crowe.

"She won't need to," Coen added, "because you will remove your presence from her mind. Now. It's making us unhappy."

When he said unhappy, the tree he was leaning against cracked, and I realised that *unhappy* was a minor understatement. The Abcurses were on edge, their powers starting to bleed out into the world. Crowe inclined his head slightly, and that digging sensation in my brain disappeared. I waited to see if the guys would relax after that, but none of them appeared to.

"You have something for Cyrus?" Yael brought the conversation back on track.

Fine lines appeared around Crowe's eyes. "Cyrus? No. The panteras are the ones I have brought this gift for." He lifted both of his hands up, palms flat, and closed his eyes for a fraction of a click. There was a pop, and then a set of chains appeared in his hands. The heavy bronze metal looked familiar, the cuffs thick and ornate with symbols carved into every available surface.

"Normally I would not hand a weapon with this level of power over to any beings—but the panteras are beyond the gods." His swirling eyes focussed on the chains. "However, now that I'm here, I feel that … they're meant for you."

He took a step forward, ready to place the chains into Aros's hands.

I let out a muffled cry. "No, don't touch them!"

It was a trap. I had finally remembered where I'd seen that type of chain before. They were almost an exact replica of the chains that had bound Sienna, locking her into the imprisonment realm. Maybe the Abcurses had forgotten? Or maybe they thought they were too strong. But there was one thing I knew: "Those chains can kill a god," I cried.

I dove forward then, snatching the chains right out

of Crowe's hands. I stumbled as I landed, but somehow kept my footing. "If you harm any of the Abcurses," I snarled at the black-robed god, backing away as I tightened my grip on the shackles, "I will kill you."

Crowe stared at me for an extended moment before he threw his head back and laughed. The sound rang out into the silence, because apparently everyone else was too shocked to speak.

"Willa," Coen finally warned, his voice almost too low to hear over Crowe's laughter. "You need to give me the chains."

"No way," I said, still furious.

"He wasn't trying to kill us," Siret tried to reason with me. "If Crowe wanted us dead, he wouldn't attack when the five of us were together. He'd pick us off, one by one."

The laughter died off then, and the God of Death was once again staring at the six of us. "He's right, you know," he told me conversationally. "I did not lie about bringing these chains to the panteras. I did not know I would meet any others here, but that is the risk you take when you deal with these beasts. You do not always understand the cost until it is upon you. Besides, if I wanted these five banished, I would have brought five chains, because if I only stole one of Abil's sons, the rest would hunt me down."

"Just so you're aware," Aros interrupted him. "Willa is included in that now. She is off limits."

Crowe hadn't taken his eyes off me since he

stopped laughing. It was very disconcerting, and even though there was no weird sensation in my mind, I sensed he was somehow searching inside of me.

"No dweller can hold my chains," he said slowly. "What are you?"

My hands were starting to ache from clutching the chains so tightly. "That's the golden question, isn't it?"

"Apparently," he said softly.

I grew bold then. "Will you tell Staviti?"

Siret let out a snort of laughter next to me. "My little soldier, so brave."

Crowe took an uncomfortable amount of time to answer. "There is nothing to tell him," he said. "I know nothing." Then he swished his cloak over his shoulder and spun to leave. "Give the chains to those who require them."

Then he was gone, and it almost felt like the world flickered back into perspective. The panteras returned, along with the noises that had somehow been blocked out with Crowe's presence. The trickling water nearby, the rustling of the leaves, and the chirping of bugs.

"I think black was a great choice for him," I said, my chest heaving in and out as the reality of what had just happened hit me. "I mean, pink sparkles would have clashed horribly with his SWIRLING PITS OF DARKNESS EYES."

My chest continued to heave as I struggled to pull air into my lungs. I had felt so brave when Crowe was standing before me, but right now fear and panic were crashing in on me. It didn't make any sense.

"You're always brave when it comes to protecting us," Coen said as he stepped closer, his hands reaching for the chains.

I snatched them away, holding them close to my chest. "Stop trying to touch them," I gasped. I would never get the image of Sienna's lifeless body out of my mind.

"Willa." Yael's Persuasion wrapped around me. "Willa-toy, you don't have to worry. These chains won't hurt us, they don't work until they're activated, and you can't accidentally do that."

I wanted to be mad at him, because his Persuasion was having some effect, even with my new resistance. Logically though, his words made sense, and with reluctance, I released the chains into Coen's hands. "I chose to let them go," I told Yael.

He ruffled my hair before caressing my cheek. "As long as you keep your defiance out of the bedroom, then we won't have a problem."

"Don't you mean pool?" I called after him as he walked away.

He flashed a grin in my direction and I was pretty much a puddle on the rocky ground.

Take the chains to Cyrus, he will understand what to do. Leden distracted me. I turned to find her close by again.

"Crowe said he was bringing the chains to you, not

235

Cyrus. So why did Cyrus send me here if he didn't know they were coming?"

The light tickle of her amusement sent a shiver down my spine. *Always with the questions. Just follow the path, sacred Willa. You will get to the end eventually.*

"We need to leave now," Aros announced. "Too much time has already passed—the last thing we need is for Staviti to discover us with Death's chains."

They started to move to their panteras, pausing only when I spoke.

"Can we stop by Cyrus's home first? I ... I need to see my mum."

The vision I'd seen in the glass was haunting me. She had looked so alone. So lost. I'd spent enough time with her since she'd become a Jeffrey to know that the blankness was simply part of whatever Staviti had done to her, but I had to try. Maybe if she was with me, she would be happier. Maybe she would smile without being ordered to.

Maybe I'd get a small piece of my mother back.

Coen looked like he was about to protest the proposed change of plans, but Siret got in first. "I think we have time for one quick stop," he said, eyeing his brother. "It's Willa's mum, after all."

Coen shifted his gaze to me, and almost in the same instance nodded. "You're right, we have time for that."

I ran at Siret and he caught me deftly.

"Thank you," I muttered. He was always on my side.

He gathered me in tighter and I savoured the familiar feel of his body before he set me down and I turned to Coen. He just managed to hand the chains to Siret before I threw myself into his arms. He wrapped me up tightly, pulling me into his body. I burrowed my face into his neck, closing my eyes as I breathed him in. "Thank you," I whispered against his skin. "Thank you for caring."

His chest rose under me, like he was taking in a deep breath, and I lifted my head to find his eyes. They were blazing—so bright it almost hurt to stare at them. "I love you," he said simply. "Your happiness is important."

Before I could kiss the heck out of him—because that's exactly what we both needed in that moment— he spun on the spot and took two steps forward, dropping me onto Leden's back.

I opened my mouth and he silenced my words with a single kiss, before pulling back, leaving us both breathless. "Save it for later," he said. "Later you're mine."

Leden took off before I had a chance to combust, and as the cool breeze washed over me, I sucked in deep breaths, trying to centre myself. Trying to focus. How in the worlds had I gotten so lucky?

You have brought much into their lives. Leden cut into

my thoughts. *I have never seen six beings mesh so seamlessly before. A bond to surpass all others.*

"I'm not sure I could live without them," I admitted to her. "It scares me, and yet … I can't walk away. I will never walk away."

Just keep fighting.

I had a feeling her words were going to become much more literal in the next few moon-cycles. An intense fear was building low in my gut. I could only stay hidden from Staviti for so long. What would happen when he figured out what I was? How could we possibly fight against the Original God?

I didn't know why—or how—but Jakan was the key. The mortal glass had shown him to me for a reason. I needed to learn more about him before it was too late.

THIRTEEN

I t wasn't very hard to convince my mother to come with us—certainly not as hard as it had been to track down the hidden entrance to Cyrus's lair again. She was still sitting on the bed when we arrived, still staring blankly at the wall. I had asked her if she would like to come with me, but she hadn't responded. She had stared, waiting, until I realised that in her current state, she probably didn't have a whole lot of 'wants'.

So, I took her—kidnapped her, if you will.

The panteras hadn't taken us all the way to Cyrus's home, because it was too near the banishment cave, so we had to walk back to where they waited. I wasn't sure how much time had passed, and I was too exhausted to ask—though the exhaustion was of a different kind to what I was used to. Before my death, so much hiking and climbing would have made my legs weak and shortened my breath. My ribs would have been aching, my stomach cramping, and my mouth should have been dry. Instead, I was only gasping as though my body recognised the habit of it. There was a hollow sort of ache throughout my body, as though the exhaustion was buried deep inside of me. I knew I needed sleep—there was no doubt about that—but I also knew that I could have easily stretched my energy for another whole sun-cycle.

"There they are." Siret pointed ahead, and I ran to catch up with him, peering through the low-hanging branches of the trees that wound alongside the river bank we were following.

The panteras had stayed behind, waiting for us at the base of the river, downstream from the waterfall beside Cyrus's home.

"Why do you think they wouldn't come with us?" I asked, as I spotted movement ahead. A flash of black fur.

"It probably has something to do with the banished servers," Aros replied. "They were originally of Minatsol, and then they were brought here, infused with the magic of this land, and then banished to a cave, most of the magic stripped away. Those souls are lost, stuck between worlds."

"Souls?" I paused, almost tripping over an extended tree root. "You think the servers have souls?"

"Of course they do." Coen was the one to answer me this time. "You've seen what it looks like to take away the full soul of a person—it renders them as good as dead. The servers are still functioning: walking, talking, obeying orders. He has preserved at least *part* of their soul."

I glanced behind at my mother. She didn't seem to be listening, though she met my eyes when I looked at her.

"Do you have a soul?" I asked her.

She lifted her shoulders in a stiff shrug. I waited for more, but nothing else came. I sighed. It was worth a try.

"Do you know what a soul is?" Siret asked her, surprising me.

"Yes of course, Sacred One," was her reply.

"Really?" I pressed. "Can you point to it?"

She nodded, and then pointed at her nose.

"Just to confirm." I stopped walking and turned fully to face her, the others pausing around me. "Your soul is … your nose?"

"Exactly, Sacred One."

"She doesn't know what her soul is," I told Siret, rolling my eyes and continuing on toward the panteras.

We must hurry. Leden's voice filled my mind, and I watched as she pushed through the dense foliage, revealing herself to me. *Your time has almost run out.*

We helped my mother onto one of the panteras, and then I climbed onto Leden, holding on tightly as she propelled herself from the ground, her wings beating against the trees as she rose into the sky. She was flying faster than usual, and it was too dark for me to make out much of the scenery, so I buried my face into her soft fur, protecting my cheeks from the sharp sting of the wind and emerging only when she began to slow again, dropping back to the ground. She had taken us back to the Garden of Everlasting, right where we had started.

"When will I see you again?" I asked her as the Abcurses all muttered their soft gratitude to their respective panteras.

Soon, Willa Knight. She nudged my face gently with her nose, and my hands reached up instinctively, flattening down over the soft fur between her eyes.

"Is there anything you can tell me?" I tried one last time. "Anything about what the cave showed me, about Staviti and Jakan, about what I am? Anything?"

If you cannot see the full picture, what must you do? she asked me, her wings stretching out in preparation for flight.

"Find the rest of the picture?" I guessed. "Find the missing piece?"

And what is missing from what you saw? she returned.

I thought hard, trying to figure out what might have been left out of the scenes, what I might not have picked up on, but my mind kept getting snagged on Jakan—the piece that didn't make sense.

Why does Jakan not make sense? Leden seemed to be hinting at something, as the other panteras rose into the sky.

I realised, then, what she meant. Jakan himself was the missing piece, because he was quite literally *missing*. I needed to find him, or at least find out more about him. Maybe one of the other gods knew something.

"Thank you," I told Leden, as she pushed up from the ground. "Thank you for everything."

"We need to hurry," Rome told me, reaching my side. "Take hold of Donald—this transition might be hard for her."

I nodded, moving to my mother's side and taking her hand. She glanced at me, and then pulled her hand out of mine.

"My apologies, Sacred One."

I blinked at her, confused, and took her hand again. She pulled it away again.

"My apologies, Sacred One."

"What the hell are you apologising for?" I finally asked, attempting to take her hand again. She kept shifting it away.

"I keep running into you," she explained.

"Gods give me strength," I muttered, before taking her hand again. "*I'm* touching *you*, Donald. It's deliberate. Stop apologising."

"Oh." She blinked. "My apologies, Sacred One. I didn't realise you were initiating intimate protocol."

"Intimate ... what now?" I managed, as she pulled her hand out of my grasp again and started walking away. "Intimate *what*?" I yelled after her, before turning on the guys. "What the hell is she talking about? What is she doing?"

Coen coughed. Aros was shaking his head. Siret looked uncomfortable.

"DONALD!" I screamed, forcing her to stop walking. She turned, waiting. "What are you doing?"

"Finding a suitable surface on which to perform intimate protocol," she informed me, before pointing to a patch of grass free of leaves or debris. "Is here sufficient, Sacred One? Shall I take off my covering?"

"Not unless you want me to gouge my eyes out," I warned her, throwing another accusing glare at the guys. I wasn't sure how, but this was their fault.

"I do not want that, Sacred One."

"Good. Keep your covering on and never say the words 'intimate protocol' ever again. You had enough 'intimate protocol' in your dweller life, you don't need any more of it."

"As you wish, Sacred One."

"I don't think I can touch her hand again," I muttered, as we gathered in preparation to go through the pocket.

"I've got her," Siret announced, reaching out and wrapping his hand around my mother's arm, right above her elbow. "Let's go, Donald. Brace yourself—this might hurt."

We stepped through the pocket one-by-one and gathered on the other side, waiting for Siret to pass through with Donald. I rushed forward as they

244

appeared, already reaching for her. I had expected screaming, crying, maybe some mechanical gasping, but instead, she was hanging limply from Siret's grip. I quickly picked up her other arm, supporting her other side. Her head was hanging down. She was a dead weight.

"What happened?" I asked Siret.

"I have no idea." His expression was grim. "We've never tried to sneak a server into Minatsol before—this might not have been such a good idea."

"Did she die ... *again*?" My voice was reaching hysterical levels, and I was starting to panic.

This was my fault. My stupid idea.

"Let's just get her back to the Peak," Rome muttered. "We can take her to a healer—and if that doesn't work, there will be a sol and Beta of healing skulking around, hiding from everyone else."

"I've got her," Siret assured me, swinging my mother up so that he could carry her on his own.

"Let me." Rome held his hands out, and Siret passed her over. She looked so small and fragile against Rome's massive frame—it was odd to witness, since my mother was several inches taller than me. I must have looked tiny in comparison to my guys.

"You make up for it in temper," Yael informed me, as we began to walk in the direction of the mountain. It was just visible in the early morning rays of sunlight, but I was still worried that we wouldn't make it in time for the beginning of that sun-cycle's training session. I also needed to eat, and possibly sleep. I wasn't sure how long my new undead stamina would hold.

We picked up our pace as the thought crossed my mind. The journey back was silent, with my attention constantly being pulled back over my shoulder, checking on my mother's state. Rome assured me often that she was still breathing, but it worried me that there were no other visible changes. She was limp, unresponsive. I needed to fix her, before something worse happened.

By the time we reached the base of the mountain, exhaustion was creeping in—a tremor finally beginning to make itself known in my calves and wrists.

"I'll take Donald to our rooms and call for a healer," Rome announced. "Someone give my student something to crush. It'll keep her occupied until I'm back."

"Can it be one of the other students?" Siret quipped.

"Don't see why not—" Rome started, at the same time as Coen spoke.

"Absolutely not."

I might have grinned if I hadn't been so tired. Instead, I could only focus on where I planted my feet. I didn't want to slip and go sailing off the mountain— that hardly seemed productive, considering all the trouble we'd just gone to. I was wearing the heavy chains around my neck and they would sail off the mountain right along with me, rendering our entire operation futile.

"Really?" Aros grumbled in reply to my thoughts. "*That's* the downside to you falling off a mountain? The fact that we'll lose the chains?"

"They're very valuable chains," I defended. "And heavy."

"They're heavy because you refuse to let anyone else carry them for more than a click," Siret pointed out. "They would have been much lighter if you'd let us keep them."

"I'll hand them off when we get to Cyrus—I don't care so much about *him* touching them. He'd be a great Neutral of the imprisonment realm."

"That's our girl." Coen laughed.

We separated when we reached the section of the mountain housing the god residences, and then separated once more when we reached the dining area. Siret and Yael were going to go ahead and meet the students while I went with Coen and Aros to fetch food for everyone.

I knew that we were quite a sight as we passed through the tables of stunned sols eating breakfast. There were no gods to be seen, and I suspected that most of them preferred to have their food served in their residences, where they wouldn't have to mix with the sols any more than necessary, outside of their teaching rotations.

Our clothing was dishevelled, our hair mussed, and

I knew that for my own part, I was toting a look of half-crazed exhaustion. There was dirt beneath my fingernails and pantera hair stuck to my shirt.

All the other sols looked fresh, fed, and ready to tackle the sun-cycle, though there was something of a harrowed look in their eyes. I didn't blame them, after witnessing where they were all expected to sleep. I'd feel harrowed too if faced with the prospect of falling through a hole in the wall and tumbling down the side of a mountain in my sleep.

"We need containers to carry everything in," I said as we approached the large serving buffet.

"Our students are supposed to be our servers while we're here," Coen informed me. "But we told them we liked to do this sort of shit ourselves."

"So you lied?" I grinned at him, and his lips twitched in return.

"Something like that. There are wooden food containers down in the kitchen. I'll grab some of those." He turned without waiting for a response and began to move through the mass of sols—all of whom jumped out of his way to allow him passage.

When he returned a few clicks later, there were at least five sols trailing him, carrying wooden food containers. He walked down the line of the buffet, pointing out foods and barking orders while they rushed to fill up the containers. I stepped back, leaning into the hard warmth of Aros's chest. His hand settled on my hip, and we watched and waited until Coen was done.

"To the training rooms," Coen grunted out to his group of followers, before striding out of the room.

The sols were almost tripping over each other in their haste to follow him.

We trailed after the group at a slower pace, walking as though hypnotised by the aromas that drifted from the containers. I could barely wait until we reached the training rooms, but I was also too tired to catch one of the sols and steal away their container, so I dragged myself after them, squeezing through the group as they all piled into the narrow marble corridor.

When we reached the rooms designated for the Abcurses and their training, I collapsed in the corner and simply waved my right hand in the air.

"What do you need, Soldier?"

"Food," I mumbled. "Need food."

I heard laughter, but after that I had no idea what happened because my eyelids lowered and then everything went dark.

Sometime later I awoke to low murmurs.

"The healer has no idea what's wrong with Donald. Even Lancaster stopped by for a look."

At those words, slow swirls of panic began to build low in my gut, but I was still too asleep to completely understand why.

"Do you think it's wise?" asked another voice.

"Having Lancaster know that one of the servers is in Minatsol? What if he informs Staviti?"

"He's afraid of Willa," said the original voice, laughter in his words. "He's not going to say anything."

My brain finally started working again, and in a rush of understanding I realised it was Rome and Coen talking ... about my mum. I gasped as I pulled myself up from the hard surface I'd been sprawled across. As my eyes opened, I registered the muscled chest below my hands. I'd been asleep *on* an Abcurse. Coen Abcurse to be accurate.

"Willa, what is it?" Green eyes bore into me as he examined my face. "What happened?"

"My mum needs me," I said, voice husky. "You have to take me to her. I healed Yael, somehow, so maybe I can help her as well."

Coen turned to Rome, who sat nearby. He just shrugged those huge shoulders of his. "Can't hurt, right?"

I pulled myself to stand, mourning the loss of Coen's heat, but knowing I needed some space to get my mind functioning again. That sleep had really knocked me out. My legs wobbled for a moment before I felt my strength returning to them and I was steady. Clearing my throat, I tried again. "You know I'm going to do this no matter what you say. You might as well give up now."

Coen rose to his feet before answering. "I'm just worried. Healing takes a lot of energy. You're still learning about your powers—their capabilities. I don't want you to hurt yourself in a quest to ... save your mother."

I *heard* the underlying truth of what he was telling me. There was no way to save Donald, she was even more undead than I was. Just a husk of soul trapped in its shell. But ... I had to try.

They must have seen the determination in my features, because no one argued with me again. "I need to deal with my sol," Rome said with annoyance. "She's being a real pain in my ass, but if you want me to come with you ... I'm there."

A quick glance told me that the Strength sol was in the corner of the next open room, smashing her fists into a rock. Her dark hair was tied back severely, accentuating the angry lines of her face. I wasn't sure if she was carving the stone into something, or just taking out her frustrations, but either way ... I didn't want to be alone with her. Ever.

She wasn't the only one who looked pissed. Despite the fact that Siret, Yael, and Aros were with their sols—all of them in their own interconnected rooms, each looking more bored than the one before— the females were still shooting angry glares in my direction.

They seriously needed to get over this shit.

"They're angry because we all watched over you while you slept. We took turns," Coen told me.

Something about that statement warmed my heart.

No one had ever done that for me before, except Emmy.

I rose up onto my tiptoes to kiss Rome on the cheek. He still had to bend down for me to reach. "Go to your sol," I murmured to him. "Before she knocks this entire building down."

He let out an exaggerated grumble, his chest shaking. "Don't stay away too long," he finally said to us. "I have this feeling we should stick together as much as possible, just in case."

He didn't say in case of what, but we all knew there were more than a couple of situations which could spring up and would require the full might of the Abcurse brothers.

"Willa Knight!" The shout had me spinning around, my hands slamming against my chest as my heart pounded hard. "You broke the rules again! *Seriously*."

Emmy stormed into the room, her long hair flowing behind her, her eyes shooting daggers. Apparently, this was the section of the marble forest designated to people who wanted to kill me with their eyes. As she got closer, I braced myself to receive the full force of her wrath. She had made me promise I wouldn't disappear without her, and then I'd gone and done just that.

"It's not my fault," I protested when she was a few feet away. "Cyrus made me go and collect something for him—that was my punishment."

At that thought, I remembered Crowe's chain, and my hands flew to my shoulders.

"They're in a safe place," Coen told me, leaning down so that no one else could hear.

I narrowed my eyes on him. "You took them the moment I fell asleep, didn't you?"

He just grinned, and I couldn't find any energy to be mad at him.

"Are you even listening to me, Willa?"

Emmy had still been talking. I had not been listening. I was the worst kind of friend and sister.

"I'm sorry," I said, interrupting her next tirade. "I know I'm being a terrible sister to you right now ... I mean, even worse than usual, and there was nothing to brag about before. But so much is going on—I can't keep up, Emmy. I ... I just need you to stick with me. Please. I'm going to try harder."

Rome chuckled. It burst from him, and I reached out to slap his chest.

"I *am* going to try harder," I said.

His expression softened. "You care too much. Emmy-dweller might be your family, but she needs to try and understand as well. You're different now. You don't always have time to pander to her emotions and feelings."

Emmy gasped loudly. Everything stilled. I tried desperately to think of something to fix this moment, all the while waiting for her to rip us all a new one. Her eyes were the only part of her that was moving; she looked at me first, and then at Rome and Coen.

"He's right," she finally murmured, shocking the hell out of me. "Never thought I'd say that about a god, but he is right."

She reached out and grabbed my hands. "I'm sorry, Will. I've been struggling to accept the changes in your life. Struggling to let you go after all the life-cycles of being the most important person in your life. But ... I realise now that I'm being unfair." She swallowed roughly, and I felt a lump form in my own throat. "You're the happiest I've ever seen you," she continued. "As much as ALL gods are pissing me off these sun-cycles, the Abcurses are fulfilling you. Completing you. I have to start accepting this reality."

I shook my head fiercely, tears springing to my eyes. She always did this: forgave me for my flaws, while beating herself up for hers. She had lost her person. She had been left to fend for herself in a world where everyone had been taken away from her. She should not have been apologising to me—I should have been the one empathising with her.

"Emmy, you're the most important person in my life, too. I can't live without you. You're as essential to me as the Abcurses, just in a different way. And I am so sorry that I haven't been there for you lately. There is no excuse for that. It kills me that my life has been taking me on a path that is no longer parallel to yours.

But our paths will come back together again. I feel that with every part of my being."

Emmy and I were the forever kind of friends. We were family. It was difficult right now with me being undead and tied to five gods, but that didn't lessen the truth of what I knew.

We were forever.

She hugged me so tightly that all breath rushed out of me. "I love you, Willa. I should say that more often."

I went so many life-cycles never hearing those words. Now, I was overwhelmed by all of the love in my life. I didn't even know how to handle it.

"I love you, too," I murmured back, before we pulled apart.

I realised, then, that she was wearing a dress. Not just any old dress either, but a very nice, well-fitted, dark purple number that swished around her ankles and gave her impressive cleavage. I tried to remember the last time she'd been out of her sensible 'work' clothes. The girl had actual boobs.

Rome and Coen both chuckled then, no doubt thinking about all the times I'd flashed mine to the world. This was a first for Emmy.

"Are you still ... uh, unemployed?" I asked her.

Gods that sounded wrong.

She grinned, bringing a hand up to wipe a few tears away. "Cyrus and I reached an agreement. At the moment, I'm a free agent. I don't have any duties. I don't answer to any of the gods. He has given me a free pass."

No one else seemed shocked by that, but I think my eyes were wide enough that there was a scary chance my eyeballs would fall out. "A free agent...?"

What the hell did that even mean? There was no such thing. Even sols weren't free.

"Cyrus might be the boss here," I finally said, "but what about all the other gods? What if they tell Staviti? How are you hiding this?"

Emmy shrugged. "Cyrus said he was taking care of it. It was his way of apologising after the drinking incidents."

I felt like I'd stumbled into an alternate reality. Was this really Emmy? Or were we once again being fooled by a sol who could change her appearance?

"It's Emmy," Rome confirmed.

There was something different about her, though. It was more than just the dress. Emmy had always been confident, but in the live-by-the-law-of-the-land way. She knew her place, and she outshone every single one of us while sticking to her place. This was more than out-shining the others, though. This was something else.

"You seem happy, too," I said slowly. "I never thought you could survive without all the dweller stuff."

She shrugged. "I don't know how to explain it, but when I quit, something released within me. Like a tether I didn't even know was there. I was so tied to my identity as a dweller, that I'd never even stopped to think about who I was without that."

Rome distracted me then by swinging his head toward the back of the room. "I'll be there in a click," he bit out in annoyance. "Just keep doing what you're doing."

Peering around him, I realised his sol had left her stone and was now standing near us. She was glaring, arms crossed as she replied.

"Stop wasting time with these ridiculous dwellers. Seriously. Do you realise that there's a possibility that all of us will die? Even you, if you can't manage to make me strong enough to ascend to godhood?"

Rome didn't look at all concerned, but her words were enough to remind me of what Staviti had declared back on his platform. If the Betas didn't make their sols strong enough to become third Beta Gods, he would kill the Betas as well.

At the time, I thought it was an empty threat, something to get them motivated. But ... who knew with Staviti. He had crazy eyes. You can never trust someone with eyes like that.

"Go," I said, pushing him gently. "Go teach her crushing stuff. I'll be fine."

I turned to Coen, then. "You should go as well. Emmy will stay with me while I see if I can heal my mum. Apparently, she's a free agent now."

"What's wrong with your mum?" Emmy interrupted, drawing closer to me.

Her concern brought my own worries back to the forefront of my mind.

"Something happened when we brought her here." My voice shook as the guilt of what I'd done hit me again. "Something about her transition into Minatsol messed with her ... with whatever Staviti did to turn her into a server. The healers couldn't help, so I'm going to see if I can."

Coen did that rumbly chest thing, which always got my attention. "It's too dangerous for you to be wandering around here alone. The sols we've been saddled with aren't the only assholes gunning for you, Willa."

I waved him off. "You know I can burn a god. I'll be fine."

His jaw went rigid and I knew there was nothing I could say to convince him. I was just about to concede when a large man entered the room, a scowl twisting his features.

"I'll escort Willa and Emmy," Cyrus said without preamble. "No one will bother them if I'm around."

What the hell is going on here? Were these rooms some kind of central hub for people to pop in and out of at random?

"Fuck no. Not happening." Coen didn't even hesitate. "I trust you less than I trust Staviti. Let's not forget what happened the last time you were alone with her."

Cyrus threw his hands into the air. "I've explained that to you all multiple times. You're going to have to let it go at some point."

I almost laughed out loud then. He was talking about us 'letting go' of him killing me in the same way one might talk about accidentally borrowing someone's clothes and tearing them.

The rest of the Abcurses drifted closer to Emmy and me, forming a wall behind us. "We will never let it go," Siret said, somewhat calmly. "We work with you because there is no other choice. But what you did … there is no forgetting."

"Okay, okay." I held both hands up. "We don't have time for this, and whether we like it or not, we're on the same team right now. We've managed to stay hidden from Rau and Staviti, we've managed not to die … again … so we're all good. Right now my focus is on Donald, and since it's my choice, I'm going to go with Cyrus and Emmy. You five …" I swung around to see them. "Go and fix your sols. Make them better."

The five sols were about six feet away, and they heard me clearly. The Pain and Strength sols flipped me off. Trickery just swung around, her purple hair flying in a pretty arc behind her. The other two looked bored. Like they were past giving a shit.

Yael started to protest, but I cut him off. "Please," I said. "Let it go just this once."

His teeth clinked audibly as he slammed his mouth shut, his face unyielding.

"Straight there and back," he finally relented. "No detours, and if anything weird happens with your mum, you get your ass right back to us. Understood?"

I exaggeratedly saluted him. "Yes, sir."

Before anyone else could start protesting again, I blew them a kiss, linked my arm through Emmy's, and then dragged her out of the room. I didn't look back to see if Cyrus followed, because I really didn't care.

As we started to walk, my stomach protested. I'd fallen asleep before I'd managed to eat, so of course now my body was reminding me of its current food-deprived state. Hopefully I'd be able to eat as soon as I healed my mum. I couldn't focus on anything before I did that.

FOURTEEN

Cyrus caught up to us when we entered the main hall. Up till that point, I'd been silently dragging Emmy along, unable to carry out any conversation with all of my worry. When Cyrus joined us in the uncharacteristically quiet hall, he broke that silence.

"How was your trip to Topia?" he asked, sounding casual. "Did you get what I needed?"

I shrugged. "Funnily enough, the panteras didn't have anything of yours. They said you must have been mistaken."

They hadn't exactly said that, but ... whatever.

Cyrus didn't react. No anger, no annoyance, no slow boil of disbelief followed by fury ... in fact, his eyes were *very* clear. Less bloodshot than usual. Maybe he really had cut back on the drinking.

"Hmmm," he murmured. "I could have sworn there was something there for me. Maybe I left it somewhere else."

I doubted he had been confused like that about anything. Which made me wonder if he'd set the entire thing up just to get me to the panteras. I mean, I never would have expected that much help from Cyrus, but it wouldn't be the first time he'd tried to be of use. In his own, unique way—a way that usually wasn't *that* helpful.

"Did you learn anything while you were there?" Emmy asked me.

"Actually, I did." I halted for a moment, so I could focus on what I was about to say. "Can you tell me anything about the history of Minatsol's royal family? How long ago was that? Oh, and ... what happened to destroy the monarchy?"

Emmy just blinked a few times at me. A quick look at Cyrus told me he was doing the same thing. I barely resisted an eyeroll. "Come on, I like to learn things every now and then."

Emmy recovered enough to snort laughter at me. "Willa, you literally fell asleep during history class every single rotation. You never missed a nap."

True. Very true.

"It just never felt relevant. Plus, it was always so *sol* and *god* focused. I really didn't care to listen about how great the world used to be for dwellers—since everyone was one in the old times—only to now be living in a world where we were relegated to nothing more than slaves. Where our world was slowly being leeched of life, and the expectation was that one sun-cycle there would be nothing left of Minatsol."

Emmy shook her head. "You're missing the point, though, Will. You learn about the past to change the future. Nothing stays the same, ever, but the past often repeats itself. History can teach us a lot. Important things."

"So teach me these important things then. I want to know about the monarchy."

She narrowed her eyes on me. "Cyrus has an entire library just off his office. I doubt he's ever stepped foot in there because I'm almost positive he can't read, but that's a good place to start looking."

Cyrus smiled. An actual real smile. His eyes were locked on Emmy. "You amuse me little dweller," he said slowly. "You would have made a very interesting god."

I caught the slight flush of pink to Emmy's cheeks before she turned away. "A god is the last thing I want to be," she murmured, before her voice grew louder. "Come on, the infirmary is this way."

She continued on without looking to see if we were following. I narrowed my eyes on Cyrus as he fell in behind her.

"Stop smiling," I muttered to him. "It's creeping me out."

The smile turned into laughter, and I threw my

hands into the air and hurried my steps to fall in next to Emmy. Creepy Cyrus was not someone I wanted to be alone with.

Emmy led us through the maze of training rooms and out into the elements. We passed down to another level of the mountain—where the dining hall was located—and then further down still, to another main hall. It was on the western edge of the cliff, positioned far back from the trail, so that you had to pass through a tunnel of rooms to get to it. I could see the ocean through the large, round windows spanning the rock wall.

"Patients respond positively to fresh air and sunlight," Emmy explained when she saw me gawking at the view. "It's very peaceful here."

There *was* a peaceful feel to the room, and I wanted to spend more time enjoying the water beyond, but my mum needed my help.

Two healers met us near a front desk.

"Can we help you?" the first one asked. She was a pretty woman with strawberry blonde hair hanging in ringlets past her shoulders.

"Uh, yes, I hope so. My mum was recently brought in ... Donald?"

She blinked at me for a click, before turning to the man at her side. He ran a hand through his inky black hair, letting it fall in disarray around his face. He had a nice face, kind of boring, but not as mean as a lot of sols. The healing-gifted ones were more compassionate in general.

"Your mum's name is Donald?" he finally asked me.

I tapped my fingers on the bench. Nice face or not, I didn't have time to mess around. "Trust me, it's better than Mole. Her name really doesn't matter. Is she back there?"

They both jumped to attention.

"Yes," the woman said, "she's right back here. We tried to heal her, but ... Donald, isn't responding to anything so far."

The sick feeling I'd had in my gut since we crossed burst back to life. "I'd just like a few clicks with her," I told them, and no one held me up any longer.

Emmy and Cyrus—who was uncharacteristically quiet, but had at least stopped smiling—followed me. My mum was in the second room along the hall; her wall had the same round windows set into the stone, displaying a calming view of the ocean.

"Just call out if you need anything," both of the healers said, before they exited, drawing the curtain across the entrance.

For a moment, when I first crossed to my mum's side, I thought she was dead. Her skin was a sickly grey, her frame sunken, and there was no sign of chest movement to indicate she was breathing. My heart thundered in my chest, and I forced myself to reach out and place my hand on hers.

She was warm, and under my fingertips I felt the faint buzz of her pulse. *Alive.* She was alive—or at least some version of it.

"What happened to her?" I murmured, hoping that Cyrus would hold some answers.

I felt him move closer, his energy buzzing along my skin. "I have no idea. Servers can usually leave Topia, as you saw when Staviti sent everyone to attack you. There's something different about your mum, something that impacted her transition to server."

I let my gaze rest on her weathered face, the flyaway hair and tired features.

"There's always been something broken in her," I whispered. "Maybe she just had too many cracks to ever be put together right, even as a server."

Emmy stepped forward to the other side, her back to the windows, and took mum's right hand. Both of us held on, fearing that we were already too late.

"She looks really bad," Emmy sobbed.

I nodded slowly. It was the truth. She looked dead already, and maybe she was. Maybe the signs of life we saw were just the last-ditch attempt of organs to keep blood pumping. Maybe there was no saving her. But I had to try.

"What are you going to do, Will?" Emmy's words were no louder than a whisper, and she hadn't taken her eyes off mum even once since reaching her side.

"I might have some healing abilities," I admitted. "I have no idea what I'm doing, but I have to try."

I closed my eyes before anyone could say anything else. I had no idea what I was doing—the last time it had just happened, coaxed out by my Abcurses, but this time I was on my own.

Heal, please. I willed my mum to heal, sending forth my intentions, the way I had with Yael. The energy swirling inside of me expanded, until it felt like my skin was heating from the inside out.

"Something's happening," Emmy said, startling me.

It was enough for me to lose that focus, and I opened my eyes, hoping that Donald would be sitting up, smiling, awake. Anything.

My heart sank ... she looked the same.

"What was happening?" I asked Emmy.

"Your hands were glowing," she said, blinking at me. "But ... the glow didn't sink into your mum. It just kind of hovered over her, like it didn't know how to break through whatever spell is on her."

"Staviti's energy is hard to best," Cyrus said from where he had perched himself against a nearby wall. "His energy keeps servers animated—you'd have to bust through it first before you could reach your mother's energy."

My eyelids slammed shut. Staviti was not going to win this one. I would not let him.

Heal. Heal. Heal. I chanted those words over and over, the energy picking up even more heat as it swirled harder and faster inside of me.

"Willa!"

Emmy's shout startled me again, but this time I didn't mind, because I was about half a click from setting my mum on fire. I jerked my hands back and the small flames that had been filling them died off in the same instant.

"Your energy was responding to your anger," Cyrus told me, stepping closer for the first time. "I think it might be best to leave your mum for now. She is stable. You need to figure out your gift, first. Then you might have a chance at saving her."

I wasn't sure I trusted Cyrus's advice, but there was some truth to what he was saying.

"So, you think I should just leave her? What if she gets worse?"

"If she gets worse," he told me, "you can try again. Until then, you need to focus on figuring out exactly what your powers can do. You need to train yourself."

I made an angry sound. "I don't have time for this. I have research to do."

Emmy interrupted our argument. "Maybe you can do both. Research the fallen monarchy and explore your powers at the same time. There is record of gods, sols, and their unique gifts." She lifted her gaze to Cyrus. "You have a copy of that tome, right?"

He shot her the smile again. I flinched, but Emmy just raised one eyebrow, her focus steady. "It might be in the library," he finally said. "So hard to know when you can't read."

"I'll be there," I announced, turning on my heel and heading out of the room.

It didn't occur to me until I was at the doorway that I didn't actually know where Cyrus's library was—or even that he had one there on the mountain. I paused, glanced back, and opened my mouth to ask.

"I'll show you," Emmy said, a wry smile twisting her lips.

"Wait." Cyrus had a strange look on his face as he switched his attention quickly from Emmy to me.

Even though he had asked us to wait, he didn't follow up that command with anything further, and eventually Emmy turned to face him, an inquisitive look twisting her features. They stared at each other for an oddly long amount of time. Not a word passed between them, until I finally cleared my throat.

"I haven't allowed anyone else in there," Cyrus finally admitted, though he seemed to be talking to Emmy.

Emmy didn't reply. I walked back to her side, peering at her face. She swallowed, her eyes on Cyrus, and for the first time since I had known her, she actually appeared vulnerable.

"I don't want to break up the unspoken moment," I announced uneasily, glancing between them. "But can this maybe wait until later?"

I wasn't even sure that they heard me—they were too busy staring at each other, Emmy looking all vulnerable and Cyrus looking all vulnerable and my mother looking all comatose.

"Will it help if I solve this little conundrum right now?" I asked, still receiving no response. I sighed, moving to stand directly between them. "Okay, here's the situation. Cyrus, big scary Neutral God, thinks that Emmanuelle, lowly dirt-dweller, has a really nice butt."

Emmy blinked, switching her gaze to me for the barest moment.

"And Emmanuelle kind of wants Cyrus to be touching all her stuff even though she complains about it, which means she kind of likes him—"

"I don't," Emmy interrupted, colour rising in a sudden flush through her cheeks. "Like him, I mean," she added hastily. "I don't like him."

"She does," I argued, rolling my eyes at Cyrus, who seemed to be coming out of his trance and was now just staring at me in confusion. "And *you* like *her*," I told him.

"No, I don't," he argued. "She's annoying."

"How annoying?" I goaded.

"So annoying."

"So annoying that you want to kiss her?"

He frowned, pressing his lips together, refusing to reply.

"So annoying that you want to maybe see her naked?" I continued, enjoying the way his eyes flared for an instant. "Yeah, I thought so. Can we consider this moment dealt with now? Can I see the secret library?"

He scowled, flicking his hand. "You may borrow the book, but you may not enter the library."

"How is she going to get the book, then?" Emmy asked, folding her arms over her chest.

"I never said that *you* couldn't go into the library," Cyrus grumbled, pushing past us and leaving the room. We stood there in shocked silence.

"He likes your butt," I told my sister, when it seemed like she wasn't going to stop staring after him.

She shook her head, striding for the doorway in a strikingly similar manner to Cyrus's recent exit. "I'll get you the book and meet you back in your rooms."

"Thank you," I told her, before catching her arm and drawing her into a hug before she could storm off. "Thank you for everything."

She relaxed for a moment, wrapping her arms around me, and then she sniffed and drew back, her eyes flicking to my mother.

"You need to find a way," she told me. "Your mum might know something about what you are. She might be the missing piece in all of this."

The missing piece.

I stared after Emmy as she walked away, her words echoing in my head. I had thought that I already knew who the missing piece was, but Emmy was right. If anyone knew what made me different, it would be the woman who gave birth to me.

After a few clicks alone in the room, with my mother unresponsive on the bed and the view of the ocean lulling me into a false sense of calm, I finally roused myself into action, leaving the healing ward and heading in the direction of the god-residences. I waited in the rooms for Emmy to bring the book—a tome as big as my head—and then I hurried back to the training alcoves, where I found each of the Abcurses huddled together in one of the small rooms, their sols gathered in another. I waited in the entry for an extended click, wondering what was happening. The sols seemed to be arguing, the Strength student gesturing wildly toward the Abcurses, the Seduction student speaking back in a low tone, her eyes narrowed dangerously.

I approached the circle of Abcurses, squeezing between Yael and Siret, until I was in the centre of them.

"What's going on?" I whispered, as a quietness settled over our huddle, each of their eyes flicking down to me.

"Something isn't right," Aros murmured, the gold in his gaze swirling lightly. "Staviti's energy is all over this place. It happened suddenly, while you were gone."

"What?" I backed up a little, but only managed to bump into Coen, whose hands landed on my shoulders, spinning me around.

"We were debating whether we should get you out of here or not."

"I can't leave, not until I've found a way to heal my—"

"You won't be any use to Donald if you're the reason Staviti has come down to the Peak," Yael interrupted. "He hasn't shown himself, hasn't announced anything to the sols or gods. He's hiding his presence."

"Where are the ..." I trailed off, repeating the question inside my head, directing it to the five of them. *Where are the chains?*

Coen swore, pulling me forwards—though he turned at the last moment, propelling me ahead of him, his hand switching to the back of my neck, directing me to the doorway.

"We need to make sure he didn't come for them," he announced, the others following closely behind us.

"YOU CAN'T JUST LEAVE," one of the girls screeched, forcing our group to halt and our heads to turn.

It was the Trickery sol: her purple hair almost seeming to stand on end in agitation.

"We aren't learning anything," she spat, the others fanning out behind her. "This is bullsen shit. You five are supposed to be helping us become better, but you're too busy babysitting this dweller slut—"

My hand was suddenly before my face, my palm facing out, and power was surging down my arm. Maybe it was the stress over my mother, or the possibility that

JANE WASHINGTON & JAYMIN EVE

Staviti might have followed us out of Topia—that he might have allowed us to take the chains into Minatsol only to sneak after us and steal them back. Or maybe I just didn't like being called a 'dweller slut'. Whatever the reason, my power was suddenly exploding into the world, and it was too late for me to stop it. The Trickery sol was bent over, her hands covering her face, a scream floating back to where I stood.

I rushed over to her, guilt flooding into me and snapping my energy back into my body with a heavy pull that had my head spinning. My legs were shaking as I bent beside her, my hand on her shoulder. She flinched away from me, and the Seduction and Strength sols crouched beside her, drawing her back from me.

"I'm sorry." I tried to get close again, but the Trickery sol kicked out at me.

"Stay the fuck away from me!" she shouted, though her voice was strangely muffled.

"I don't even know what I did," I pleaded, searching her body for scorch marks, or any sign of fire damage.

She lowered her hands from her face, revealing two blood-shot eyes and a ...

"Well ... I did not expect that." Siret was behind me, his voice somewhat amused.

"You ... *oh*." That had come from Rome, also sounding amused and a little horrified.

I swallowed, torn between an absurd urge to laugh, and an even stronger urge to cry. A strangely manic emotion was trickling through me—possibly a result of the sudden rush of power and adrenaline, but just as likely a result of the absurd vision before me.

Dickhead.

I had been thinking it just a micro-click before I lashed out at the girl, along with a range of other insulting curses. I had been thinking it, and then ... *I had manifested it.*

There she stood: purple-haired, red-eyed, with a penis protruding from her forehead. A real, live penis.

"How do you know it's alive?" Siret was really enjoying this moment. I could already tell I'd improved his sun-cycle immensely with my ability to make a literal dickhead.

"I don't know!" I exclaimed. I was squinting at it, trying to see if I recognised it.

I was hoping that it didn't look like it belonged to any of my guys. It was too small to be Rome's, and it wasn't anywhere near as nice-looking as Siret's or Yael's.

"Nice looking?" Yael choked out.

"You mean you ... you ... *manifested* a cock, and it isn't even one of ours?" Coen's tone was hard, almost pissed-off.

"WHAT HAVE YOU DONE?" the Trickery sol screamed, her hands darting up towards the thing dangling from her face.

Every single one of us flinched.

"Oh gods." The Strength sol had her hand over her

mouth. She looked a little sick. "Please stop touching it."

"Why?" The Trickery sol was growing pale, her eyes widening in panic. "Is it doing something?"

"It's not doing anything," I assured her, even though I was actually avoiding looking directly at it. "But still probably don't touch it. You might get pregnant ... and I think that would make me the father of your baby."

The sol began to wail, then. Long, loud, and mournful.

"Ahhh." I broke away from the guys, kneeling in front of her again. "Please stop, just let me try to fix it, okay? I'm sure I can."

"Really?" Rome asked from behind me, sounding doubtful.

"*Shh*!" I shot him a look over my shoulder, before re-focussing on the sobbing girl. "I'm sorry, okay? I wasn't aware that this was something I could do. I mean, they don't exactly teach you about penis-manifestation in the dweller schools. It's more about cleaning and bowing and scrubbing pans. Will you let me fix it?"

"FIX IT!" she screamed in response, her hands balling up into fists.

"Alright, jeez. Calm down, it's just a penis. We all have them."

"You do?" the Seduction sol asked, her eyebrows shooting up.

"Well yeah," I waved a hand behind me. "I have theirs. So technically I have five of them. But that's not really important. Can you please take her arms so that she doesn't punch me?"

The Seduction and Strength sols obeyed, and I suspected it was mostly because they also didn't want to suddenly gain dangly bits from their faces. I held my hand out again, palm facing outward, my eyes closed.

Neuter, I thought, my face scrunching up in concentration. *Neuter her face.*

Behind me, there was a crash, and I opened my eyes in shock, my gaze whipping back to Siret and Aros, who were leaning on each other, their hands over their mouths, trying to stifle the laughter that had begun to shake their entire bodies. I scowled, glancing over at Rome, who had fallen onto one of the couches, laughing. The thing seemed to have cracked apart beneath him.

"So immature," I muttered, rolling my eyes and then turning back to refocus.

"Says the girl currently trying to neuter someone's face," Aros shot back, laughing even harder.

"Like you five haven't ever made any mistakes!" I closed my eyes again, turning my palm up one more time.

I need to fix this, I told myself, drawing in several deep gulps of air.

"Oh hell no," someone muttered—one of the

students. It was a small, sweet voice. The Persuasion sol, I thought.

"What?" I replied, keeping my eyes closed and my concentration locked onto the task at hand.

"I looked at it," she moaned out in regret. "It has purple hair on it."

I shuddered, shaking my head. "No. No. No. Don't say that while I'm sitting this close to it. I'm trying to fix it. Stop distracting me!"

"Wait!" one of them said loudly. "It's changing. I think it's getting smaller!"

"You should leave her with a little bump," Siret suggested, as I attempted to double-down on my focus and tune them all out. "Leave her with a reminder of the fun time we had here this sun-cycle, so that she can always remember you fondly. Willa Knight, the dweller with the cock power."

A tickle of laughter built up in the back of my throat, but I swallowed it back, working instead to focus the power flooding down my arm, fuelled by panic and nervous energy. I needed to fix this. I needed to prove that I could do more than set things on fire and break people. I needed to prove that I could control something. Anything.

"You're doing it, Willa-toy." Yael was beside me, the laughter gone from his voice, his breath tickling my ear. I could feel the heat of his body curling around me as he crouched just behind me, his hand on my arm. "Keep your focus. Breathe. Yes, you're actually doing it." There was incredulity in his tone, and a sudden silence in the room.

Elation filled me. With it came a sudden rush of power, so strong that dots of light began to dance behind my closed eyelids.

"Unbelievable," Coen muttered, a click before everything went black.

"Dweller-baby."

There was a voice reaching to me, trying to draw me through a tunnel of immense darkness. I wanted to lift my arm—to reach for the voice. It was smooth, deep, familiar ... but my arm was too heavy.

"Sweetheart."

A different voice this time. Huskier. It reminded me of burnt sugar plants, and I finally managed to blink my eyes open a little bit. The room came into focus slowly, beginning as a hazy blur before gradually solidifying into solid colours and shapes. I was in our bed. There were two thick thighs on either side of my body, a muscled torso behind my head, and a golden arm wrapped around my waist.

"You're awake." I turned toward Aros's voice—he was sitting on the bed beside whoever's lap I was cuddled in.

"Hi," I croaked out. "Did I make it go away?"

He cracked a smile, his eyes lightening to a pale gold, only a few little tendrils of green visible.

"You made it go away," Coen's voice replied, the chest behind me rumbling with the words.

"Where are the others?" I asked, tipping my head back against his chest to see his face.

He glanced down at me, his touch shifting so that his hands were at my waist, lifting me up a little. Suddenly, my lips were only a breath away from his. He had been about to answer my question, but his movement seemed to shock both of us. The words died on his lips before he even had a chance to speak them, and his eyelids dropped down, his gaze lowering.

"I don't even remember the question," he groaned. "What is happening right now?"

Something *was* happening, I realised. A need was building up inside me. My body was sinking back into his, my skin suddenly aching to be pressed against one of my guys, my hands desperate to touch them. It didn't take long for me to close the distance between our mouths. I kissed him quickly, need thrumming through my body, and then pulled back. Pain shimmered across my skin, his hands contracting where they held my waist.

A touch against my chin had my head turning, then, and gold eyes locked onto my gaze, Aros's lips pressing into mine.

The second kiss was more deliberate than the first,

his hands shaping to the sides of my face, his fingers threading into the hair at the sides of my temple. I could taste him, and it was as though I needed that taste to bring myself back to life. I was so desperate for it, I could have cried.

Aros pulled back, his eyes searching my face.

"Can you feel it?" he rasped out.

I thought that he was talking to me, but Coen was the one who replied.

"Yes, she's trying to absorb our energy. Open to her."

That made sense to me, on some level—but I couldn't seem to properly analyse what it meant. Not with the sudden need that clouded my mind and swept through my body. I couldn't think.

My fingers were tangling in Aros's shirt, pulling him back to me. His lips took mine again, a groan vibrating from his mouth to mine.

Pain fissured down my spine in a sharp sting, forcing my mouth open. Aros's tongue swept past my lips, his hands dipping to my shoulders, and then to my hips, drawing me out of Coen's arms and into his. Pleasure rushed through me as soon as I collapsed onto his chest, sending him falling back against the mattress. His hands were beneath my shirt, sweeping up the curve of my spine. I felt a body hovering over me, and then a large hand threaded through my hair, turning my face suddenly to the side.

I saw a golden stretch of skin right beside my head

—Coen's arm—and then the hand in my hair was forcing my mouth to his, and the pain was sweeping back down the length of my spine. The longer we touched, the stronger the buzzing sting of his power got. I shuddered, and Aros's hands seemed to trace the reaction of my body, skimming over my back. Pleasure chased the Pain, soothing and stimulating at the same time.

Coen must have been holding himself off me so that he wouldn't crush me, but the hard pressure of his kiss was enough to have my body turning.

I had never felt so restless before. So completely unable to stay in one spot. I needed them both, and I needed them too desperately to be content with any of their touches or kisses. Aros helped me to turn, and then suddenly I was laying on top of him, my back to his front as Coen lowered himself over my front, just enough to put pressure along the length of my body, but not enough to weigh me down. Both of his hands were now holding him up, and his kiss deepened, broken up only by the small growl emanating from the back of his throat.

His Pain grew heavier, then, but it was countered almost immediately by a rush of heady pleasure, enough to force my body into an involuntary arch. I gasped, breaking the kiss, my head falling to Aros's shoulder. His hands slipped up over my hips, and Coen lifted a little of his weight. I could feel Coen's eyes on me, the attention almost like a physical touch as Aros's fingers pushed beneath the waist of my pants. The Trickery-designed cloth was tight, unwilling to allow him access, but he only applied a quick, downward tug of pressure, and I heard the tear of material as it gave way. His hand pushed beneath the hem of my underwear, his fingers finding my core. Coen watched my reaction: the way my mouth dropped open on a gasp, the way I strained to push up into the body above me while still pushing down against the fingers that stroked me. I needed more.

"Fuck, I can't stand this," Coen groaned, his mouth falling down on mine, his body shifting slightly to the side, his weight dropping down to his left elbow.

He wasn't covering me anymore, only pressing into my side, but I couldn't complain—not with Aros's heavy breath against my neck and the feeling of bliss building up quickly through my body.

"Watching this is torture." Coen sounded angry, but I didn't have time to respond before my shirt was pulled away and flicked up over my head, breaking our kiss for only a breath before we came together again.

"Need. Both," I managed, but I wasn't sure if either of them heard me.

"I need her." The words had come from Aros, muttered heavily as his fingers pushed into me.

"I fucking need her," this had come from Coen, the words dashed against my lips.

Both of them pulled back, swearing. This felt like new, uncertain territory, and I wasn't sure why. My body was suddenly turned again, but this time they seemed to have taken on my restlessness, their hands pulling at the scraps of clothing that still remained on my body, casting them from the bed as though personally offended by them. I was turned toward Aros, Coen now warming my back, and both of them were grabbing a hold of my body, dragging it in opposing directions. Coen had filled his hands with my breasts, pulling my upper half against him as small tendrils of pain licked down my chest, merging into a stinging haze of need as it neared my belly. Aros had taken my hips, dragging them against his, before his hand slipped down over one of my thighs, drawing it up and over his hip. His hardness was suddenly nestled between my legs, and I pressed against it, feeling overwhelmed by their warring powers even though I still strained for more of them.

Aros was swearing again, pushing against me.

"Choose," Coen growled out, his touch growing rough, his cheek dragging across the back of my neck. "Quickly, before I make the choice for both of us."

Aros shifted, sliding my leg back down again. His lips pressed hard to mine, before drawing back.

"Willa." He was demanding my attention.

My eyes were heavy, slow to blink open, unwilling to break the haze of pain and pleasure.

"How do you want to do this?" His voice was strained. "We really need to know, because I don't think we can hold on any longer."

JANE WASHINGTON & JAYMIN EVE

"Both," I muttered, a small gasp escaping my throat. Coen's fingers had slipped between my legs, his grunt against the back of my neck telling me that he didn't so much care about the semantics.

Aros took my mouth again, shifting his hips back a little. He pulled my leg out again but placed it against the bed instead of slinging it over his hip, and then his hands were on my face and Coen was drawing his fingers away. I cried out, reaching for both of them, but Aros quickly smothered the sound with his lips, flooding his power into me as pain shimmered across the backs of my thighs. There was another sensation there, too. Something hard, pushing between my legs from behind. A hand was on the back of my thigh, pushing the leg that Aros had positioned further up the bed, and then Coen was sinking his length into me. Aros swallowed up each of my sounds, but there was no masking the rough curse that Coen released against the base of my neck as he drew back and pushed forward again, deeper this time.

I clutched at Aros, the pain-power seeming to surge through me with each of Coen's movements, even though my body was loving every moment of what he did to me.

"Both," I finally managed to demand, though I wasn't exactly sure how that was going to be possible.

It wasn't until Aros shifted further up the bed that I realised how they were going to manage it. Once he had moved up far enough, I reached for his pants, working them down over his hips and taking his hard length into my hands. I caressed him lightly and heard the breath hiss out from between his teeth. It wasn't until Coen tightened his hold on my hip, surging into me with more force than before, that I was spurred into action.

I dipped forward, Aros moving at the same time, and my mouth opened as he pressed between my lips. He seemed to be trying to move slowly, to allow me to adjust, but I tried to swallow all of him, and he groaned, his hands quickly shifting to the back of my head, his hips flexing forward.

We quickly developed a rhythm: pain and pleasure at war in my body as Coen drove me closer to release.

Aros growled out a rough sound. "I'm going to come, Willa," he told me.

I figured it was a warning, but I definitely wasn't going to stop. I tried to pull him in deeper, and he groaned, releasing into the back of my throat.

Coen shifted me around as Aros eased out, lifting my body higher for greater access. He slammed harder into me, a tingling sensation ricocheting through my body. The sparks of pleasure had faded now that Aros was gone, but I was too far lost to care. Right then, pain and pleasure were two sides of the same token.

I cried out, and Coen groaned into my neck, his sounds muffled as we rode out our pleasure together.

I wasn't sure how long we lay tangled together afterward, but the haze of bliss took a long time to fade

JANE WASHINGTON & JAYMIN EVE

from the edges of my mind. I was buzzing with energy suddenly, my eyes wide awake, my mind alert. I assumed that not too much time had passed, because light was still streaming in through the windows high in the stone wall.

"Wait ..." I tensed, drawing a grunt of acknowledgement from one of the inert bodies at my side. "You were waking me up? Did something happen?"

I pushed myself up into a sitting position, but a strong arm very quickly wrapped around me, pulling me back down.

"Not now," was the sleepy grumble that accompanied the arm. "Later. After sleep. And more sex."

My body buzzed in response, my toes curling involuntarily. Sex. It seemed like a very underwhelming word for what I had just experienced. Another groan answered that thought, this time from the other body.

"Don't tempt us, we're not *that* drained."

"Shit." I tried to disentangle myself again, finally managing to gain my knees. *Drained.*

Two huge, beautiful gods lay sprawled before me, completely naked. I didn't even remember them taking off their clothes.

"I drained you both. I stole your energy." My tone was accusatory, but I was only accusing myself. I felt terrible.

"Yes." Coen opened one eye sleepily, fixing it on me. "Now come here and drain me again."

I snorted out a laugh before I could stop myself, and the sleepy smile that turned up the corners of his mouth had my heart melting into a puddle in the centre of my chest.

"I can see everything." Aros sounded like he was complaining, but his hand was already slipping up the inside of my thigh, his eyes both open and burning into me. "You're going to either have to put some clothes on or give us back our energy so that you can steal it from us all over again."

All of the laughter died out of me. I was aching again, my thighs tensing around his hand. I felt thoroughly satisfied, but the sudden tightening of my body was enough to suggest that I would never have enough of them.

"Keep looking at me like that," Aros warned, his hand inching up higher.

I began to part my knees, just a little, but a sudden sound wailing through the room had us all pausing. It sounded like an alarm of some kind. A horn, blasting in a succession of sounds.

"What the hell?" I scrambled from the bed, the others moving even faster.

They had their clothes on before I had even managed to locate my pants. Not that they were much use, considering the fact that they were torn beyond repair.

"Here." Aros was pulling a shirt over my head, but it wasn't one of mine. It fell to my knees and drowned my form, though it did manage to smell clean.

"Thanks," I muttered distractedly, as we all hurried to make our way out of the room.

I only had one boot on, whereas the other two were fully dressed and didn't even seem to have a single hair out of place. I wouldn't have cared in any other situation, but I didn't particularly want to be caught in the middle of a battle with only one boot and no underwear.

Aros stopped walking, causing me to collide with his back. Coen has also stopped. Both of them were staring at me while the sound of the alarm continued to blast through the corridor around us.

"You didn't put on underwear?" Coen asked, his eyebrows inching up.

"Is that really important right now?" I had to raise my voice over the sound of the horn.

The two of them glanced at each other, and then back to me, both sets of eyes dropping to the hem of the oversized shirt I wore.

"I feel like it's important," Coen admitted, while Aros nodded.

I swallowed, my mouth going dry. Suddenly, the alarm didn't seem so ... *alarming*.

"Let's go," Coen ground out. "The next time I have you won't be in a damn stone hallway."

"*Why not*?" I called out after him, as he took off at a run. Aros was close on his heels.

I was a little further back, on account of my shorter legs and the way my belly was clenching with annoying need. I hadn't always been so needy. It seemed that I grew worse with every encounter. I'd heard about sex addictions back in the seventh ring. Maybe I was developing a sex addiction ... although that didn't seem quite right, because I only wanted to have sex with my Abcurses. That had to count for something. I *only* wanted to have sex all the time with each of my five boyfriends. Sometimes at the same time. No, definitely at the same time. *Both is better*—that was my new motto.

"Wil-la." Aros drew out the word, his voice a mix of frustration and strain. "There's a crisis going on, you need to stop making me want to drag you back to that room."

"Right. Crisis." I nodded, my breath puffing out as we ran up the steps toward the top of the mountain.

I wasn't sure *why* we were running to the top of the mountain. I was following Aros and Aros was following Coen. I supposed it seemed like a smart place to go, considering the main hall was the largest area for people to gather in.

Siret, Yael, and Rome were already waiting at the top—though they were half-hidden behind a few towering pine trees, visible only from the direction we approached them in. We reached the top of the stairs just in time to witness the *second* strangest thing I had seen that sun-cycle.

A group of sols were pushing through the entrance ahead of us, herded by several Topian servers.

"What the hell is going on?" I whispered, as Coen suddenly froze, snagging me by the waist and pulling me over to the other Abcurses.

Aros was already hidden, his back to the trunk of a tree beside us, muttering lowly to Siret. We all peered out at the servers: they were holding pitchforks, which they occasionally prodded at the sols they were herding into the main hall.

"I have no idea," Aros answered, "but considering Staviti's energy was all over this place before you passed out, I'm going to say it's nothing good ..."

We all paused, Aros's words dying off as a sound rang through the hall, floating out toward us with an eerie echo. It had been a man's laugh: high and maniacal.

I knew that laugh.

I would have known it anywhere.

"Rau," I whispered, before breaking away from Coen. He reached out and re-caught me before I had even taken a step.

"No," he said, "you're not going to storm in there and confront Rau."

"This is because of me," I argued, as a form became visible before me, running up the stone steps of the mountain toward us. "Wait ... that's Emmy, let me go!"

"Willa!" She was screaming, having spotted me at the same time as I spotted her.

I tried to signal to her that she needed to keep quiet, but she wasn't paying any attention.

"Stop!" She was still screaming, even though we were clearly stopped already.

"Shhh, Emmy," I was motioning to her frantically now as she reached me and I pulled her into the cover of trees.

She was bent over, trying to draw in painfully deep gulps of air. *Where had she run from*? *Topia*?

"You. Can't." She paused for air again. "Go. In. There."

"Take a click, Em, you're about to die," I advised, before further shouting had my eyes flicking over to the building again. The servers standing at the entrance had disappeared, and the front had been left bare, the doors hanging open. I side-stepped the guys, moving toward the opening without thinking. One of the Abcurses cursed from behind me as I reached the door, positioning myself behind it and peering through the hall. It was surprisingly empty, other than the lines of sols leading right through the hall and to a set of doors at the other end. The servers were still policing the lines with their pitchforks, prodding the sols toward the other doors.

Through the hall, and beyond the doors, I could barely make out Rau standing on a wide expanse of clifftop, his back to the ocean.

"All sols will line up there," he shouted, his voice carrying through the doors and echoing around the hall.

The sols that were already facing him were mostly shaking and grey-faced. "You will all go up against me, one by one, until my Chaos sol shows herself. She is the only one who can save you."

"Willa Knight," he shouted out, just as the realisation sank into me. "You are the only one who can save them."

Oh, shit. Why was I always the one called into battles? One look at me should have told everyone concerned that I wasn't much of a fighter. Not that it mattered. I couldn't just stand back and let all of these sols die for me. And maybe it wouldn't be so bad? I had brand new powers, after all. Rau was about to find out what it felt like to have a real live dic—

"Willa!" Emmy's cry cut off that train of thought, and I spun to her. Her breathing was now calm enough for clear speech. "Don't even think about it. You cannot take on an Original God. Not to mention ... you need to go to Donald."

I hadn't expected her to say that at all. I had expected the warning about Rau and how he was probably going to rip my undead head off, but ... my mother was supposed to be comatose.

"She woke up, and immediately started malfunctioning," Emmy continued. "She's currently trying to stab people with her imaginary weapons.

When I left, she was using a pitchfork, but who knows what's next."

"Are you worried it might be a real pitchfork next?" Yael asked, the right corner of his lips tipping up slightly.

Emmy shot him a glare, and he held both hands up in surrender. The smile grew, though.

"I can't let Rau kill them all," I whispered to Emmy, because we were close enough to be overheard. Luckily, the Chaos God wasn't looking in this direction yet. He was too busy ordering sols to their possible dooms. "Just strap her down or something, she always liked that in her human life."

Never walk into a room at the local bar while your mum is entertaining. I'd learned that lesson the hard way. There were just some things you couldn't un-see.

"I will handle Donald and watch over Emmy." Cyrus's voice was loud—he clearly didn't care about rousing the attention of the pitchfork-wielding servers. "But you should think on whether the best course of action is for you to run into Rau's little trap here. You don't understand your powers yet. Feels like a great way to get yourself killed. Again."

"Are you stalking us?" I bit out, wondering why he was always around.

His eyes flicked to Emmy, before coming back to rest on me. *Ah,* he was stalking *someone.*

He was right, though, about getting myself killed again. We didn't know if I could die or not and going up against Rau was a huge risk, but I knew he wouldn't stop until he got what he wanted. We needed a secret weapon.

The chains.

"We need Crowe's chains," Coen said at the same time as the idea occurred to me. "I'll be right back."

He took off so fast that it was almost like he disappeared.

"Don't let my mum or Emmy get hurt," I said, locking my eyes on Cyrus. "You've been a mostly unreliable bastard since I met you. Random as hell. Choosing sides where you see fit. But this is something I'm trusting you on."

For once, there was nothing hidden in his face. He almost looked ... dependable. "I will protect them, Willa."

Realising that I didn't have much of a choice, I turned to Emmy. "Stay safe and stay out of sight," I told her before pulling her in for a hard hug.

Her face was pale and drawn when she pulled back. She was going to argue more, I could tell, but Cyrus scooped her up before she could say anything. Her worried face morphed into one of pure astonishment; it was almost comical. It wasn't until the Neutral god was nearing the top of the stairs again that I could see her fire return as she started to argue with him. By this time, though, we were too far away to hear what she was saying. No doubt it would be colourful.

"Focus here, Soldier," Siret said, bringing my

attention back to Rau and his quest for sol domination. Every single sol was now in his line. It filled the hall entirely. I noticed the gods now, standing along the sides of the hall, appearing to be mostly bored, even though they really should have been worried about their sols dying. If their sols died, so did they, according to Staviti's new rules.

Maybe none of them believed it, or maybe it wasn't even true.

"You first, Bestiary," Rau ordered, gesturing toward the female at the start of the line. She had long chocolate brown hair, reaching her mid-back. It was dead straight, not a flyaway strand to be seen. Her skin was a similarly brown shade, and she had flashing blue eyes that locked onto Rau, like he was prey. She stepped forward confidently.

"I like her," I said sadly. "She has sass."

"You've never even met her, and she probably hates dwellers," Yael reminded me.

"True, but that doesn't mean we can let Rau kill her."

Rome wrapped an arm around me, probably for comfort, and also to keep me from running off. They knew me very well. "Just wait for Pain," he told me, pulling me even closer. "He'll be back soon."

He would, I knew that without a doubt. But would it be in time to save the Bestiary sol?

Rau watched as she stalked toward him, her hands lifting up in front of her like she was summoning energy into them. Behind the Chaos god, storm clouds started to gather, and I tried not to freak out. I'd been caught in one of his storms before. If this was anything like that one, everyone on top of the cliff was about to be swept out into the ocean.

Lightning cracked the ground where the sol was standing, but she managed to jump back just in time to avoid being burnt to a crisp. She slapped her hands together and the ground shook beneath our feet before a small fissure appeared and a bunch of creatures poured out of the rocks.

"Gah!" I jumped back even though I was nowhere near the animals. "Are those ... *sleepers*?"

"Yes, their breeding grounds are usually found deep within mountains," Aros informed me.

I swallowed the lump in my throat before wiping my damp hands across my shirt.

This movement seemed to draw the Abcurses' attention away from the multitude of poisonous, eight-legged, multi-eyed, scary-ass creatures that were swarming en masse toward a relaxed Chaos god. They ran their gazes across me. Starting at the top of my mussed sex-hair, right down over my shirt, and finishing on the single boot I wore. Aros had already seen me in this chaotic state, but the others were finally noticing.

"Are you wearing underwear, Soldier?" Siret asked me, his eyes centred on my chest.

I shook my head hard. "No time for that, I had to make do with what I had."

He just shook his head, his expression almost pained. "This is not the sort of attire you want to fight a god in."

"Might give her an advantage," Aros said, his eyes practically the colour of melted gold as they met mine. "I'd definitely lose."

Rome's voice sounded strained. "One: we do not want Rau looking at her like that. Ever. Two: we would all have to kill him on the spot, and that would just get messy."

Killing a god wasn't something they could easily achieve, but we all knew what he meant. "We have the chains now, Willa," Yael reminded me. "Killing just got a hell of a lot easier."

My attention was drawn back to the scene on the cliff again. Rau was still just standing there, the first lot of sleepers about to reach him.

"There have to be thousands of them," I murmured. We didn't have them in the seventh ring— one of the few good things about living in the outer areas of Minatsol. But I'd heard the stories. The venom in one bite was strong enough to kill ten sols. That's how deadly they were.

Warmth moved down my spine; I recognised the Trickery straight away, and barely even flinched. I didn't turn from the scene to see what Siret had clothed me in. It really didn't matter, it had to be better than what I'd had on.

"Got it." Coen's low voice caused me to jump. I spun around to find him looking a little windswept, the engraved chains in his hands, before a scream from behind had us all whipping back toward where Rau and the Bestiary sol were facing off. Fire had ripped across the top of the cliff, engulfing all of the deadly creatures, as well as the Bestiary sol who controlled them. Before anyone could say anything, I snatched the chains off Coen and dove for the doorway.

Strong arms wrapped around my biceps, halting me mid-step.

"No, Willa!" Yael snapped. "You'll get yourself killed running in like that. Give the chains to us."

With a shake of my head, I wrapped both arms tightly around them. "No. I'm the only one who has a chance of getting close enough to Rau to use them. I need to stop this now."

I knew there was no way they were going to let me just walk over to him, but I couldn't listen to the screams of that sol for another click and not do something.

Freeze them. The thought pushed through my mind with force, almost seeming to slam into the Abcurses. I knew the only reason I got away with it was because the last thing they expected was for me to use my powers against them. So they had no shields against me. *Freeze them!* I mentally screamed this time.

All sounds faded away.

Even the birds that had been screeching in the sky went quiet. I managed to wiggle myself out of Yael's hold. Thankfully, he'd been trying to swing me around, so his grip was loose. Taking in the scene, I scrambled into the hall. Everyone was frozen. Not just the Abcurses, but all of the sols, gods, and … even Rau.

Holy fucking shit. This was my shot. My chance to take him down.

I sprinted forward, stepping my way around burning animals, the fire eerily still. I was running as fast as my legs could move, eyes locked on the prize, chains clinking in my hands. I had no idea how long my freezing power would last. Probably not long enough, but this was my only shot. All of the gods would be on guard against this sort of attack if they had even a moment to recover. If I'd learned anything from those bitches who could change their appearance, it was that you might fool a god once or twice, but the moment they caught on to what you could do, there was no way to fool them again.

From the corner of my right eye, I caught movement—it was already wearing off. I cried out in pain, pushing my body faster and harder than I had ever thought possible, reaching Rau just as his eyes snapped to me. I took one of the cuffs and slammed it around his right wrist. As I went to click the left into place, his arm shot out, the movement blurred with speed. Before I could do anything, the second cuff clicked into place.

On my wrist.

"Activate," he said, the maniacal hint of a laugh underlying the word.

SIXTEEN

Having my soul torn from my body and catapulted through time and space into a banishment realm was far less painful than I'd anticipated—but it didn't seem to be the same for Rau, whose high-pitched screams kept me company until my eyes opened again.

There was some disorientation, and it took me some time to understand why everything was muted, the colours dull and washed out. The landscape also left something to be desired, taking its inspiration from the outer rings of Minatsol. Barren of life.

Maybe this was another dimension of Minastol? Like a plane of existence that sols and dwellers couldn't see, but that existed side by side with ours? The way Topia and Minatsol did?

The rambling of my thoughts appeared to be getting worse.

"How dare you use Crowe's chains on me." Those hard words snapped me out of my delirium. My reality rushed in, slamming into me with the force of an enraged bullsen.

Rau. Banishment realm. Fuck.

I spun around to face him, moving much faster than I would have been able to in Minatsol. My hands were up in front of me in the same instant, as I prepared myself for a fight.

I felt solid and alive but looking down at my skin and clothes, which were almost grey in colour, I realised I was just as washed out as the rest of this land. And I was back in the shirt, because apparently Trickery clothing did not travel across realms.

Rau stalked closer, looking the same, only a little blurred around the edges. "I don't care if you are my Beta," he declared as he got closer. "I'm ending this now. Gods might not be able to die in the other realm, but they can *here*."

He lunged for me, and I let out a shriek, throwing my hands into the air. My powers weren't swirling inside like they normally did, but my instincts were to try and use them.

Rau slammed into me, and when I got thrown off-balance by his weight, my body jerked backwards, my head slamming into his, knocking him off me.

I groaned, holding my hand against my forehead as I peeled myself up off the ground. I spun to where Rau had been, only to find that he was no longer there.

Movement from my left had me spinning again, but the sad face staring back at me was not the god of Chaos.

I stilled. "Hello," I greeted hesitantly. The male was smaller than me, fragile looking, with an innocence in his features. He looked no older than four. A child.

A god child.

My heart immediately clenched and I wanted to vomit. The panteras told me that the Abcurses were not the only children to be born of gods. They were just the only ones that Staviti didn't kill, for whatever reason.

"Hello," I tried again. "What's your name?"

I was trying to keep an eye on my surroundings, to figure out what had happened to Rau, but I couldn't seem to tear my gaze from the young god.

"I … don't have a name," he finally stuttered out, sounding even younger than he looked.

Another shadow presence stepped in then. Female, looking like she was no more than four as well. "I don't know my name either."

"None of them know their names." The deep voice was so instantly different that I jerked myself toward him, hands up again, forehead ready for more headbutting.

It was a man. Tall and imposing. Well, as imposing as one could be when they looked like water had washed away all of their colour. "Who are you?" I asked, cautious, moving closer to the two children. My instinct was to protect the young, no matter their undead state.

"Are these ... the god children?" I asked, choking on the words.

He nodded, face solemn. "Yes, Staviti had them all banished. God children are not babies for long. Their parents managed to hide most of them until they were seven or more sun-cycles old. But their powers grew too strong after that."

I wondered if one could cry in this realm, because I sure as hell felt like I was about to. My throat and chest and eyeballs hurt. My body burned, and if I had been capable of fire right then, I would have been nothing short of a volcano.

"Are you telling me," I said, when I could finally speak, "that Staviti has a room or cave or dungeon filled with chained god babies. All of them stuck between two worlds?"

The man nodded, his hair bouncing across his shoulders. I would guess the colour was blond, but it was next to impossible to tell.

He was handsome and clean-cut. He looked like a sol: rich and assured. It wasn't possible, though. He had to be a god, if he was in the imprisonment realm.

"Who are you?" I asked.

He looked like he was about to answer, but in that moment, Rau made his second appearance. He must have disappeared to find a weapon, because he was charging me with a long spear in his hand.

The god children turned slowly, their eyes listless as they stared at the crazy screaming god. I, on the other hand, did not just stand there. I started to run, because I might have a tough head, but it was no match for the sharp point of a spear.

"Do powers work in here?" I shouted at the man as I ran in his direction.

He shook his head. "No, we are stripped of godhood in this realm."

Well, that was just great. I was going to have to run for it and hope that I was faster.

Before I made it past the man though, he reached out and latched onto me, almost toppling both of us over.

"You cannot run from him," he warned me as we straightened. "He will never sleep or stop, there's nothing else for him to do in this realm other than hunt you down."

"Do you have a better idea?" I screamed. I was getting sick of being handled by all of these men. I needed my powers back, it was nice to be able to kick ass on my own.

Something heavy dropped into my hand then, and I focused long enough to see a glint of silver. A dagger, just like the one Rau had tried to kill *me* with.

"You should get out of the way," I told the man, keeping my body half-turned to hide the knife.

Rau was almost upon us, and the man backed away, leaving me to twist to the side as the spear neared my torso. The sharp tip followed me, Rau anticipating my movement, but my foot snagged on a rock and I lurched suddenly forward, the spear bouncing across my back, missing its true mark.

I didn't pause to think through my actions, only shoved the dagger upward as Rau collided with me, sending us both to the ground. His weight landed heavily over me, the hilt wrenched from my hands. I kicked him off, scrambling away, but he wasn't trying to fight me anymore. He was slumped over the rock I had tripped on, his hands trembling around the hilt of the knife, which protruded from his chest. His fall must have pushed it all the way in, because he was staring at it as though he had somehow stabbed *himself*.

He let out a horrible gurgling sound, his eyes travelling up to mine.

"This isn't over." He forced the words out through gritted teeth, the words struggling to form around the immense pain that he was obviously in.

"If this isn't what *over* looks like, then I no longer trust the meaning of the word," I retorted, still out of breath. I motioned to the wasteland around us, populated only by banished ghosts.

Rau's eyes were fixed steadfastly to mine.

"Why were you not torn apart?" he rasped out, his eyelids flittering briefly, his body crumpling back. He was losing strength. "The crossing to the realm. It should have torn your soul into two—the chains are only enough to carry the weight of ... of ..." He started coughing, but the movement only ended on a moan of pain.

He was silent, then, hunched over himself, blood pooling along the ground around him.

"The weight of what?" I prodded, taking a few steps away from the spreading pool of blood. I didn't want to get my boot dirty, seeing as it was the only one I had.

"The weight of one soul," a voice replied.

The voice from earlier.

I turned, finding the maybe-blond man behind me again. The children had gathered around him, all of them staring at Rau. I wanted to cover up the god of Chaos, to shield the image from their view ... but what was the point in protecting their innocence? They were already dead. You couldn't be more mature than a dead person.

"But two of us came here," I muttered, the man's meaning finally catching up to me.

"Two parts of two souls travelled here," he countered, "equalling the weight of a single soul."

"You mean ..." I turned back to the slumped over, washed-out image of Rau. "He's not dead?"

"A sliver of his soul has died, absolutely, but the rest remains."

I groaned, stalking away from the body, back toward where the black chains lay, still in the dirt several feet away. "Just my luck. I finally beat that asshole in a battle, and it turns out I was only battling a *piece* of him. Not even the real him. Wait ... does that mean I'm not even the real me? What was he saying, about my soul not being torn?"

The man had his head cocked as he watched me, walking slowly toward where I crouched beside the chains.

"Your soul had already been separated," he informed me. "The sons of Abil and Adeline guard the splintered pieces, forming a bond between the six of you that cannot be broken, even in death."

I froze, grabbing the chains and standing again, my gaze sharpening, trying to make out any further details in the shadowy visage before me.

"How do you know about that?" I asked, swallowing. "Who are you?"

"We can see through the eyes of what we left behind," he replied cryptically, motioning to one of the children. The girl hurried over to him, casting a wary look at me.

"Where is your body?" he asked her. "What can you see?"

The girl closed her eyes, and her body immediately seemed to shrink, to recoil away from us.

"It's dark." Her voice was shaking. "And cold. There are others here, but I can't see their faces. There are chains—they're heavy, and cold. Water is dripping on my leg. There are bugs crawling on me." She started crying, and the man whispered something to her. She opened her eyes again and threw her arms around his neck, sobbing.

I realised, then, that she was talking about the body she had been imprisoned in, and I wanted to throw up again. I waited until the girl calmed down, and the man sent her back to the others, rising to his feet again.

"We can still see," he told me. "And I have seen you before, Willa Knight."

I stared at him for a long time, sure that I had never seen his face before, though there was an inkling of something familiar about him. I thought that it was in the shape of his eyes, or the wideness of his smile.

"Wait ..." My voice was shaking, shock tumbling through me. "*Sienna*?"

He blinked, unsure how to answer for a moment, and then he was laughing. The sound wasn't as full as it should have been, as though laughter wasn't allowed in this place of dust and shadow.

"No," he replied, when his laughter had died off into a chuckle. "I am not Sienna."

"Then how have you seen me before? Did you die in Minatsol?"

"I didn't," he replied, a smile twisting his lips. "I died in Topia, at the hand of my brother. He locked my body away, but the panteras drove him from the spot. They now guard it, and he cannot return. I lay behind the mortal glass, my body preserved from age and decay, so that I might see the secrets of the world, both past and present. I watch as the world changes, unable to do anything about it, unable to change myself. I watched you while you watched me. Do you remember?"

I stumbled forward, one of my hands reaching out toward him involuntarily. "Jakan?" The name was only a dry whisper, barely escaping my lips.

He nodded, and then he captured my extended hand. It felt natural for my hand to fit into his, and I wasn't sure why. Maybe it was because we both lacked substance in this realm, but longed—with whatever substance we did have—for a connection to the other realm. Or maybe it was because he knew everything there was to know about me, through the glass, and I had seen his birth with my own eyes. We were connected, in a very strange way.

"I should be scared of you," I found myself saying, as I pulled back from him, my hand falling to my side again. "You are Staviti's brother. A god, just like him."

"A god of creation, just like him," Jakan confirmed, "though my powers have been stripped away."

"Why did he kill you?"

"He killed me because he wanted to be the only one. He will kill you for the same reason."

"I'm as good as dead." I tossed my hands out, indicating where I stood. I had been too busy fighting off Rau before, for the reality of that statement to properly sink into me, but it did now.

There was a part of me that would never die. A part of my soul that had splintered away from me and latched onto each of the five Abcurses, the beings who surrounded me after Rau's curse tore me apart. But the rest of me? It was lost. Limp and lifeless, as Sienna had been.

"That's not entirely true," Jakan argued. "You're not dead. Not yet. Since a part of you remains, you can use the chains as a tether. A pathway can always go in both directions: forward, or backward. They brought you here, so they can take you back."

"Come back with me," I blurted, the plea barely even making sense.

There were children that needed saving, not to mention Sienna, and countless others. I wasn't sure how I was going to bring back all of the children, though, especially if Staviti would only banish them all over again.

Jakan smiled. "I cannot. My soul here is whole, it would tear me apart to go back with you. Remember, you can only carry the weight of half a soul ... though I think you will want to save that space for someone else. Someone who has been waiting to speak to you for a long, long time."

He held out his hand, and I took it again, allowing him to lead me down a dusty, dirt-cracked path. We didn't seem to be heading in any particular direction. The landscape seemed to go on forever, with no place to stop or rest. It was dust as far as the eye could see. I realised after almost half a rotation of walking that there wasn't even a sun, or a sky. The dust had merged with the horizon, providing no source for the dull light that illuminated everything, and no sense for where we were in the sun-cycle.

"She is usually here," Jakan told me, his voice lowered. His tone was softer now, his eyes downcast.

The woman was standing at the crest of a hill, staring listlessly off into the distance. She was familiar to me, even through the washed-out greyness that was painted over her profile.

"Mum?" I choked out.

She turned, her hand raising up. "Herd," she said.

I froze in my scramble up the hill, confused. "Herd?" I asked, turning to Jakan, repeating the word. "Herd? What does that mean?"

He shrugged lightly. "She says strange things, sometimes. Her body is still functioning. I don't know where it is right now, because you took it from Topia."

"Herd," my mother repeated, her hands now seeming to grasp something invisible in front of her. She made a stabbing motion. "Herd. Herd."

"Oh gods," I moaned. "She's copying what Donald is doing in Minatsol. Emmy mentioned that Donald was malfunctioning, trying to herd her with an invisible pitchfork. Is this why my mother hasn't ever seemed quite ... *right* in the head?" I asked the question of Jakan, who had moved to stand beside my mother, leading her shadow gently down from the hill to where I stood.

"You don't understand the feeling," he told me.

"You are never apart from the pieces of your soul that have been ripped from you. Your mother has been incomplete for a long time."

"Will this fix her?" I asked, reaching out and taking her wrist. She was still trying to stab things with her other hand.

Jakan smiled again, but the gesture was sad, somehow ... different to a real smile. Tainted by something that I didn't yet understand.

"Does she really need fixing?" he asked. "Can't she be perfect in her incompleteness?"

I stared at him, uncomprehending. "Are you trying to say you're going to miss her, and that you don't want me to take her away?"

"What I have to say no longer matters, Willa. You must return immediately. The other pieces of your soul are in danger."

I snapped one of the cuffs onto my mother's wrist before the full weight of his words had even sunk into me. It must have been the sudden shift in his tone, or the way that my mother stopped trying to stab at things, her whole body going slack, her head hanging from her shoulders as though partly unhinged.

If the other pieces of my soul were in danger, that meant the Abcurses were in danger. I snapped the other cuff to my other wrist, and watched as Jakan covered both cuffs with his hands, his eyes settling on the shadow of my mother, before shifting to me.

"This will not be easy," he told me. "Staviti is your

enemy. He does not want any beings in Topia other than the ten perfect beings that he created. He will do everything in his power to kill any sol who has a chance of ascending to godhood, and any god who has already ascended. If he could put a stop to ascension in itself, he would."

I nodded, my brain absorbing the information and storing it away somewhere to be dealt with later. I had one thing on my mind, and one thing alone.

I needed to protect my Abcurses.

"Thank you," I murmured, as our eyes met again.

"Close your eyes," he replied. "Reach into the chains as though they are a rope, and when you think you can see it, grasp that rope and pull. It will resist you. Keep pulling. Eventually, you will find your way home again."

I did as he told me, my eyes closing, my consciousness directed toward the chains. It was easier than I had thought it would be, since everything in me was already reaching out for the Abcurses and the other pieces of my soul.

I clasped the invisible tether, and the chains hummed with power against my skin.

"Jakan," a clear, bright voice rang out. My mother's, I realised. I had never heard her sound so coherent, so ... *alive*.

"Jakan!" she cried out again, in despair, this time. "No! I want to stay with you!"

Shock barrelled through me, because I had never

heard her speak any beings name like that. Like … *she loved him.* Did that mean that Jakan might be more important to me than just Staviti's brother and something the mortal glass wanted me to unravel? Could he possibly be … my father?

I cried out for him as well, but it was too late. We were being pulled back the way we had come, and I could feel the jarring *snap* of my soul crashing back into my body, before everything went dark.

SEVENTEEN

I woke up to the sounds of screaming. When I blinked my eyes open, the cliff-top that Rau had challenged the sols upon had drastically changed. There were scorch marks along the grass, and a giant mess of charred, twisted rubble where the main hall had been. There was a god standing amidst the debris, his feet safely balancing on a single, un-blemished plank of wood, his robe still somehow pristine as it fluttered about him, pushed by some invisible breeze.

All around the rubble, the sols and gods had gathered, each of them turned toward a woman who had collapsed on the ground, her screams of agony filling the air.

There were five broad backs spanning out in front of me, positioned to protect my body. I was laying on the grass, an inert body beside me, the chains linking us together. For just a moment, I thought that it was my mother, but that was only wishful thinking. The blood-red robes that enveloped the form belonged to Rau. He remained still, his eyes open, as though he was dead. I shoved the cuff off and scrambled to my feet, rousing the attention of the guys. Each of them spun around, and I was suddenly tangled in the embrace of too many arms.

"We could still feel you," one of them muttered.

"We knew we hadn't lost you," another added.

I was still disoriented, still dizzy and trying to get my bearings, but it felt right being momentarily crushed and then repositioned, only to be crushed again as they fought with each other to hold me properly. A kiss landed on my lips, another on my cheek, another on my neck. I basked in the warmth of them, the solidness of them. Each unique scent, and the brightness of their colouring. It was shocking, after being stuck in the world of grey dust, but it was a welcome shock.

"Staviti is trying to kill everyone," I muttered, as we turned to watch the woman again.

I didn't recognise her.

"What do you mean by everyone?" Coen asked, claiming my right side, his eyes on the god standing above everyone, his voice almost a whisper.

I squinted at the god, and then almost fell back a step in shock. It was Staviti. On the Peak. Watching a woman break down. From the remains of the hall.

This was apparently too much information for my

brain to handle, because the only word that I could manage to form was, "What?"

"She means *everyone*," Rome supplied. "I heard it in her mind before she started freaking out. He wants to kill all of us."

"Everyone but the Original Gods," I clarified. "His brother told me."

"His brother ..." Aros trailed off, turning away from the scene before him to stare at me, his brow crinkled. "You mean Jakan—"

I leapt forward, quickly covering his mouth, but it was too late.

His brother's name had captured Staviti's attention.

"Willa Knight," his voice boomed out, cutting over the sounds of the sobbing woman. "You have taken something from me."

"If you lost something, you should probably check that mess there," I found myself responding as I pointed to the broken pile of building that he stood on, my voice almost loud and confident ... if you ignored the tremble of terror undermining everything.

He smiled, his head shaking slowly from one side to the other, and then he was moving toward me. With each of his steps, a wooden plank shot out from the rubble, providing a smooth and unblemished step to aid his descent.

"You have taken one of my creations," he said, when he was before me.

I could feel the tension coursing through Coen and

Rome on either side of me, and I knew that all five of my Abcurses were a click away from jumping in front of me and starting a fight with Staviti just to distract him.

"We're even then," I said, trying to force my voice into a semblance of calm, the way he was doing. "You took my mother from me. I took Rau from you."

"I *saved* your mother," he crooned, his voice soft, placating. The way you might speak to a child who was getting upset over ghost stories. "She was incomplete when I visited her. I only wanted to ask about you." He smiled, the gesture almost gentle. "I was curious, that is all. I wanted to know what made you special, but she barely seemed to know anything about you at all. I killed her, but I fixed her, don't you see? She's better now. And I let you have her back, didn't I?"

There was no reasoning with that level of crazy. I should have guessed that he would be insane; a god who killed children just to keep his own power was not a benevolent sort of god. I had to try, though.

"She's not better," I told him. "You need to understand that most of the things you've done to 'improve' the worlds have only served to hurt them. Don't you care about your creations?"

Obsidian eyes examined me; he almost looked curious. "How are you alive, Willa Knight?" He disregarded my questions as easily as he disregarded his creations. "I was watching you. You died. And then you were no longer in my vision. So, tell me, how this is possible?"

I opened my mouth, but the words died on my lips as he continued. "Your mother told me you weren't special. She was very insistent about that. She seemed to truly believe that there was no way you could have had the Chaos power. She called herself the lowest of the dwellers, and placed you right alongside her. You were supposed to be nothing more than a burden. A mistake. A blight on Minatsol. So, explain to me how you have been hit with Rau's curse, skewered by Cyrus's blade, and retrieved from the imprisonment realm ... and yet here you stand. Still *alive*." He finally pulled that unnerving gaze from me, letting it rest on the Abcurses, who were at my side. "How do you command such powerful gods? The power within you, how was it given to you?"

There was no right answer. I knew that. He was just playing with me before he struck, because his intentions were to kill me—along with everyone else who wasn't an Original God. He must have needed something from the lesser beings. The weaker sols and the dwellers who posed no threat to him. He must have needed their worship, their beliefs, otherwise he could have just destroyed all beings on Minatsol instead of trying to pick away at the strongest. I just needed to stall long enough to figure out what to do.

"You've been so easily fooled," I blurted out.

Real smart, Willa. Insulting him would *definitely* stop an attack.

I hurried on: "Siret has been using Trickery to convince Rau, and all of the gods, that I have a Chaos power. He even tricked Rau and Cyrus into thinking that I died that night. My mom was right. I'm nothing special."

Someone made an angry noise beside me, and my heart warmed, because I knew that there were at least five people here who disagreed with Staviti and my mom.

Staviti took a step closer. He was about ten feet away now. "And, yet, somehow you managed to take Rau from me." He flicked a hand toward the god who was still on the ground, unmoving. "One of my creations. One I do care about very much."

Interesting. My words before had registered with him, even if he did choose to ignore them.

"It's time you felt the same loss," he announced, his tone cold.

His entire demeanour had changed, and now I felt the threat that he presented. I felt it right to my core. He was about to attack. I tried to figure out how to protect my boys, power swirling inside of me with more force than I'd ever felt. Heat was already pouring out of me. I'd just taken a step forward when a scream rang out. It was not the woman from before, but a new cry of pain. Emmy flew through the air, stopping just before Staviti, hovering there, her face a mask of pain and suffering.

"This one is precious to you," he said, almost conversationally. "This is one you treasure. One you will mourn more than the pathetic mother who has no love for her daughter."

For a brief click, I wondered if I should pretend not to know Emmy. Pretend that she meant nothing to me. But in almost the same instant, I knew that would be a futile endeavour. Staviti knew so much about my life. He had been studying me, trying to figure out the riddle of who I was.

He knew how much I loved my sister.

I released my hold on the power inside. My skin was awash in flames, because for Emmy, I didn't care if Staviti knew about my powers. For Emmy, I would burn Minatsol to the ground.

"If you hurt her, I will never stop hunting you down," I told him, taking a step forward. Five gods stayed closer by, or as close as they could without getting completely incinerated. "I will kill every single god you created. And when I'm done killing them, I will kill you."

I meant that. With every fibre of my being.

"I'm offended," said an amused voice off to the side of where I stood with the Abcurses.

I pulled my gaze from Emmy long enough to find Abil, relaxing against what remained of a half-destroyed wall. "And here I thought you enjoyed my company, daughter-in-law."

I blinked at him, some of my fire dying off as I tried to figure out what he was doing there, and what he was talking about.

"You just threatened to kill all Original Gods," Siret informed me.

"We all say things when we're angry," I muttered, turning back to Staviti.

He was still holding Emmy's prone figure in the air before him. "All Original Gods except Abil and Adeline," I added, the fire flaring to life around me again. I took another step forward. "Let. Emmy. Go."

When it came to my family, I no longer feared death. For them, I could be brave.

Staviti's eyes flicked across to Abil. And then to the five Abcurses around me. Then they returned to me. "Trickery ... can it make fire like this?" he snarled. Losing control for the first time. "Are you really nothing more than an insignificant being who happens to have some very powerful friends? You need to understand that a debt must be paid. I will take the debt owed me and then return to Topia. Do not rest easy, however. I will be back, and I will finish what we started here this sun-cycle ... in a more *opportune* setting."

All I heard was *take the debt owed.*

I leapt forward, letting my powers free, urging them to wrap around his legs. I could burn a god, I already knew that. I was too late, though. Before my fire could touch him, Staviti had turned his hand, and with a crack, Emmy's neck twisted at an unnatural angle, her face falling still.

A scream ripped from me, followed by another as I continued to charge. I saw nothing but the Creator. I would kill him if it was the last thing I ever did. He doused the flames that had leapt out ahead of me, but he would not be able to douse me. The power was within, and I would push it all out until he was no more. Just as I dove at him, however, a strong and unnatural wind blew me to the side. I crashed to the ground with a hard thump, extinguishing the flames almost immediately, as I had nearly landed on Emmy's body. Rolling over, I wrapped myself around my sister, holding her close. A flash of white drew my attention, and I realised that it was Cyrus.

Sweet gods on the mountain. He was glowing. His entire figure bore such a white light around it that I almost couldn't stare directly. He attacked Staviti, energy flinging from him and slamming into the Creator, knocking him down. He didn't stop there, his feet hovering from the ground as he glided forward, his face devoid of any emotion except wrath.

He gripped Staviti around the throat, hauling him up and holding him in the air in front of him.

"You have broken the balance," Cyrus said, his voice deep and echoing. "You will pay for your crimes."

His head swung toward me, and I was suddenly

locked in the gaze of a pair of blinding white eyes. "Emmy?" I heard the question in that one word.

I shook my head, pulling her closer to me.

Cyrus roared then, a low guttural sound that sent goosebumps across my skin. Staviti must have realised that he had made a mistake; Emmy wasn't just important to me. He launched into action, knocking Cyrus back a few feet with some kind of invisible force that was strong enough to send the other's body several inches into the packed dirt. This gave Staviti enough room to gather a storm around him, wind and rain popping into existence from nowhere, battering everyone on the mountain.

Cyrus pulled himself up again and pushed through it, sending blasts of white light at Staviti, who countered these attacks with jagged bolts of deadly lightning, fissuring the Neutral power into harmless droplets of rain. Their fight continued on, back and forth, while the rest of us held on for our lives.

"Give Emmy to me," Siret's low voice pleaded. I realised that I was surrounded by my Abcurses; I had no idea how long they'd been there, my focus had been entirely on Emmy, and then on Cyrus.

"No!" I shook my head, pulling her limp body even closer. "No. I can't let her go. I won't let her go."

A scream ripped from me as I sobbed. My breathing was so fast that I was about to hyperventilate, but I just couldn't accept that she was gone. I had seen her neck snap. I had seen the light fade from her eyes, and I still couldn't accept it. Rain slapped at my bare skin, stinging with its assault, but it was nothing compared to the pain inside my chest.

She's alive. She's alive. She's alive.

I chanted this in my head, over and over, each chant bringing another sob. Hands touched me, but no one tried to steal her away. They just gave me their energy. Their love.

It wasn't enough.

My power swirled with the same force as the storm outside. *Live, Emmy. Live.*

"Please," I sobbed out loud.

I closed my eyes and pressed my forehead to her chest, my arms wrapped tightly around her as we lay together. My head started to swirl, the same way my energy did inside my body, and within a few clicks I grew light-headed, dark spots flashing over my vision.

"What the fuck is she doing here?" Coen's question should have been concerning to me, but I was struggling to focus on anything other than the dizzying sensation in my head.

"Pica never leaves Topia." This time, it was Aros speaking. "Fuck. She might be here to help Staviti."

I missed parts of the conversation as my precarious hold on consciousness started to slip.

"... Hates him," someone else was saying. "There's no way she's here to help. She's here because of Rau."

"Pica ..." I recognised Staviti's voice, but the tone confused me. I was barely managing to regain consciousness, and I lost whatever else he said, though he seemed to be shocked. A woman replied, and then he was angry. Betrayed. Blackness pressed in on either side of me and I wondered then if maybe I was dying of a broken heart. Everything hurt and my energy was slipping from my body.

"Willa!" Aros's shout barely even registered. "No, you can't …"

The darkness sucked the last of my breath from me, and then everything was still.

EIGHTEEN

I wasn't sure if I died again that sun-cycle, but when I finally regained consciousness, I sure as hell wished that I had. Pain was everywhere. There wasn't a single part of my body that didn't hurt. I groaned as I tried to open my eyes.

"Willa." That whisper of my name was from Yael. I'd know his voice anywhere. He brushed a hand lightly over me and I flinched. The pain was just so intense, it was almost unbearable.

I felt the rim of a cup being pressed against my lips and then liquid on my tongue, at the back of my throat, soothing and cool. "Drink it please, you need to rest some more."

That voice was definitely not one of my guys, unless one of them had gotten decidedly feminine in the last few rotations—or however long I'd been out for. Whatever was in the liquid, it worked almost immediately, and whatever hold I'd had on reality faded away again.

The next time I woke, the pain was almost at a manageable level, so I pushed through the fuzziness in my head and forced my eyes open. The first thing I saw was an arm: bare, bronze, and well-muscled. It was not my arm, but it was an arm that was very close to my heart. Literally and figuratively.

I wiggled up in the bed, pausing when I realised that I was in bed with five sleeping gods. All of my gods. They were sprawled around me, keeping me at the centre of them all.

Coen's arm was the large one I'd first seen. Yael's was close to his.

I started to cry. Tears flooded my eyes and trailed down my cheeks as I sat there and watched the gods. It wasn't until a calloused thumb wiped away one of my tears that I realised they weren't really sleeping anymore. No one said a word as they pulled themselves up, surrounding me, pressing in closer. I ended up with Siret behind me, Yael to my right, Coen to my left, and Aros and Rome in front. I was the centre, the Abcurses a circle of heat around me.

"Where is Emmy?" I acknowledged the most pressing pain in my heart. Tears ran unchecked down my cheeks, wiped away by a different Abcurse each time, their hands pressing to my face as they touched me.

Before anyone could answer me, a tall, thin woman

walked into the room. It only took one glance to assure me that it was a god. She was stunning, her hair extra-long and perfect, her eyes sparkling with beauty, her cheeks so damn rosy. Unnatural. Her beauty was unnatural.

There was no wariness in the boys, but there was something familiar about her that I couldn't place.

"Pica," Aros said.

Oh, Pica. Wait a freaking click … *Pica*? Like, the one god Staviti was in love with? The literal Goddess of Love? Her name was ringing some sort of bell for me … was she at the Peak? Had someone said that?

For the first time, I noticed my surroundings. We weren't in our rooms. I was in a huge bed—clearly, because it fit five massive gods with ease—but the room beyond that was unfamiliar. There was a lot of pink, however. Bright pinks, pale pinks, even a nice purple-pink floral design near the door.

"What's going on?" I asked. "Where are we?"

Rome cleared his throat, laughter in his words when he said, "This is Pica's home. She … invited us to stay with her for the next little while."

Pica hurried forward then until she was standing right at the end of the bed. "I've waited a long time to meet you, Willa."

I just blinked, waiting for my brain to figure out what she meant. "You've waited to meet me?"

She nodded, her eyes wide and bright. "Oh, yes, I think of you as the daughter Staviti stole from me."

Say what now?

"Uh, I'm really confused," I finally admitted. "What happened on the Peak? Where is Staviti? How are we not all dead?"

The moment I said *dead*, the mental image of Emmy sprang to mind. Those lifeless eyes would haunt me forever. My tears were still flowing. I couldn't seem to shut them off.

"Someone tell her already," Rome finally bit out. "If I have to see her cry like this for one click longer, Pica will be building herself a new kidnapping room."

Kidnapping room? I thought she'd invited us.

"It was sort of a 'impossible to refuse invitation,'" Yael admitted, reading my thoughts.

"Emmy is alive, dweller-baby," Coen announced, distracting me from that disturbing statement. He lifted a hand and gently wrapped it around my face. "You saved her life. You ..." He cleared his throat, sharing a look with the others before he finished. "You turned her into a god."

My world stilled. Even the breath that had been rattling in my lungs stopped. I just stared at him.

"She's in shock," someone murmured. "Get the dweller-Emmy so she can see for herself."

I don't know who left, or what happened, because I was still frozen in place.

It wasn't until familiar blond hair appeared in my vision—along with familiar blue eyes, and a familiar smile—that the icy hold on me cracked.

"Emmy," I sobbed, caving forward on myself, arms wrapping across my chest like I could hold my heart inside from where it was trying to burst out.

She pushed through the Abcurses before basically crawling into my lap. She enclosed me in her arms, and I sank against her. "How is this possible?" I cried against her neck. "I saw you die."

"You saved me, Willa." Her voice was low, serious. "You shared your energy with me. You brought me back to life."

"And almost goddamned killed herself in the process," Siret muttered from nearby.

"Emmy is a god," Pica trilled. Damn woman was so chirpy; she was making it really hard for me to cry in peace. "We don't know what she's a god of, yet, but we're all expecting big things."

I pulled back, then, to get a closer look at Emmy. "But, you look the same?" I questioned. "Shouldn't you look different?"

Emmy shook her head, and the most breath-taking of smiles spread across her face. "You look the same. Becoming a god doesn't change your outside, but I promise, I have never felt so strong in my life."

"Cyrus?" I had no idea why he was the first name that came to mind, then, but the last thing I remembered was him being all bright and fighting Staviti.

My spine straightened. "He's okay, right? Staviti didn't kill him?"

Emmy's cheeks went a little pink. "He's fine. The moment Pica and Adeline showed up, Staviti must have realised he was overpowered, and he took off."

That was great news, but … he wouldn't have given up so easily. Jakan had been very clear in his message. Staviti was on the path to destroying all of the gods. All of them except his precious Originals. Only…

"Why did you help us?" This question I directed to the Goddess of Love, who was busy flitting around the room, rearranging the four billion accessories that were on every spare inch of space. "Staviti loves you, and you turned against him."

She spun toward me, holding an ornate crystal lamp. "I LOVE lamps," she said with enthusiasm, before smiling down at it fondly. "Don't you love lamps?"

I flicked a side-eyed glance at Coen, who just shook his head. *Okay then, crazy-pants it was.*

"Lamps are … great, sure. I really enjoy their … light."

"I know!" she shot back instantly. "I love light. It's so warm. I just love it."

"She loves everything, right?" Emmy said, her voice low, edged with laughter.

"Every-fucking-thing," Yael said, low and derisively.

"Ask her the question again, Willa," Coen encouraged. "She gets easily side-tracked."

Right. "Why did you help us, Pica?"

The lamp was gently placed down and she

gracefully crossed to be closer to the bed. "Because he killed my son, many centuries ago. I loved my son more than any of my other loves. More than I love the stars and moon and the air and breeze and the lamp—"

"We get it," Aros cut her off, his voice rougher than usual.

"Your child is one of those in the imprisonment realm?" I asked her, my voice trembling as I thought back to those blank-faced children.

Some of the dreaminess left Pica's face then, and she focused on me properly. "Yes, Judas, my one and only baby. Mine and Rau's. For this, Staviti will be punished. He will suffer. I've been waiting for the moment another who could challenge him would come along. I knew the moment Rau found you that you were the one. I waited for you to ascend when you died, but you never did." Her full lips pressed into a pout, and she blinked dramatically like she was going to cry. "I've had this room set up for you for so many moon-cycles."

She spun in a circle, her face lighting up again. "Do you like it?"

"Am I allowed to ... not like it?" I asked, thinking back to the still-unresolved mystery of how Pica had kidnapped us.

"No!" She replied, smiling—though I was pretty sure she really meant the 'no'. "You're only allowed to love it!"

She stood there, her hands held out to me, her smile wide and disarming. *Holy shit, she was the most frightening of all the gods.*

"Alright," I acquiesced. "I like it. So much. It's … so pink."

"Pink is just so *lovely*!" she exclaimed.

"You scare me," I muttered back, causing Emmy to choke on a laugh.

"What was that?" Pica asked, leaning forward a little, the smile still stuck in place.

"I said you have lovely hair," I amended.

"And yours is just *divine*," she shot back, pawing all over me, her hands wrapping in my hair. "It's so yummy I could eat it! Num num num!" She mimed chomping down on my hair and then drew back, laughing.

I stared at her. Wide-eyed. Horrified.

"Num num num," I repeated, in a daze. When I had recovered, I tried to speak again. "So … it's really nice in here and everything, but … how long do we have to stay?" I asked, trying to be delicate about a situation I had no understanding of.

"Apparently, this is where you live now," Rome muttered out of the side of his mouth.

"Oh, silly Willy!" Pica spun around, opening the door for me. "You can leave anytime you want!"

"How long has she been calling me Willy for?" I whispered to Emmy.

"For as long as you've been here," Emmy whispered back.

I extracted myself from the bed and stood, my head swaying for a moment as I tried to gain my balance.

"And how long have I been here?" I asked this question a little louder, directing it to everyone.

"Fourteen sun-cycles," Coen replied. "Pica took you after Staviti left the Peak. She told us she knew how to heal you, but she grabbed you and jumped through the same pocket as Staviti, closing it behind her."

"I did do that," Pica confirmed, smiling jovially. "It was time to bring you home, Willy."

"Right." I fixed Coen with a stare, widening my eyes a little. He cringed in response, and then answered my unspoken question.

"It didn't take us long to find you. This was the first place we checked: Pica's platform. She was having a tea party with you, right out in the open. Invited us to have a cup."

"A tea party?" My brow furrowed in confusion. "I don't remember that."

"Oh yes!" Pica clapped her hands together beneath her chin, donning a whimsical expression. "It was so lovely."

"You were unconscious," Yael supplied.

"Oh." I was officially terrified of Pica.

I made my way to the door and carefully edged past her, walking into the hall. Her residence was made of marble, as with most of the god-homes, but there was so much pink fabric hanging everywhere that it was a little hard to recognise our space as one of the typical marble houses that I had grown used to in Topia. Nonetheless, it wasn't too hard to navigate my way out the pink nightmare. I opened the main door and stepped out into a small garden, surprised enough that I paused to look around. Soil had been piled into marble garden boxes, fruit and vegetable plants overgrowing from the sides. Everything looked so ... *well-loved*. I shuddered, hurrying out of the garden.

"Oh!" Pica called after me, causing me to turn around.

The Abcurses had followed me silently, Emmy right behind them. Pica pushed past them, making her way to me.

"I forgot to mention," she said, linking her arm through mine and squeezing tightly. "You can go anywhere you like, just as long as you don't leave my platform. I can't protect you if you do, and I can't let anything happen to you, Willy. I fear so badly that if I let you out of my sight, Staviti will snatch you up and destroy you as he did my beloved Rau."

Suddenly, it made sense for Rau to have been with the Goddess of Love. She was just as crazy as he was.

"Staviti ... killed Rau?" I asked hesitantly, my eyes flicking to Rome for a moment. He shook his head, the barest of movements.

Pica doesn't know.

"He has been jealous of Rau since the beginning of our creation. He created me, the perfect vision of love, but I did not love *him*, as he had intended. He made a few mistakes with me, being his first creation. He couldn't understand why, but ..." she laughed, suddenly. "Whoever does understand love?"

"Right," I agreed. "Nobody. Love is ..."

"Crazy," she inserted. "It's crazy, isn't it?" She laughed again, the thought apparently delighting her.

"You said it. So, what happened when you didn't love him back?"

"He got lonely, he created the others—new and improved companions, without the glitches—to keep him company. Rau, Abil, Adeline, Terrence, Lorda, Ciune, Gable, Haven, and Crowe. I knew I loved Rau from the moment I laid eyes on him."

She sighed. It was a dramatic and dreamy kind of sigh. "He was such a contradiction. So caring, so cruel!"

"So cruel," I agreed.

"He was everything good and everything bad, do you understand?"

"So bad." I nodded. "Totally understand."

Help, I called out in my mind.

I had intended to call for one of the Abcurses, but the last thing I expected was an actual answer. In my head.

What do you need help with, Sacred One?

340

I squealed, jumping away from Pica. I spun around, trying to figure out where the voice had come from.

"Whatthehellwasthat?" I rushed out, my words running into each other.

"What was what?" Yael asked, glancing around.

"Nobody said anything, Will," Emmy added, looking confused.

I glanced at Pica: she was pouting, her lip quivering. Had I ... upset her?

"Uh," I scratched my head. "Are you okay?"

A tear quivered at the edge of her eye before plopping down onto her robe. She sniffed once, twice, and then broke. Suddenly the crazy woman was sobbing. She threw herself at me, her arms wrapping around my shoulders, her head falling against me as she cried.

"You pushed me!" she wailed.

I had no words. I lifted a hand, patting her awkwardly while directing a look toward the Abcurses.

Did I really?

Did you really what, Sacred One? The reply was instant, and I jumped away from Pica once again, leaving her to crumple to a heap on the ground, still wailing.

"What the hell!" I exclaimed, spinning around again. "Who keeps doing that!"

"Doing what?" Rome strode forward, grabbing my arms, forcing me to still, to focus on him. "What's happening, Rocks?"

"Someone keeps speaking in my head! You five can't hear her?"

"Your thoughts are still a little tangled," Rome answered.

"It's a female?" Siret was beside Rome, a frown twisting his face.

"It was ..." I paused, realisation slamming into me. That voice had been familiar. I sucked in one breath, and then another. "Donald," I finally said, my wide eyes travelling over to Emmy. "It was Donald. Where is she?"

"Pica sent her somewhere," Emmy replied, moving to help the god up from the ground.

Pica allowed herself to be helped up, her crying beginning to quieten. She wiped away her tears with a section of her sleeve, before patting Emmy on the cheek.

"What a lovely girl you are. Where is my Willy? I must apologise to her. *Willy*?"

I cringed, shaking my head at the Abcurses. "I'm not here."

Siret smirked. "She's going to find you in about one-eighth of a click—"

"Willy!" Pica had peeked beyond the Abcurses, finding me huddled before them. She wrapped her arms around me again, and I wondered if I should just go ahead and push her a third time, because things were always better in thirds.

"Sorry I pushed you," I managed to force out.

"No, it was my fault." She patted my cheek as she had patted Emmy's. "Whatever you do to me is my fault, lovely girl. Now, shall we have some tea?"

"I ..." I shook my head. There would be time to tackle her frightening misconceptions later. For now, I needed to find my mother. "Yes, I would like tea. Can my server make it? Donald? You have her here somewhere, don't you?"

"Oh, very well." Pica swept away, clicking her fingers as she went. "Follow me, pumpkins!"

"Can I crush her now?" Rome asked, his mouth twisted down in a disgusted expression.

"She's the Goddess of Love," I replied. "There's probably some kind of defence mechanism that kicks in when you try to hurt her, and you end up falling in love with her or something."

"You pushed her over," Aros countered. "Are you in love with her?"

"No. I want Rome to crush her."

Aros grinned, pulling me under his arm as we moved to follow the trailing magenta material of Pica's robes. "We'll get you out of here soon, sweetheart, I promise."

"Maybe you shouldn't," I replied with a sigh.

"She's right," Emmy agreed, before I even had a chance to voice my argument. "Staviti was going to kill everyone until Pica showed up, crazy with grief over Rau. She threatened to kill herself to join him, and Staviti looked like ..." She shook her head, her expression pitying. "He went white as a sheet, told her that he would leave, and then he made this ripping motion in the air, stepped into it, and disappeared. Cyrus told me that it was a pocket—Staviti is the only one who can create them in Minatsol."

"So, this is potentially the one place that I'll be safe from Staviti," I concluded, as the others walked beside us silently.

"At least Rau isn't a concern anymore." Yael sounded tired, and I turned to watch him pull his hands through his hair. I wondered if they had been sleeping much for the past fourteen sun-cycles.

"Pica has been letting you all stay here?" I asked.

"For now," Coen replied. "We told her that our parents abandoned us."

"Did they?" I asked, surprised.

"No." He laughed. "They're hiding out in Cyrus's residence, where they can be safe from Staviti."

"I bet Cyrus is loving that," I muttered, sneaking a look at Emmy out of the corner of my eye. "So many people getting all up in his business, touching all his things. He's very particular about his things, isn't he, Em?"

She turned to glare at me. "I'm not one of his things!"

I grinned. "I was talking about his *actual* things. You know, that row of books above his bed and the funny little shelf of penis-shaped ornaments in his closet."

She stopped walking, her eyes blinking. "I ... don't remember that shelf at all."

"Ah-ha!" I exclaimed, pointing a finger at her as several of the guys chuckled. "So you *have* been in his bedroom! Emmy-freaking-Knight, the brand-new Goddess of Giving it Up to the Neutral!"

Her face flamed red and she stalked past me, rushing over to where Pica was bent over a small round table of cups and saucers.

"Pica!" she exclaimed, when she got there, her raised voice carrying over to us. "Willy is upset! She said she missed you!"

"Oh, my Willy!" Pica straightened, turning about with urgency, searching me out. "I'm right here, darling! Come here. Come here into my arms. That's a good girl."

She was holding her arms out dramatically, trying to wave me into them.

"Can I pretend I'm dead again?" I asked quietly.

"I think not," Coen replied. "You might just encourage her to resuscitate you in some weird way."

"Gods help me," I muttered back, bracing myself for another hug.

I was almost to her when there was a small *popping* sound and my mother appeared, just a few feet away. I stopped, turning to face her, my heart suddenly threatening to jump out of my chest. I wasn't sure exactly what I had expected, but it certainly wasn't for her to be the same person I'd been seeing since her death. The same ... Donald.

"How may I serve you, Sacred One?" She directed the question to Pica.

I felt as though I would collapse, then. Loss was crashing through me all over again. It should have been different. I had brought back a part of her soul—it should have healed her. It should have changed *something*.

Mum? I called out, appealing to the voice in my head again.

Six people all turned to look at me. My Abcurses ... and my mother.

"I'm sorry, Sacred One," she said out loud. "I don't understand the command."

"She didn't say anything," Pica said, a smile lighting her face. "What a funny little server you are. I always liked the faulty ones better than the functioning ones. There's something so ... charming about a flaw. Now, tea, please." She clapped her hands, waiting.

"Yes, Sacred One," my mother replied, before *popping* out of existence.

Tea. Tea. Tea. Tea. Need the cup. Cup. Cup. Cup. Cup. Need the water. Water. Water—

"Ugh," I clutched at my head, shaking away my mother's inner monologue. I had no idea why it was being broadcast into my mind, but I had a whole new appreciation for the Abcurses having to listen to *my* thoughts all the time.

"That must be it," breathed out Aros, his eyes lighting up. Apparently, he had been listening in on everything going on in my mind. "You say you brought back part of her soul?"

I nodded, not trusting myself to reply, because Pica was casting us glances from where she had seated herself at the little table.

"You didn't return it to her." Coen finished Aros's thought. "You kept it—assimilated it—the way we all did with the pieces of your soul that latched onto us."

Fell into the water. Need new covering. Covering. Covering. Covering. Can't find covering. Late. Late. Late.

My mother reappeared, dripping wet. She was holding a tray piled with three little teapots, which she placed on the table before Pica.

"Why are you wet?" Pica asked her, appearing perplexed.

Lie, my mother's thoughts projected to me clearly, a moment before she opened her mouth.

"It was time for my bath, Sacred One. I must stay clean and presentable."

Pica laughed. "You are just *so* delightful! Lovely, just lovely!"

"You know what else would be just *so* lovely?" I asked Pica, moving over to take a seat beside her, the brilliance of my sudden idea spurring me into immediate action.

"Tell me!" Pica bounced about excitedly, forgetting

about my mother as she waited for my reply, her eyes wide and unblinking.

"If I had my own little residence here, on this platform, with you!" I exclaimed, trying to match her level of excitement. "I could be like ... a grown-up god. Living here with you. We could live like a connected family ... in our own separate houses! I could have my own house over ... there!" I pointed in the opposite direction to her residence, not even bothering to check what I was pointing at. "And I could have my own server ... how about Donald? You like her so much, so maybe she can be my server now ... in my new house ... over there ..."

I trailed off, waiting for a reaction. I didn't know Pica very well, but from what I did know of her, the chances of her bursting into sudden tears were as good as her approving of the idea. The guys also seemed to be waiting, sharing glances with each other and me. Barely any of us were daring to breathe, until finally, Pica exploded out of her chair.

"Oh YES. What a LOVELY idea!" She seemed even more excited about this than she had been about the lamp. "We must organise this immediately ..." she was wandering off in the direction I had pointed, talking to herself—or possibly to me, though she didn't check to see if I was following.

Silence remained in her wake, until finally all of us started to laugh. Siret cracked first, followed by Rome and Aros. Yael and Coen only chuckled, shaking their heads. Emmy was grinning at me, and Donald was standing there, expressionless.

New home.

The thought hit me, spoken in my mother's voice, and I could feel the clench of my heart.

"New home," I confirmed, looking at her.

To be continued …

ALSO BY JANE WASHINGTON

Standalone Books

I Am Grey

The Bastan Hollow Saga

Book One: Charming (Dec, 2018)

Book Two: Disobedience (Jan, 2019)

Book Three: Fairest (Feb, 2019)

Book Four: Prick (Mar, 2019)

Book Five: Animal (Apr, 2019)

Curse of the Gods Series

Book One: Trickery

Book Two: Persuasion

Book Three: Seduction

Book Four: Strength

Book Five: Pain (Oct, 2018)

Seraph Black Series

Book One: Charcoal Tears

Book Two: Watercolour Smile

Book Three: Lead Heart

Book Four: A Portrait of Pain

Beatrice Harrow Series

Book One: Hereditary

Book Two: The Soulstoy Inheritance

ALSO BY JAYMIN EVE

Secret Keepers Series

Book One: House of Darken

Book Two: House of Imperial

Book Three: House of Leights

Book Four: House of Royale (September 15th 2018)

Storm Princess Series

Book One: The Princess Must Die (September 1st 2018)

Book Two: The Princess Must Strike (October 1st)

Book Three: The Princess Must Reign (November 1st)

Curse of the Gods Series

Book One: Trickery

Book Two: Persuasion

Book Three: Seduction

Book Four: Strength

Book Five: Pain (October 2018)

NYC Mecca Series

Book One: Queen Heir

CONNECT WITH JANE WASHINGTON

Website:

www.janewashington.com

Email:

inquiries@janewashington.com

Facebook:

@janewashingtonbooks

Instagram:

@janewashingtonbooks

Twitter:

@TheAuthorPerson

CONNECT WITH JAYMIN EVE

Website:
www.jaymineve.com
Email:
jaymineve@gmail.com
Facebook:
@JayminEve.Author
Instagram:
@jaymineve
Twitter:
@jaymineve1